The Warm Feeling

Also by Merle Miller

NOVELS

A Day in Late September
A Gay and Melancholy Sound
A Secret Understanding
Reunion
The Sure Thing
That Winter
Island 49

NONFICTION

The Judges and the Judged
We Dropped the A-Bomb
Only You, Dick Daring (WITH EVAN RHODES)

The Warm Feeling

by Merle Miller

COWARD-McCANN, Inc.

NEW YORK

48,030

Part One

—FLYING INTO THE SUNSHINE—

Chapter 1

❦ "I don't want to fall in love again," Sybil was saying. "I've got enough enemies."

Lydia saw that, as always, Sybil was charming everybody she set out to charm, which was everybody. If she weren't my oldest and best friend, thought Lydia, I'd hate her. It is, after all, *my* going-away party; Sybil is only the hostess.

But there. In the years Sybil and I have known each other I have with regularity hated her, disliked her, loved her, liked her, felt indifferent toward her, been jealous of her, forgiven her her trespasses, been silenced by her intelligence, awed by her wit, baffled by her stupidity. I have indulged her, endured her, been bored by her, and enjoyed her. And, on a very few occasions for a very few minutes, I have even come close to understanding her.

As is usually the case in any relationship, the arrangement has worked both ways; it has been vice as well as versa.

"It's always the same," said Sybil. "They say, 'love you. I cannot live without you; therefore, you must die.'"

Her remarks appeared to be intended primarily for Teddy Lipton, who was carefully not looking at Sybil, who was carefully not looking back. That meant their affair was well underway. It also meant that Sybil was about to add to her collection of abstract paintings. All of her young men were abstract expressionists.

At the moment the walls of the huge front room were crowded with the work of a young Mexican Sybil had met in Yucatan the previous summer. Federico was half Indian.

"He'll never be able to mix a color as beautiful as his skin,"

Sybil had said. "I couldn't help wondering if he was that color all over."

He had talent, too, and when Sybil sponsored an exhibition of Federico's work, it was well received.

Unhappily, one of the visitors to the exhibition was a famous actor who took Federico to Hollywood. "He would never be happy in a cold climate," the actor told Sybil.

Teddy Lipton did not look as if cold weather would bother him much, and in introducing him Sybil had said, "He's wildly talented." That, thought Lydia, is possible; Sybil does know her abstractions, but young Mr. Lipton isn't nearly as good-looking as Federico. Teddy Lipton's face and lengthy body looked as if he hadn't yet decided whether he wanted to take out a long-term lease on them.

Of course, thought Lydia, that may only be youth. I have reached an age where not only policemen look like children; so do several U.S. Senators and one or two members of the Supreme Court.

But Teddy Lipton looks as if he weren't more than nine years old, ten at most.

I do hope he is wildly talented, but it's too bad he isn't one of the Liptons with all the money. Money is always handy when the fire has cooled down, and it will. All of Sybil's affairs are forever, and the longest lasted almost six months.

"I can solve everybody's problems but my own," Sybil was saying. "I'm thinking of buying a comb for my hair and starting a column called 'The Eternal Duenna.' "

Lydia saw, without joy, that Robbie Martinson's new wife was starting toward her. The latest but by no means the last Mrs. Robin Martinson was carrying a potent-looking highball in her tiny right fist. A rattle would be more appropriate, thought Lydia. Robbie's new wife looks like an elderly baby in a fright wig, and I'll bet you dollars to donuts that if she were to fall downstairs, she'd go bumpty-bumpity-bumpity.

"Isn't this just one of the nicest parties ever?" said Peggy Martinson, spilling a little of her drink on Sybil's white wall-to-wall.

Seeing that there was no escape hatch in the immediate vicinity and not a rabbit hole anywhere, Lydia slipped on one of her Lady Bountiful masks and said. "It is nice."

"Robbie says you're going to Portugal. I've never been, but we used to have Portuguese fishermen in Rhode Island, where I'm originally from, and they were always so good-looking, and I dated this one boy named De Souza until my mother got after me."

Your gift for syntax is almost as extraordinary as your talent for the fresh phrase, thought Lydia, and one, this one anyway, would like to ask where you developed it. One's mind is abuzz with confusion and questions . . . Twenty Questions. Truth or Consequences. Spin the Bottle, and I'll bet Peggy got straight A's in Post Office. So what if she didn't do too well in preschool arithmetic. When she has finished with Robbie, she can hire people who know how much two and two add up to.

"It's sad, their singing the wha-ya-ma-call-it," said Peggy.

"*Fado.*"

"Huh?"

"I believe you mean the Portuguese *fado*," said Lydia.

"Could be," said Robbie's child bride, looking with disappointment at her empty glass and at Lydia's half-full one.

"I freshen your drink?" she asked.

Lydia shook her head, still wearing the Lady Bountiful mask.

"I think I'll have one more for the road. *Excusez-moi;* I'll return in a jiffy."

Lydia continued smiling. If I don't, she thought, I'll burst into tears, and now that I am queen and have a room of my own, we mustn't. Because we don't cry. Although we can't help wondering why Robbie always marries the same awful girl.

And she thought, with the exception of the girls he marries and one other person, everybody is fond of Robbie, and for once, everybody is right. Robbie is a dear man, and in one of my dark periods, he saved my life.

Robbie is fond of me, too; he may even love me, but I am not the kind of woman he would ever marry.

Too tall, for one thing. All of Robbie's brides have been

shorter than he, which has taken a little shopping around, because Robbie is only five feet, three.

All four of Robbie's wives have had acquisitive natures, and I doubt that any of them would have consented to marry Robbie if his family didn't own most of Baltimore, Maryland. Look at the way Baby Peggy is fondling that Cartier diamond; she's almost as fond of that as she is of bourbon.

Robbie's wives have all been deeply religious, too. Peggy is Catholic; Reba, number three, was an Episcopalian; Lacey, number two, was an admitted member of the Ethical Culture Society; and Ellie, the first, was a devout Communist.

Ah, yes. The stylish stout in the upper balcony wants to know who besides his wives does not like Robbie. Why, Robbie himself, of course. Isn't it always?

Another question, dear heart? Well, it's awfully late, and most of us have trains to catch. However, just a short one. That's what I thought. In what way, besides being too tall, am I not qualified to be one of Robbie's wives? Because I am born agnostic and because I married for love.

How did I make out? Some other time, madame, some other year, some other lifetime.

And now the meeting is dismissed; any contributions will be gladly . . .

Sybil was saying, "There's always a tear in her eyes. It's a tear that never falls; it just stays there and catches the light."

Sybil was now on the familiar subject of her mother, who was due to arrive in New York the following Monday for a stay of indefinite length.

"I can hear her now," said Sybil. " 'Bring on the branding iron. We might as well get this all over with at once—the castrating, the branding. Head them into the corral.' "

Sybil's mother was an awesome woman all right, but Sybil's lively imagination had made her more terrifying and, for that matter, more interesting than she really was. She was not, decidedly not, a Carleton from Roanoke.

It had been twenty-five years since Sybil had come, uninvited, to a faculty reception given by Lydia's father.

"I'm Miss Sybil from Louisville," she announced to the muf-
fled roll of drums, "and my mother is a Carleton of Roanoke."

Her accent had been more Southern than the one Vivien
Leigh had used in *Gone with the Wind*, and her manner was
that of wealthy matron distributing Thanksgiving largesse to
the needy.

"It's sweet of you-all to ask me," Sybil had said to Lydia's
father. "I didn't realize you even knew I was on the campus."

Sybil had a trim figure; she walked gracefully. She had untroubled blue eyes, an imp's nose, and a guileless smile that
caused a great many people to underestimate her.

Lydia was not among them; she hated Sybil on sight. At the
time Lydia was an overweight seventeen, giggled a good deal,
carried her left shoulder somewhat higher than her right, was
forever adjusting the seams of her stockings or some inner gar-
ment, and couldn't seem to remember to pick up her feet.

Sybil kissed Lydia's mother on the cheek, which no student
had ever done before, and after she had introduced herself to
Dr. Wylie, head of the English department, she said, "They say
your course in the nineteenth-century novel isn't open to fresh-
men, but I felt that if you had a moment to spare and we could
chat, I might persuade you to change your mind. I've read just
everything, and I adore Thomas Hardy, and—"

Dr. Wylie, who had made a pilgrimage all the way to Dor-
chester to shake Hardy's hand, blushed. "Why, of course, my
dear. How about tomorrow afternoon in my office. At four?
We'll have tea and talk."

Next, Sybil turned to Lydia's father and announced that she
had read both of his books "several times over, and I was absolutely overwhelmed."

She quoted various passages, and Lydia could see by watching her father's face that Miss Sybil Lee of Louisville, whose
mother was a Carleton of Roanoke, had a faultless memory.

"Dr. Lyman," said Sybil, "you and Descartes are alone among
the philosophers in feeling that the purpose of language is to
communicate and not to obscure."

Lydia's father adjusted his pince-nez, touched his mustache
as if to find out if it was still there, thrust his chin forward in a

manner that reminded some people—mostly Republicans—of Franklin Roosevelt, and said, "That's very kind, but to compare me with Descartes, whom, as you may know, I greatly admire—"

Lydia, who was rapidly becoming a woman, found herself saying, "But, father, since Miss Lee has read your books, she certainly *knows* about your admiration for René Descartes."

"You must be Miss Lydia," said Sybil. "I've heard that you're just as bright as a button."

Lydia gave Miss Sybil Lee a sanctimonious smile that she had practiced in front of a mirror, knowing it would come in handy someday.

"Are you pledging one of the sororities?" asked Sybil.

"Not as long as I remain in reasonable control of my faculties," said Lydia.

"That is an extremely witty remark," said Sybil, looking pained.

Then, turning back to Dr. Lyman, she said, "I've read that all great men are modest, and now that I've had the privilege of meeting one, I can see that it is absolutely true."

Lydia's father once more checked on the status of his mustache. It was still intact; so was his pince-nez.

"You're a remarkable young woman," he said. "Were you educated in the public schools of Louisville?"

"Mother wanted it that way," Sybil said modestly.

"I'm sure you were an outstanding student," said Lydia's father, who had an I.Q. of 167.

"I was valedictorian of my class," Sybil said, a note of reluctance in her voice, "and I was offered scholarships to Vassar, Wellesley, and Radcliffe, but when I heard about the brilliant faculty here at Briley—"

"Excuse me," said Lydia.

"Are you feeling all right?" asked her father.

"As well as can be expected under the circumstances," said Lydia.

"I certainly do hope we can be the best of friends," said Sybil.

Not unless you can run faster than I can, and although I was by no means valedictorian of my class, I was captain of the girls' track team, an honor not lightly given, thought Lydia. She said, "I think that would be ginger-peachy."

As she gavotted from the room, Lydia heard her father, who had an honorary degree from Columbia University, say, "It seems almost impossible to believe that Miss Lee is only a freshman."

Dr. Wylie, who was the author of the definitive biography of Thomas Hardy, said, "I see no reason at all why the rules cannot be amended to accommodate a mind of the caliber of Miss Lee's."

Professor Hayes, who had lectured at the Sorbonne, said, "All of my classes are open to those interested in the languages of the Mediterranean, the cradle of civilization."

Lydia did not sleep at all that night; she kept wishing that when she had been in Haiti the summer before, she had taken up voodoo.

The old woman who offered to teach her had said, "You can learn to destroy any enemy."

At the time, thought Lydia, in the last summer of my innocence, I didn't have an enemy in the world.

But that has changed, a lot.

The next morning at breakfast, Lydia's father, who had the unfortunate habit of being cheerful in the morning, said, "That Miss Lee is certainly an impressive young woman, wouldn't you say, Lydia?"

"You betcha," said Lydia.

"She has real wit," her father continued, "and wit is rare among the young. It is only developed by suffering."

"So I hear."

"Miss Lee has charm as well, don't you think?"

"Indubitably."

"Whatever charm is. Somebody once said that it's a word we all know the meaning of but none of us can define. I may have said it myself."

"How true."

"You aren't eating enough to keep a bird alive," said Lydia's mother.

"Not only that," said her father, "Miss Lee has a remarkable critical perception. And intelligence. I very much hope, Lydia, that you and she can become better acquainted."

"I shall lose no time in doing so," said Lydia.

Several mornings later, when Lydia walked into the coffee shop of the student union, she saw Miss Sybil Lee of Louisville, whose mother was a Carleton of Roanoke, at a table across the room.

Lydia started in the opposite direction, making use of her training on the track team, but she had not even completed a fifty-yard dash when Sybil reached her and somewhat breathlessly said, "Miss Lyman, may I buy you a Coke?"

"That certainly is sweet of you, but I have a class."

"You don't have another class until eleven, Chemistry One."

"Do you tell fortunes, too?" asked Lydia.

"No, but when I was at your house the other night, your schedule was on the table in the hall, and I memorized it."

"For heaven's sake, why?"

"I thought it might come in handy, and it has."

"Oh," said Lydia.

"It wasn't very nice of me, but then I'm not a very nice person."

At last you've said something I agree with, thought Lydia. She said, "I don't like Cokes. However, you could buy me a chocolate frosted."

Over the frosted she said, "Would you read somebody's personal letters if they were on the library table?"

"I don't ordinarily *steam* letters open," said Sybil. "Because no matter how careful you are in resealing them, they never look right. But if a letter is already open, and I'm pretty sure I can get away with it, of course I do. Don't you?"

"I haven't so far," said Lydia.

"Then how do you ever find out about people's secrets? Everybody's got closetfuls of disgraceful secrets."

"Including you?"

"Especially me."

"We might be friends at that," said Lydia.

"I think that would be ginger-peachy," said Sybil.

"By the way, what happened to your Southern accent?"

"It comes and goes, like hives. I learned when I was a mere slip of a girl that if you have a vomit-making Southern accent, you can get away with practically anything."

"Is your mother really a Carleton of Roanoke?"

"Ha, ha, ha," Sybil replied.

"And were you really valedictorian of your class?"

"I have no objection to telling the truth if it's useful," said Sybil.

"And how about all those scholarships?"

"You'd be an awfully good lawyer," said Sybil. "How about another frosted?"

"No, thanks. You'll have to come and have dinner at our house some night. My father liked you a lot."

"I thought maybe I was laying it on a little thick, but I guess you never can, not even with college presidents."

"Especially with college presidents," said Lydia. "How about tonight?"

"I'll have to glance at my engagement book, but I believe it's just possible."

"We have dinner at six thirty, but my father has cocktails at five thirty, and you and I could have ginger ale."

"I ought to tell you my name isn't really Lee. It's Levy."

"Why don't we meet outside the fine arts building at five?"

The house in which Lydia was born and grew up and in which her mother still lived was at the end of a wide avenue that led into open country. The street was lined on both sides with larch and beech and maple trees, which in some places joined in an irregular arch overhead.

A few leaves had fallen, and Sybil picked up one, a red maple.

"It's perfectly formed," she said. "I don't see why if God could take such trouble with leaves, He couldn't have worked a little harder on people."

"Don't you like people?"

"Not remotely. Don't tell me you do."

"I think so. I don't mean all of them, but most people I like. You know, parts of them."

"Especially boys," said Sybil, "parts of them."

"You have a dirty mind."

"Of course. Everybody has, but most people don't admit it."

"I hated you the other night."

"I hated you, living in that beautiful house and having a famous father and the way you look. You're the kind that gets better looking the older she gets."

"Do you really think so?" said Lydia. Then she said, "Even I haven't read *all* of my father's books."

"You don't think I did, do you? I spent an hour and a half in the library memorizing the stuff I said. He's tough to read, impossible really. I asked one of the librarians. What's the one with a face like a fig?"

"Miss Desmond."

"I asked Miss Fig Desmond what philosopher your father liked, and she said Descartes. She told me about Dr. Wylie and Thomas Hardy, too, and about that old poop, Professor Hayes. He's a big feeler. Did you know that?"

Lydia greeted what was news to her by saying, "Everybody knows that."

"It's a good idea to bone up on people before you go to a party," said Sybil, "especially if you haven't been invited."

"It seems sort of deceitful."

"So what else is new?"

"I don't think you really believe half of what you say."

"If we're going to be friends, the sooner you get over thinking that, the better. I mean every word I say."

"I like you a lot," said Lydia.

"Bright as a button my foot," said Sybil.

They laughed and shuffled their feet through the fallen leaves.

"My grandfather and grandmother met during the Battle of Atlanta," Sybil was saying. "He was sixteen, and she was fifteen. When he asked her to marry him, naturally she said yes. Later she told me, 'It was a hot day, honey, and there wasn't much else to do.' "

Her audience was enthralled. With the possible exception of the undersigned, thought Lydia, and I have heard the story once or twice before. The fact that there isn't a word of truth in it is of small importance since, by now, Sybil herself probably believes it. And anyway, Atlanta is a lot better place for your grandfolks to meet than St. Petersburg. Unless you're a Chekhov heroine, which Sybil isn't exactly.

But I must away to another part of the forest, particularly since I see Baby Peggy toddling in my direction, holding a glass in which there appears to be the better part of a bottle of bourbon. I wonder if Robbie has to burp her occasionally.

As Lydia opened the door leading to the terrace, she saw that Teddy Lipton's knee was lightly pressed against Sybil's. I give it four months, and then it will be necessary for me to nurse Sybil through the anguished aftermath. The last time, following Federico, the suffering lasted a little longer than usual, almost thirty-six hours.

Sybil's young men, Robbie's baby wives. We keep repeating our mistakes because, as the French say—*excusez-moi*—the more we remain the same, the more we remain the same.

Except for me, naturally. I don't repeat my mistakes because I never make any. That's the reason my husband went off into the sunset with a twenty-three-year-old named Penelope, long for Penny, short for faithful. Wherefore, on the morrow I am going to Europe in a flying coffin, unaccompanied and alone, and I am a woman who likes accompaniment. . . . We will now have have an interlude of hearts and flowers on the mighty Wurlitzer organ.

The guest of honor closed the terrace door behind her, and nobody noticed, nobody anywhere.

I have given up weeping, thought Lydia; I have had enough of the taste of my tears. Besides, it is a beautiful evening. Let us concentrate on the softness of the April air, on the moon that is full and orange, on the blue and green lights on the fountain in Sybil's garden, on the soft sounds of early evening coming from the street.

"Hello," said a voice, and Lydia turned.

"Hi, Jack," she said. "I didn't see you come in."

"I didn't, not in there. Does a Christian volunteer to enter the Coliseum during the lion act?"

Jack Bernstein looked into the crowded room, in particular at Teddy Lipton, whose knee was still pressed against that of Sybil.

"I didn't used to mind Sybil making a fool of herself," he said, "but I do wish that just once she'd choose a man. Surely she must get bored with those epicene kindergartners."

He smiled at Lydia, the smile of a boy who desperately hopes you'll like him but is pretty certain you won't.

"At least I think that's what I wish," he said, "or tell myself I wish, but most of the time I don't care."

He did, though, care about something anyway; something hurt, maybe only his pride. Wounded pride is a lot more prevalent than, say, heartburn or the loss of love. As Sybil had said of the latter, "You may kill yourself over it, but you won't die from it." What she had said about pride or heartburn Lydia had forgotten. Sybil must have said something, though; if not, it was one of the few subjects she'd neglected. You could go through the Encyclopaedia Britannica from *A* to *Zygote,* and you would find remarkably few items on which Sybil did not have an opinion, and she was not one who was able to hoard. A thought thought was a thought expressed. You didn't even have to ask.

"I've got a magnum of champagne in the fridge," said Jack. "Will you share it with me?"

"I'll probably get all gooey," said Lydia. "I've already had considerable to drink."

"You could never get gooey," said Sybil's husband.

Then he said something quite unexpected. He said, "There are times, quite a few of them, when I wonder what would have happened if when I had a blind date with a girl at Briley, it had been with you instead of Sybil."

Chapter 2

❦ Jack was in the kitchen, getting the champagne, and Lydia was in the dining room, thumbing through a book of poems.

"I've tried to be good. I brush my teeth every night. I haven't had sex for a month. I object. I'm a liberal. I want everyone to be happy."

On the record player Johnny Mathis was singing "Taking a Chance on Love."

The brownstone in which Jack and Sybil had coexisted for ten years was not a house; it was houses. There were separate entrances, separate living rooms, separate kitchens, baths, bedrooms, and in their separate houses, Sybil and the man she had married lived separate lives.

Sybil's way has been briefly observed and will be again, more at leisure—a life of young men who were not epicene (Jack was wrong about that), of expressionist paintings, of exhibits sponsored and attended, plays gone to (the most serious; to Sybil the theater was a lecture hall), concerts attended (she had no ear for music and could have heard Beethoven's Fifth a thousand times but on the thousand and first hearing would say, "What's that?"), parties attended (particularly those at which money was raised for one worthy purpose or another. Sybil was always among the first to volunteer a contribution).

That will do for now. Except to add that on the rare occasions when Jack did wander into the lion's den he was either not noticed at all or, if introduced, was at once forgotten.

Sybil had her house redone at the beginning of each new affair; interior decorators loved her, platonically, of course. Jack's house had been painted only once, coffee-colored, every room, including the baths. It was carelessly furnished, too, as if the pieces had been chosen hurriedly from a poorly lighted warehouse.

There was, however, an enormous record player that seemed to have as many knobs as the instrument panel of an airplane. Lydia had never touched it, never would. There were records, thousands of them, tens of thousands maybe, all kinds—Mozart and Mathis, Sinatra and Schwarzkopf, Haydn and Herman's Hermits. That will give you some idea.

Books were everywhere—on shelves that, fortunately, covered a great part of the coffee-colored walls, on the mustard-colored carpets, not wall to wall and thin, on beds, in unused bathrooms, in closets, on tables. All kinds of books, the predictable sets of Dickens and Balzac, contemporary novels, nonfiction, science fiction, dictionaries, encyclopedias. And magazines, great piles of them, mostly British—*Punch, Encounter, The New Statesman, The Spectator, London Life, Animals.* And newspapers. As many newspapers as there were records and books. Lydia often thought of the Collier brothers, those odd, misanthropic millionaires who died in Brooklyn (wasn't it?) in a gloomy mansion filled with newspapers and the smell of death.

But Jack Bernstein was not misanthropic, not a hoarder or a miser; he was, to the contrary, a generous man. As for the newspapers, Lydia felt that he hadn't so much saved them; he had simply neglected to throw them away. When she was in the house, however, she was wary of lighting a cigarette. Besides, there were no ashtrays.

And that, thought Lydia, is all I know about the house that Jack's parents—grandparents?—built. Are mysterious strangers received in the dark of night? Are revels reveled here? Orgies orgied? I doubt it. I wouldn't swear (can you ever?), but I'm pretty sure that Jack Bernstein is a loner.

At the moment the record player had Johnny Mathis singing "Don't Blame Me."

But on the subject of Jack Bernstein, what else is there to say? Well, he's a kind man, and he's quiet; and at my time of life I appreciate quiet. Like Bach. When I was young and twenty, Johann Sebastian's music used to bore me, but now that there are silver threads among the gold (or would be, if it weren't for Mr. Kenneth), it delights me. Away from the madding crowd, from loud noises, sudden or otherwise; let me slumber in the corner by the chimney here. You want me to try on a glass slipper, you say? Look, buster, stop interrupting my nap. Let Cinderella try it on, and if it doesn't fit her, try either or both of her ugly sisters.

But I wander, I wander, another sign of galloping senescence. Jack Bernstein. He is a graduate of the Harvard School of Business (that's important?), and he once in a while pays a short visit to an austere office in the Empire State Building. What he does there and whether or not it is necessary is another mystery. It will remain unsolved. There are a number of loose ends that will not be tied up in this particular narrative, but so are there in what is often referred to as real life.

Finally, and perhaps this should have come first, Jack Bernstein is rich, very. That fact came first with Sybil.

It was the year of Pearl Harbor, but in October who except for a few high-ranking Japanese naval officers knew that?

Lydia and Sybil were juniors at Briley and shared an unremarkable furnished room on College Avenue. Lydia's father and mother were spending a few months in Europe; the reason need not concern us. Lydia spent her spare time hiding behind a book in the college library or lurking in the darkness at the Odeom Theater in Briley, and she went to a great many athletic events, always with other girls who were not likely to be the belles of any ball.

So much for the essentials.

On the third Saturday night of the month—you can look up the date, but why?—Lydia came back from the basketball game she'd gone to with two other girls. (They wound up doing graduate work at Radcliffe and never married.)

Sybil was still up, sitting under one of those goosenecked lamps, writing busily.

"Hello, there," she said. That was also the year Sybil, for reasons not even her best friend could understand, confused her identity with that of Katherine Hepburn and started talking through her nose.

On that October Saturday night—it was almost twelve, late for those days—Lydia could see that Sybil had the look of a canary-eating cat, but she had no intention of asking why. For two reasons. First, if she did, it would give Sybil the upper hand, which is never desirable. Second, Sybil would volunteer. I'll wait a minute, thought Lydia. She said, "You can't be doing your homework; it's only Saturday."

"I've been making a list of my bridesmaids," said Sybil. "You're first, naturally."

"Oh, sure. You bet."

Lydia went to her half of the closet and got out the black lace nightgown that she would never under any circumstances show to her mother.

"We won," she said, "eighty-six to forty-six. Basketball players all have ugly legs. Have you ever noticed, all that hair?"

"So don't ask me how was my blind date."

"How was your blind date? Is he the one who asked you to marry him and you said yes? He must be a dreamboat."

"He wears horn-rimmed glasses about the size of dinner plates, and he's a chubbo and the world's worst dancer, and he talks so low you can hardly hear him. I think he's shy."

"I can see why he asked you to marry him, but why did you say yes?" said Lydia, starting to brush her teeth.

"He hasn't actually asked me yet, but he will. His name is Jack Bernstein, and his family has got more money than the Rockefellers, just as much, anyway. They own about nine thousand department stores."

"I wish you'd learn to hang up your toothbrush," said Lydia, yawning. "I'm going to bed. Gretchen and Tina and I are going to a swimming meet tomorrow."

"Oh, go chin yourself," said Sybil.

"Is it all right with you if I don't hold my breath until the wedding?"

"So it'll take a little time. All successful campaigns do. Sherman didn't just waltz through Georgia. It'll take planning, too, and I have to make sure that if there's any blood shed, it isn't mine. His parents are going to hate me, but that's to my advantage."

"How do you figure?"

"Because nobody likes their parents; it's only natural. So what they hate, you like. Jack Bernstein'll like me because of their opposition, not in spite of it."

"I like my father and mother," said Lydia.

"You're sick."

"And they like me."

"So what else is new? I was born in original sin."

"But I didn't think you were religious, Sybil."

"The original sin is to be born poor, and you have to spend the rest of your life purging yourself of it."

"You won't be happy if you marry for money," said Lydia.

"Sometimes I wonder if you're really eighteen. I bet you still believe in Santa Claus."

"No, but I'm not sure about Easter bunnies."

"Now tell me about your evening. Did you and the goon girls get all goose-pimply and cheer your little lungs out over the idiot goings-on of those hairy-legged Neanderthals?"

"Good night, please."

"He's asked me to New York next weekend, and while there I shall, if it is humanly possible, get myself compromised."

"I'm asleep," said Lydia.

"Wish me luck," said Sybil, "seriously."

"I wish you luck, seriously."

Jack and Sybil were married the following January in an unaired office of a justice of the peace in White Plains. There were no bridesmaids and no witnesses, and less than a week later the groom, who had a commission in the U.S. Navy, went off to the wars.

The baby was born, prematurely, it was said, in late May. It was male, and it lived for a little less than two hours.

*   *   *

Jack came in from the kitchen with the champagne; he had two thickish goblets in his hands.

"I keep meaning to get glasses," he said, "but I always forget. Anyway, champagne—I'm told this is a good year—presumably tastes the same even if the glasses did come from Woolworth's."

He poured the champagne, lifted his glass, and said, "Bon voyage."

"It tastes better in glasses from Woolworth's," said Lydia.

"Has anybody told you how well you're looking?"

Lydia shook her head, although earlier in the evening several people had told her that, most of the women with envy.

"There were several times this past winter when I came close to jumping in the car and driving up to see you," said Jack, "but then I figured you'd work it out alone. Which I gather from the look of you, you have. You've come through the door, and I guess you've discovered that there aren't any road maps."

"I've come through the door."

"What are you going to do in Europe?"

"Spend some time in Portugal, at Armação de Pêra," said Lydia. Then, seeing Jack's face, she wished she hadn't spoken, but you can never turn back, so she said, "That's where Sybil stayed last year."

"I'm aware that Sybil stayed there last year, at a hotel on a cliff managed by a young man named Bernardes."

"And then I'm going to Madrid," Lydia said hurriedly, "mostly to look over Christopher's bride-to-be and maybe examine a few things in the Prado."

"I envy you the Prado. It's one of the few museums in the world that's all one piece, like some people. Of whom you are one." He lifted his glass again. "Have a good time."

"I think I will. I'm a little scared. I've practically never gone anywhere except Poughkeepsie alone."

"You'll make out, and you won't eye handsome young waiters in the restaurants or the handsome young managers of the hotels. Have some more champagne. It'll get flat."

Lydia said yes, she would have some more champagne. Mathis was singing "Dancing on the Ceiling."

"I wouldn't worry about Christopher's wife," said Jack. "I'm sure he's chosen well. He's a smart boy and even rarer, a nice one. Day's nice, too, but then how could the two of them not be? They were smart enough to choose the right mother."

Somewhere a clock discreetly announced that it was ten o'clock.

Lydia rose. "I think I'd better get back," she said.

Jack kissed her gently on the lips and said, "You may never come back, of course. You may marry a duke or a count or one of those people. It happens all the time in the movies and, I'm told, on television. They're usually impotent, though, aren't they? Try not to marry an impotent man."

"Good-bye, Jack," said Lydia, "and thank you for the champagne."

He swayed a little, and Lydia wondered if it was like that every night.

"I'm very fond of you," he said, "very."

"I'm very fond of you," said Lydia, meaning it but realizing that what she meant and what Jack Bernstein meant were not the same.

"You married a man who wasn't good enough for you," he said. "I promised myself I'd never say that, but now I have. I'm drunk. Go now; hurry, but if you ever need me, I'm here."

"Good night, dear Jack," said Lydia, and she thought, I'm a liberal. I want everyone to be happy.

Chapter 3

❦ Teddy Lipton was, not surprisingly, the last to leave the party. He said an overly polite good night to Lydia. For a moment she thought he might be going to kiss her hand. Instead he said, "I met your daughter once, and I wondered where her beauty came from. Now I know."

Sybil went into the hall with him, and Lydia walked around the room, emptying ashtrays. I am an emptier of ashtrays, she thought. When others say good night to their youthful lovers in dark hallways, I virtuously clean up the debris from the party that is now over. I have the soul of a housewife, and the only trouble now is that although I still have a house, I am no longer a wife, and that's the way it's going to be from here on in.

There were soft mutterings, like doves, in the hallway. Sybil's voice, "Good night, baby," and the other, "[something, something], darling . . . call you . . . [something]."

The street door closed softly, as if in shame, and after a moment Sybil came back into the room in which all of the ashtrays had been emptied.

"It was a lovely party, Syb. Thanks," said Lydia.

"It wasn't bad. Nobody got falling-down drunk, and there probably aren't more than half a dozen new cigarette burns. And you seemed to have a good time. Everybody said you looked wonderful, which you do. Teddy said you were extremely intelligent as well as beautiful, and that's rare. He's usually critical of everybody. You'd better watch your step with him. I may have to scratch your eyes out or pull your hair."

"I'm a great step watcher," said Lydia. "Robbie Martinson told me a whole new life is going to open up for me. 'You're a new woman,' he said. I hope so. I'm tired enough of the old one, but I'm inclined to think that at my age nothing much is going to change, and I'd better make do with what I have."

"Philosophy One," said Sybil. "Mondays, Wednesdays, and Fridays at nine. Let's have a nightcap."

Lydia, who didn't want another drink, nodded. A slight libation was one of the lesser prices of friendship.

As Sybil mixed the drinks she said, "I've written to Bernardes, the manager of the hotel at Armação de Pêra. He'll have a car waiting for you when you get to Pêra. I've told you about him."

"You've told me about him."

"And I'll see you in Madrid in exactly thirty-one days. We'll have a great time, you and I and Christopher and his girl. What's her name?"

"Candice," said Lydia.

"You and Christopher and Candice and I. Bullfights and *flamenco* and the singing of the *cante*. And we'll have garlic soup and roast pig and visit El Greco's house in Toledo and stare at all the beautiful young men who look like El Greco paintings. And we'll go to the Prado and look at naked *contessas* and at those happy pictures of joyous dwarfs and flattering mirrors by Velázquez."

Sybil handed Lydia her drink. "I hope the girl Christopher chose is a winner," she said.

"She will be. Christopher has very good taste in girls."

"They're fine, but to me they're like so many Chinese. I can never tell them apart."

It's true, thought Lydia, there have been remarkable similarities in Christopher's girls. Height, always tall. Legs, always long and good. Voices, modulated, finishing school voices. And their talk. Talk of summers at the Jersey shore or on the Cape. "The lifeguard was positively ugly and the color of a ripe tomato, but I felt my life was absolutely safe in his hands, unlike some of the handsome ones." Talk of music. "I'm not sure Bartók holds up all that well." Talk of books. "Did you know that all of the girls in *Remembrance of Things Past* are really boys? Like Shakespeare. Can you imagine a boy playing Lady Macbeth?" Talk of weekends in the city. "I've got two tickets for *Waltz of the Toreadors*. Saturday matinee. I may invite you if you'll take me to Sardi's first. Or, if you're feeling lush, Twenty-One."

Pleasant girls, girls with bodies built for motherhood, girls trained to be good wives, well brought up girls. And they all had one other trait in common. They could not stop looking at Christopher. But who could blame them? Christopher is one of the handsomest young men anywhere, maybe the handsomest. And I can think that without being immodest, because Christopher inherited all of his looks from his father. As did his sister Day, despite the flattering but inaccurate observation of Teddy Lipton.

Christopher had been dating girls from Vassar and Bennington and Wellesley and Smith and Sarah Lawrence since he was sixteen, but he had announced to his mother and probably to the girls, "I'm not planning to get married until I'm twenty-five."

He announced it in the same way that he had said he was planning to go into the foreign service.

Why?

"I should like to combine my interest in travel with my wish to do some good in the world," he had said solemnly. He had been a solemn boy, a predictable boy, a boy who never ever cried, a boy who seldom displayed a feeling of spontaneous joy.

Now, predictably, he was twenty-five, a promising young man in the American embassy in Madrid, and he was engaged to a young woman named Candice from Missoula, Montana. They were to be married in the presence of the groom's mother in mid-June.

Although Lydia had never met her and Christopher had written only that "She's special," Lydia felt that she knew certain things about Candice, her height, that her legs would be long and good, etcetera.

"I'm sure Christopher can tell them apart, which is really all that matters," Sybil was saying. "Of course, you won't admit it, not even to yourself, and you wish you didn't and try not to, but you can't help loving Day a little bit more than you love Christopher."

Lydia said, "One would think that with a permanent, incurable case of running off at the mouth, from which you suffer, that once in a while you'd make sense."

"It's perfectly natural, of course. At least, so I've read. Mothers in general prefer the problem children."

Lydia said, "The fact that we have remained friends for so long is a tribute to my saintly nature."

"Christopher never went through any of those rebelly stages. He's the kind of boy who'll probably hold in all his inhibitions and hostilities until he's about forty, and then, wham. He might do away with his wife and children, sell secrets to the heathen Chinese, or play tic-tac-toe with hydrogen bombs."

"Sybil, shut up."

"What you don't realize is that beneath that blond, bland, and beautiful exterior is a very vulnerable young man, very tender."

"Could we drink sitting down, or would that interfere with your monologue?"

"It won't interfere," said Sybil, leading the way into her sitting room. The walls were painted in varying shades of blue. Lydia seated herself on a small sofa that had been covered with denim.

"I'm going to have all this redone," said Sybil, "but I can't decide what color."

"Of course you are. How about puce?"

Sybil, who was changing into a dark green dressing gown, said, "This is the best time of any party, after the guests have gone and you can sit around with your best friend and take the guests apart. Like Robbie's new wife. Isn't she ghastly?"

"I thought she was sweet and a brilliant conversationalist."

"You're a bitch. You didn't either. I saw you duck out when she started your way."

She leaned over and kissed Lydia on the forehead. "I was

proud of you tonight. You were more relaxed than I've seen you in years. The time will come when you realize that the day you and Simeon called it quits was the luckiest day of your life. By the way, I've been meaning to ask you, did Simeon take the Eames chairs?"

Lydia nodded.

Sybil took a sip of her mahogany-colored drink. "That's not fair. You should have had the Eames chairs."

"Syb, stop picking at the scabs."

Lydia tried to suppress a yawn but didn't succeed.

"I've got to get my beauty sleep," she said. "I'm taking the eight-o-five to Briley in the morning and coming back to Kennedy at seven. It's going to be a long day, and then I'm flying off into the sunshine, which will be a long flight. So if you'll excuse—"

She started to rise, but Sybil took her hand and with an unfamiliar urgency in her voice said, "Don't go yet."

"I won't go yet," said Lydia, once again unable to hold back the yawn. "Syb, are you feeling the miseries for any reason?"

"Of course not. I'm happy as a lark, assuming larks are happy. How in the world do they know? I've heard of dog analysts, and I saw in the paper the other day a cat analyst is setting up in business on West Fifteenth Street. But how many lark analysts have you met up with lately? I'm going to have another drink, but why don't you go to bed if you want to?"

"I'm not sleepy. Besides, I'm not going to see you for thirty-one days."

Near the end of the second drink Sybil said, "What did you and Jack talk about?"

"Nothing much. We had a couple of glasses of champagne, and he said he envied me the Prado, nothing much."

"Did he say anything about—anybody else?"

"Nope, unless you count his mention of Christopher and Day."

"You know what I mean, another woman."

Sybil finished the drink and leaned closer to Lydia. "Do you think—could there be one?"

A moment, then Sybil said, "That's a silly question, isn't it?"

"It would be silly of me to answer it, since I haven't any idea."

"As if you could know if there were another woman. If I don't, I mean."

Another moment passed, slightly longer, and then Sybil said, "If there were, I think I'd kill myself."

What do you say? What do you ever say?

"Now go to bed," said Sybil, "and have the most beautiful time ever."

"Thanks, and in thirty-one days we'll meet in the Ritz Bar in Madrid, Spain. You'll recognize me by the red rose in my hair."

"We're two very smart ladies," said Sybil, "but most of the time that doesn't seem to help much, does it?"

Chapter 4

❧ After Lydia got under the covers, she stretched lazily, and then because she didn't want to think of Sybil, the smart lady in the room below, or about Jack Bernstein, the poor little rich boy in the lonely house next door, or about herself, she said silently, "I shall sleep soundly tonight because I have a big day ahead of me tomorrow. I shall make my mind a blank."

"She made her mind a blank." If I've read that once, I've read it a hundred times, and I've certainly met up with a few blank-minded ladies and, for that matter, gents, but with me it never works. The mind of the girl of the limberlost here may not be up to much, but blank it never is, especially when I want it to be. Chug-a-lug, chug-a-lug, always in there, panting away. Except when I want to be brilliant. Then it blows a fuse, not a thought in a carload.

Lydia thought of sheep. What do you think of sheep, Mrs. Brady? Not much. What do they think of me? She counted a few sheep, but alas, she thought, and alack, I have run out of fingers and toes.

Look here, Charlene, she said to herself, this is going to be one of those sleepless nights, and there's nothing to be done about it. Or about the fact that tomorrow at the airport people will mistake you for Whistler's mother and start pestering you for autographs.

Think of beginnings. The beginnings of things are always the best. Think of the spring you turned nineteen and fell in love with Simeon Brady or with the idea of being Simeon Brady's girl and, as soon as he asked you and if he didn't you might ask him, his wife.

It has been mentioned that at seventeen I was by no means Queen of the May. At nineteen not much had happened except I'd put on more weight, carried my shoulders at a 90-degree angle instead of 45, and still didn't pick up my feet.

So what if my father was head of the whole shebang? Boys still stayed away from me in record numbers; the mere mention of my name was likely to empty an entire fraternity house. "You mean the bat girl is coming, Frankenstein's daughter? Look, I'm fleeing town that night, a slow boat to China."

It was Simeon—credit where due—who first said to me, "You've heard, no doubt, about leg men and about breast men. Well, I'm a walk man. Did I ever tell you about Sarah Bernhardt? They say when you watched her walk, it was as if a slight wind were blowing at the small of her back." *Of course* I practiced walking, days of it, nights of it, enough to earn a Ph.D. in it. I straightened my shoulders, started to pick up my feet, and, to be sure, felt a slight wind at the small of my back.

And Simeon at the Royal Kandy Kitchen in Briley: "A double chocolate malted for the young lady and a large Coke for me. I've got to watch my boyish figure; chubby professors are out this year."

Me: "I've changed my mind; I think I'll have a Col.e, too, a small one."

Simeon: "You're going to have a wonderful figure, once you get rid of that baby fat."

He was an educator, and on our first date, after the movie, Simeon said, "I'm sorry to have inflicted that hogwash on you."

Me: "But I liked it. I cried—well, you know, practically half a box of Kleenexes."

Simeon: "That's the point. If you're going to cry, don't do it over the simulated death of some second-rate actor. Do it over the fate of *The Brothers Karamazov*."

Me: "Do you really think John Garfield is second-rate?" The observant reader will have noticed that I didn't mention *The Brothers*. In those days, and now, the Russian novelists eluded me, and so did quite a few of the French, Proust, for instance. I'm more a *Three Musketeers* type.

Simeon: "John Garfield is a fifth-rate actor. Next week I'm going to take you to New York to see Ferrer and Robeson in *Othello*." You see, Simeon was a wonderful teacher for me, but I graduated, and Simeon wouldn't give me a degree. That happened later, though, more than twenty years later.

But I'm ahead of myself; Simeon and I haven't met yet.

It had been a lonely spring. I read a lot, in one six-week period all of *The Grapes of Wrath, Anthony Adverse,* and *Gone with the Wind.* Then I read *Gone with the Wind* over again. And in my spare time I kept up with the novels of a Miss Viña Delmar, all of which appeared in *Liberty* magazine—*Kept Boy, Kept Girl, Kept Boy Meets Kept Girl,* and so on. Stendhal? Balzac? Not in the same league.

And I went to movies, lots of movies, especially movies with John Garfield; I was in love with him. For one thing, he was very, very sexy-looking, although nice girls (I was a nice girl, never asked to be otherwise) didn't talk about s-e-x. For another thing, John Garfield was Jewish, and at the time I thought everybody nice was Jewish. Like Sybil, my best friend. Like Norman Lefkowitz, who kept saying how he was sorry that he'd been too young to fight in the Spanish civil war. Norman taught me to sing, "We are the peat bog soldiers, marching off to war, dum-de-dum-dee-dee. . . ." My memory is going, one of the first signs of senescence. Let us once more to the days of my innocence and ignorance.

I had a few dates with Norman, during most of which he talked about things like electronics and the style of Karl Marx. I never got beyond the first page of Karl Marx's suspense novel, and Norman wasn't much help. He kept saying, "You have to read it in German to really appreciate it."

At that moment I had the feeling that our romance wasn't going to flourish, despite the fact that Norman was Jewish. Besides, although you weren't supposed to say so, he had demonstrable lack of chin and his face supported a bumper crop of hickeys.

Then—that was the age of miracles; I don't care what anybody says—the phone rang in my father's house. I picked it up and said, "Miss Lyman here." I was also a great admirer of Noel Coward, although I didn't consider him in the same class as Vina Delmar.

A male voice said back, "Good evening, this is Simeon Brady."

I said, "Who?"

"Simeon Brady."

"Yah. Sure." I was majoring in English and art.

The voice said, "I'm sure you won't be, but are you by chance free Friday night?"

I said, "Gee, yes." See how my gift for repartee was already fully developed?

"Could I persuade you to go to a movie with me?"

"Gee, yes." They just don't write dialogue like that anymore.

"It's a little horror—I'm sure it's a little horror—called *Four Wives*. It might amuse you, though. You haven't seen it, have you?"

"Gee, no."

This last was not completely accurate; I had seen *Four Wives* twice. Who wouldn't? Not only was John Garfield in it. So were Rosemary and Priscilla and Lola and Barbara Lane. I had gone through a box and a half of Kleenex.

I decided, however, that seeing the movie with Simeon Brady would be a totally different experience, so in a way I was telling the truth. (It's easy to get used to telling lies to yourself, and it's the one addiction they can't pass laws against. But it is habit-forming, no question about that.)

A few words about Simeon Brady in the golden days.

He was twenty-six years old, and although it was his first year at Briley, he was already the most popular professor on the campus, standing room only in all of his classes in English literature.

The girls were all in love with him, especially with the voice, a husky combination of the accents of the Piedmont region of North Carolina, where he was born and grew up, of Magdalene College at Oxford, where he spent two years, and of Harvard, where he got his Master's. His thesis was on the Trollopes, Frances and her son Anthony, and was considered brilliant.

Not only that, Simeon Brady was divinely handsome. Everybody said so, and I heard one girl say he looked like an English poet. But which? W. H. Auden? Geoffrey Chaucer? Elizabeth Barrett Browning?

Simeon had fine blond hair worn a little long, large dark eyes, a wide amused mouth, and the kind of nose that was once described as aristocratic.

He had sold a poem to *The New Yorker* magazine. His biography of the Trollopes, a revision of his Master's thesis, had been bought by a publisher after only four chapters were completed. The same publisher had read and accepted with enthusiasm a novel of which Simeon had written an outline. Simeon was at work on the libretto for a musical comedy based on Mrs. Trollope's trip to Cincinnati, *Domestic Manners,* and he was composing—he played the piano beautifully—a concerto that Toscanini was rumored to be enthusiastic about.

My father had said, "We're very fortunate in having young Brady on the campus. I consider that he has the potential of being extraordinary." Potential, indeed.

And so it was that Simeon Brady and I began the first of twenty-four springs we spent together.

My state of mind—is that the phrase—was apparent to one and all, and a great many girls who had looked the other way when I lumbered down College Avenue now claimed they were delighted at the sight of me.

"Is Professor Brady as exciting in private as he is in public, and have you ever . . ."

We hadn't, ever. There was premarital bed-going in those days, too, but we didn't talk about it as much as is the custom now. I'm inclined to think that in this area as in many others, silence is the best policy. I've never thought sex was a conversation piece. Anyway, as I say, Simeon and I didn't.

Sybil, for one, was not quite as happy as I was over my romance. She said, "He's charming all right, but after a good many hours of listening to him carry on about the Trollopes, I've decided that charm isn't enough."

"Did I ask for your opinion?"

"I've been scared ever since I first saw that dewy look in your eyes. I just hoped it would pass. Besides, he's no spring chicken. He's twenty-six."

"Simeon is writing a beautiful new poem. It's called, 'I am a man who marches without moving.' "

"It sounds terribly autobiographical. May I point out that Keats had been dead a year when he was twenty-six? Simeon Brady is an also-ran. As they say in the sports pages, he's the kind who'll never come through in the clutches. Mark my words."

"What makes you so sure your judgment is better than mine?"

"Because I'm not in love with him, dear heart!"

Me: "You're jealous."

Sybil: "Did I say I wasn't?"

With my mother it went like this:

"Could we have Simeon Brady for supper tomorrow?"

"If you like. And how about inviting Sybil, too? You haven't had her for quite a while."

"Not this time."

"All right. I can't help noticing, of course, that this is the third time in eight days for Mr. Brady."

"For heaven's sake, if you're going to keep *track,* we can eat at a restaurant."

"I'm not keeping track. You're getting very fond of Dr. Brady, I think."

"So maybe I am. Is that against the law?"

"I remember when you and I could discuss things," said my mother. "I like Professor Brady, and I love you, but you're nineteen years old."

"Just don't worry about me, please."

"I'll worry about you because I want the best for you, but I'll try to keep my peace unless specifically asked not to."

She kissed her mother on the cheek, but the golden intimacy between them was gone.

Lydia turned over the pillow; the linen was soft and felt cool. It was a little after four, and on the city street below, garbage men were banging various things and shouting at each other, displaying their understandable resentment at being awake and at work at such an ungodly hour. A murderous car raced around a corner, a carouser whistled tunelessly, and there were the menacing sounds of hurried footsteps and of furtive laughter.

In the country at this hour, she thought, there would be the sound of the first birds exchanging the gentle gossip of the night, usually a robin, but then blue jays are early risers, too, and, like the garbage men, they don't want anybody to sleep if they're awake.

And then, thought Lydia, there was the question of how my father would react to the fact that Simeon Brady and I were going steady. My father was not a predictable man.

On the morning in question Lydia was reading *Adam Bede,* which for some reason was required in the English Novel. She was not reading it with pleasure; she doubted if anybody except the author and a few very close friends had ever done that.

"Consequences are unpitying," read Lydia. "Our deeds carry their terrible consequences, quite apart from any fluctuations that went before—consequences that are hardly ever confined to ourselves."

At that point she heard her father bounding down the stairs. There are such days, quite a few of them as the years roll on. For a moment Lydia thought escape might be possible, but, no, too late; Dr. Henry Lyman was already in the hall.

Her father was at his heartiest early in the morning. The mustache, which had been inspired by an early reading of the novels of P. C. Wren, bristled; the brown hair was artfully combed over a bald spot on the peak of his left temple; the pince-nez had been freshly polished, and his cheeks glowed with eau de cologne and benevolence.

As usual, the *Times* lay, unopened, to the right of his plate; a large glass of freshly squeezed orange juice was to the left; directly in front was the electric toaster in which were two slices of whole wheat bread. A little farther away were the jars of lemon marmalade and black raspberry jam, a stick of sweet butter, and the electric coffee pot.

Exactly at eight, as always, Dr. Henry Lyman, philosopher,

educator, world traveler, and in many ways the most sensitive of men, leaped into the dining room as if warming up for a cross-country run. He looked out the open window, took a deep breath, and said, as always, "And how are we feeling this fine day?"

Lydia always had several nifty answers on the tip of her tongue, but she usually said, "Oh, fine, Dada," or else she smiled, like Amy of *Little Women.* She loathed Amy. Why couldn't she have been the one to die?

"Come, gentle spring," said her father, taking several more depressingly deep breaths. "Ethereal mildness, come!"

Lydia sighed; she placed most of the blame for her father's morning behavior on Count Leo Tolstoy. Dr. Lyman had read somewhere that the count "exchanged merry quips with his family at breakfast."

No wonder she had never been able to get beyond Page 102 of *War and Peace,* Page 87 of *Anna Karenina,* and had gotten no further with *Resurrection* than she had with *Das Kapital.* She had, however, read all of *The Kreutzer Sonata* and thought it nonsensical. The count may have known a great deal about big wars, but he knew nothing at all about the more important brushfire wars that occur between men and women.

Besides, anybody who exchanged merry quips with anybody at breakfast was bound to have a screw loose somewhere. How about that pair of socks he didn't change for four years? To Lydia it was not at all odd that the count took off to the woods with his secretary; the wonder was that Countess Tolstoy tried to get him back.

Lydia's affection for her father was subdued in the mornings; she wouldn't have cared who he went where with. As long as he came back before dinner, that is.

On the day we're concerned with here, the dining room was filled with the insistent smell of the lilacs planted just outside.

After a moment and more breathing from the diaphragm, Dr. Henry Lyman, using the voice that was so familiar to students of his Survey of Western Civilization, said, " 'Oh, to be in England now that April's there.' What nonsense! England happens to be particularly distressing in April. It rains almost every day; the air is musty; there is no central heating, or if there is, it doesn't work; and the suicide rate is astronomical.

"I go along with those historians who believe that the British Empire was possible not because the English are warlike —they're not, except in self-defense—or ambitious. Or particularly clever. They were simply trying to get the hell out of England."

"Should I write that down?" asked Lydia, who was pouring her father's coffee. "You may want to use it in one of your lectures."

"I already have, several times, but if I were you, I'd have a notebook in my hands at all times when I'm around. Where would Boswell have been without Dr. Johnson? And, for that matter, where would Dr. Johnson be without Boswell?"

"I don't have a class until ten," said Lydia. "That will give you plenty of time to tell me what's on your mind."

She returned to her book, wondering if anybody had ever really liked Mr. Adam Bede. Perhaps Mrs. Bede; Dinah was not overly endowed with gray matter.

Half an hour later, having finished the orange juice, the toast, and four cups of coffee, having commented on several unsettling items in the *Times,* and having ascertained that his wife was, as usual, shopping (she claimed that things got "picked over" after nine o'clock in the morning), Dr. Henry Lyman looked at his watch, fingered his Phi Beta Kappa key, fondled his mustache, cleared his throat, and said, "I had quite a talk with Simeon Brady last night."

"Oh," Lydia commented.

"He seems to think he's in love with you."

"Oh."

"Are you in love with Simeon Brady?"

"I think so."

"You *think* so. I'm not at all sure that love has anything to do with thought. Indeed, it usually appears to be the opposite. How would you define love, anyway?"

"Is this a quiz? Because if it is, I ought to warn you, I haven't done my homework."

"Since you ask, I'll tell you what I think it is. It is the satisfaction one person finds in close association with another."

"You are a romantic, Pop. More coffee?"

"Thank you. Simeon didn't get around to it, but I gather he is going to ask for your hand in marriage."

"I think he has more than my hand in mind."

Her father laughed. "Suppose I said no? You'd do it anyway. You're nineteen. I think that's ridiculously young to be married, but, after all, it's five years older than Juliet. I hope you make out better than she did.

"One thing occurs to me. You've never lived alone; maybe you should. You might find out things about yourself that you haven't even suspected. Robbie Martinson thinks that you have some talent as a painter; so do I. Why not finish up here? Then I'll stake you to a year at the Art Student's League. Get an apartment in the Village. Maybe you'll be corrupted. I'll take a chance you won't."

Her father rose and stood at the open window once more. "I go along with the fellow who said that in his old age he wanted to regret the things he had done, not the things he hadn't. I have a feeling the bitterest regret of all is not to find out how good we could have been. That's my feeling, of course, not necessarily yours."

"Thanks, Pop. I'd rather marry Simeon."

Lydia looked at her father's loved face and wondered, as she had before and would again, if he were a disappointed man. She would never know. Her father was a private person; he kept his failures to himself. He was a reticent man, and there is not, she thought, an epidemic of that going the rounds these days. She thought, I grew up in a happy household, and those are not exactly overabundant either.

"I've told you," said her father, "I think Simeon has the potential of being extraordinary. But will he be? Aesop, who was in general a pretty smart cookie, placed his bet on the tortoise

rather than the hare. And while it's true that the race is not to
the swift alone, that's the way I'd place my bet."

He kissed his daughter tenderly. "I wish you luck," he said.

"Any last words of advice, like the secret to a happy marriage
is to have a lot of large ashtrays?"

"I've never been an advice giver. Only the people who make
the worst messes of their own lives ever feel qualified to tell
their children how to manage theirs. My own theory about
children is that you spawn them, love them as much as you are
able, kiss and bandage their skinned knees, sympathize with
their unbandagable internal injuries, and try never to lie to
them."

Her father smiled at her, not the public smile of the class-
room, of the college president who was so successful at money
raising, of the author of two highly regarded books of philosophy, not even the smile he bestowed on his wife. It was a smile
that belonged only to Lydia.

He took her hands in his and for a moment held them very
tight. "Here comes the advice I promised not to give. Don't try
to improve Simeon; don't try to remake him in your image of
him. Accept him as he is, warts and all. And I wish you luck; I
wish you all the luck there is."

The following Saturday Simeon took Lydia to the Music Hall
to see *Mrs. Miniver*. He explained to her before, during, and
after the film that it was *drek*—the acting bad, the direction
deplorable, the sentiment mawkish.

Lydia fought back the no-doubt mawkish tears and nodded
vigorously.

Later, she asked if they were going to stay for the Rockettes.
Simeon said, "If you want to, of course, but I can't imagine
why—"

"I don't want to," said Lydia, who loved the Rockettes. "I
can't stand them; they're so tasteless."

"Taste is arguable," said Simeon. "They are without talent;
that is not arguable."

"I don't have much talent, I'm afraid."

"If you had, I wouldn't love you," said Simeon, and then, because that didn't somehow sound right to either of them, he said, "You have an enormous talent for being a woman, which is not to be sneezed at."

Later they went to Sardi's. There was only one those days, on West 44th Street. The bar was crowded with soldiers, sailors, and Marines, drinking heavily. A few of them were, no doubt, on their way to a rendezvous with death, but the majority were on their way to permanent stations at 90 Church Street or Governor's Island, and a very large number were from the choruses of various service shows that were then running on Broadway, an assignment that no doubt had hazards of its own.

Simeon, who had a heart murmur, looked at the servicemen enviously. "For my generation's Hemingway, it's a pity I'm missing the war, but I'm not going to let it throw me the way it did Scott Fitzgerald. They say the fact that he wasn't sent overseas is why he turned to the bottle."

"Nothing's going to throw you," said Lydia.

Simeon leaned across the table and kissed her lustily. "If it weren't for my wobbly heart, I might never have come to Briley and met—what did you say your name was? Will you marry me, Miss Whatsyourname?"

"You're crazy," said Lydia. "In case you don't know, on Saturdays the last decent train is at twelve forty. The next one, the milk train, is at two ten, and it stops everyplace, even the cemeteries."

Simeon reached across the table and took her hand in his. "I ask a girl to marry me, and she talks about trains."

"I didn't think—you're not serious, are you?"

"Dead serious."

Lydia thought of a line she had read somewhere—Viña Delmar?—"She loved him completely." She thought, I love Simeon Brady completely, and I shall continue to love him completely until the day I die, and when I walk down the street, people will point me out. "That's Simeon Brady's wife," the way they would have pointed out Mrs. Michelangelo if there'd been one. Mrs. Simeon Brady, who loves her husband completely. He's the genius, you know, a writer, a musician. My dear, there's nothing he can't do. She has very little talent herself, except for being a woman, which is not to be sneezed at, but she's learned a lot from him. They say he's a wonderful teacher.

She said, "Darling Simeon, of course I'll marry you. I love you, and I'm proud of you, and I hope I can help you, not that you need any help."

"Yes, I do," he said. "I need a lot of help. Beneath this brash exterior lies a mountain of jelly. I'm a great big open, bleeding wound."

"No more bleeding," said Lydia, "no more wounds."

As Simeon paid the check he said to the waiter, "My name is Simeon Brady, and if I were you, I'd keep it in mind. It will soon be on every lip. And this is my child bride, Miss George Sand."

He kissed Lydia again, and: "I'd like to have the Trollope book and the novel published on the same day. *And* a book of poetry *and* have Toscanini conduct my symphony *and* have an exhibition at the Museum of Modern Art.

"You will, my love," said Lydia, "and they'll all get glowing reviews."

"They'll all get lousy reviews," said Simeon.

It turned out they were both wrong, but that is how it began. The ending comes later, as endings do.

A sliver of light was now visible at the window, and from outside came the sounds of people on their way to work, of trucks and buses, of a new day.

Lydia rose heavily, went to the window, pulled up the shade, leaned out, took a deep breath, and said aloud, "And how are we feeling this fine morning?"

She answered the question, *sotto voce,* and then got up the courage to look in a mirror.

I don't look at all like Whistler's mother, but there is in my faded features a remarkable resemblance to his grandmother.

Chapter 5

❧ Three hours later, Lydia turned into the graveled drive leading to the Colonial house with green shutters in which she had spent the first nineteen years of her life.

The house had been built by her grandfather, who had founded Briley College. It was a beautiful house; the rooms were large, high-ceilinged, and gracefully furnished, without ostentation. In the living room, for one, there were two Morris chairs that went back to her father's undergraduate days, the Danish moderns that her mother had brought back from Europe on the first of her many trips there (she made the first when she was sixty-eight), the red leather hassocks that she had found in Marrakesh, and the coffee table with the marble top from Palermo.

Two walls were covered with books, sets of the predictable classics, the two books that her father had written, and those autographed by the famous authors who had lectured at the college and, naturally, paid homage to the son of its founder and himself its president.

On each side of the comfortable, nondescript sofa were the two Chippendale chairs that had belonged to her grandmother. There was an upright piano on which Lydia had practiced endlessly and monotonously as a girl. She had become a good pianist, not good enough to be a concert artist but, certainly, if worst came to worst, good enough to be a teacher. If ever I have to, I am well equipped to make a living for myself discussing Beethoven's last quartets, the philosophy of Kierkegaard, or teaching young ladies their do-re-mi's.

Lydia thought, the house in which I was born and raised is a peaceful house; it is a house in which voices are not raised:

"Lydia, dear, stop screaming; we keep our voices down."

"But my knee hurts."

"I know, darling, but we do our crying in private."

"Why, Grandma?"

"Because it's done, that's why."

Lydia's grandfather had died the year she was born, but her grandmother had lived fifteen years longer, until she was eighty-nine, a small, plump woman who always wore handsome black dresses and a blue cameo from Naples that she left to Lydia when she died.

Once, maybe when Lydia was six, maybe eight, she heard her mother call from the kitchen, "It's time to get up, Lydia. You'll be late for school."

"Let the girl sleep; life begins soon enough."

Lydia's grandfather had once been sent to the Philippines as an educational adviser, and during what in those innocent days was known as an uprising, her grandmother had held off twenty insurrectionists at gunpoint.

"Grandma, if they'd tried to force their way into the house, would you have shot them?"

"Without question."

"All twenty?"

"I only had ten bullets."

Lydia parked the car in front of the terrace on which she and Simeon had stood on the windy August afternoon they were married. From the music building, which was several blocks away, had come the sound of a girl's shaky voice embarking on an aria from *La Bohème,* and from a house down the street a radio announcer was saying that American troops had landed near Casablanca.

As the minister said the solemn final words of the ceremony, the nest of a Baltimore oriole fell from the branch of a massive oak Lydia's grandfather had planted.

When Simeon kissed her, he whispered, "Did you see that nest fall?"

Lydia said she had, and Simeon said, "If I were one of the symbolism fellows, I'd be scared. But I'm not a symbolism fellow."

Lydia kissed him back. "We're going to be very happy together."

"And rich and famous. We'll be on the cover of *Time*. 'America's foremost writer. And wife.' "

"Mr. and Mrs. Simeon Brady. It will be on every lip."

The terrace had not been much changed by the years, and neither had the hills beyond. Then as now, in late April, there were translucent new leaves on the beech and linden trees, white blossoms on the wild apple, and here and there, like frosting on the cake, pink dogwood.

"I'll be back," Lydia promised the hills and the trees. I belong here. I like this house, this town, this college, these people. Don't tell anybody, though; if word got around, I might be picked up as a fanatic of some kind.

Lydia's mother set a basket of hot scones on the vermilion tray she had brought back from her trip to Japan two years before.

"How was Sybil's party?" she asked.

"Nice. A lot of people sent you their love, including Robbie Martinson, who was there with his new missus. They're driving to New Haven on Sunday and may stop by."

"Good. I like Robbie. What's the new one like?"

"A little taller than the other three, maybe three foot, two."

Lydia and her mother laughed. Simeon had once said, "When you and Helga get together, you're like two thieves."

"Robbie's such a nice man," said her mother. "Why does he go out of his way to marry such peculiar women?"

She placed a plate of tiny jelly sandwiches on the tray, and Lydia asked a question she'd probably had in mind asking for some years. "Did you and Father ever think of splitting up?"

"I thought of it. Who human does not? But I never really *considered* it for very long. Your father did leave once, though."

Lydia looked at her mother, surprised.

"You and Simeon and the children were at Berkeley for the summer session, and I told everybody around the campus that your father was doing 'research' in the city, which had an element of truth, I suppose.

"He was gone six weeks, and when he came back, his tail between his legs, he begged forgiveness. And I forgave him. He wanted to tell me all about it, but I wouldn't listen to a word. Not even who it was. I imagine he'd discovered that it's one thing to spend a few nights on a bearskin rug—bearskin rugs were very popular in those days—and quite another to settle down on one. They must be scratchy.

"And breakfast, however you spend the night, is not easy unless you are fond of the other person. I was fond of your father, but I managed, whenever possible, to avoid having breakfast with him. Then, of course, there are lunch and dinner and, usually, some very long evenings and nights. I've always felt that, at most, you can't make love more than an hour or so out of the twenty-four. Suppose you work eight and sleep eight and eat two, that still leaves five hours to fill, which can be an eternity with someone you don't love."

"Did you ever wish Pop hadn't come back?"

"Momentarily, now and again, but he was, all in all, a large man, and I managed to make a place for myself at his side, quite happily most of the time. I'm afraid—I can say it now; I never could before—that Simeon is not so large a man.

"When they were looking for a successor to Dr. Bronson, two members of the board came to see me, unofficially, of course, and asked whether or not I thought Simeon was big enough to be president of the college.

"I knew how desperately he wanted to be and how much you wanted it for him, and so I hemmed and hawed and beat around the bush, but, finally, I had to say what I thought. I said no."

"Let's have our coffee in the backyard."

Lydia picked up the tray and she thought, the trustees didn't come to me, and perhaps it's just as well.

That morning Simeon had gotten bravely out of bed, had bravely kissed her, had bravely eaten a great breakfast—three eggs, Canadian bacon, toast, and wild strawberry jam.

"*Wild* strawberry," Simeon had said. "What did you have to do to get that at I.G.A.?"

"What goes on between Mr. Geonomo and me is our own affair, but all for a good cause."

"Besides, he probably thinks that now that I'm going to be president, I'll throw some of the college's business his way."

In Simeon's mind, thought Lydia, the meeting of the board of trustees is already over, and the victory is won. And then she thought, no, he doesn't think that. Now with the memory of so many defeats in the past and none of any victories. He's as edgy and frightened as I am.

She said, continuing the mood of a victory won, "Darling, we'll have to get some painting done, the living room off-white, don't you think? After all, the house of the president and his first lady can't appear dowdy. Not even shabby-genteel. We have to be all bright and shining, inside and out." Please, God, just this once let there be a happy ending. He'll be a very good president. I promise, and I'll be a proud, persevering wife, stalwart and strong, shoulder to shoulder, trusting and true. Check one.

"And I've got to get some clothes," said Simeon. "It won't do to have the president of Briley go around in a shiny suit. And you have to, too."

"From here on in I'll wear only Paris originals."

A few minutes later, Simeon, whistling, started to his nine o'clock class.

"I'm praying," said Lydia.

"It's a shoe-in," said Simeon. "We've got those trustees in the bag."

"Darling," said Lydia, "if they're foolish enough to make a mistake, I love you very much."

"They're too smart for that," said Simeon.

Lydia got through the day; you always do. There are closets to be cleaned, dresses to be pressed, shampoos and baths, and reading to deaden the mind: husband-holding, how to; adorable at fifty, how to; not a line in my face at ninety-four, how to; not a thought in my head at sixty, how to. You can always get through the day. How to.

She was on the porch when the boy brought the afternoon paper.

The name in the headline was not Simeon's, and she could now admit what she had known all along; there had never been a chance that it would be his. "Dr. Once Over Lightly," his colleagues called him. "The professor of nothing very much," "a specialist in superficiality," and, kindest and cruelest of all, "Simeon Brady is brilliant but unstable."

There was the taste of ashes in her mouth, but Lydia did not cry; she went into the kitchen and made the dinner that she sensed would never be eaten. The rib roast and Yorkshire pudding that were to have been the victory dinner were baked funeral meats instead.

Simeon got home shortly after midnight, smelling of Scotch and an unsubtle perfume, smelling of defeat and despair.

Lydia looked up from the unread page of the unread book. "Hi," she said. "Have you had dinner, darling?"

"They wanted a numbskull, not an educator, and that's what they got," said Simeon. "It's the beginning of the end of Briley."

"They'll learn. Wouldn't you like some roast beef? A sandwich?"

"You have the mind of a retarded two-year-old. Can't you raise your mind above the level of a roast beef sandwich?"

"I'm sorry," said Lydia. "I think they've made a mistake."

He turned on her, with drunken hatred in the foggy eyes. "You never thought I'd get it, did you?"

"I hoped you would."

"But you didn't believe in me. You've never thought I was half the man your father was, have you?"

"I love you, Simeon," she said, and for the first time it was a lie. Or perhaps—it happens that way—it was the first time she knew it was a lie.

There were tears in Simeon's eyes, and she held his hand and looked at him. The image was blurred, but she saw him more clearly than she ever had before or ever would again. She saw that Simeon was drowning and knew that she could not swim well enough to save both of them.

And she thought, poor, weak, defeated, defeating Simeon, the hare who has once more lost to the tortoise. And she thought, the boy who had the potential of being extraordinary is at fifty only a boy.

"Poor baby," she said, "poor, dear baby."

And she thought, what is the sound of a breaking heart?

As her mother poured another cup of coffee for Lydia, two bearded boys who looked to be in their middle teens raced past the house on their bicycles, screaming friendly epithets at each other.

"They're from the new dormitory," said her mother. "At the garden club yesterday afternoon, Mrs. Russell wanted to get up a petition against the students who're running it. Apparently they advocate asking all kinds of dangerous questions about the existence of God, the possibility of error in certain of our foreign policies, and so on. Mrs. Russell says the entire community has been contaminated."

"You live much closer to it than she does," said Lydia. "Have you been contaminated?"

"Unhappily, no. Mrs. Russell further says that all sorts of 'shameful shenanigans' go on there. I urged her to be more specific. After all, I'm seventy-four years old, and it's high time I found out what a 'shameful shenanigan' is. I might want to participate in one. She wouldn't say, though, either wouldn't or couldn't."

"Mrs. Russell is a busybody and a gossip," said Lydia, feeling virtuous.

"I take a certain active interest in the affairs of others, but I call it analyzing people instead of gossip. The semantics are all-important in these matters. And I wouldn't think of trying to interfere. Are you packed?"

"I have been for a week."

"You were always an early packer. You get that from me. And getting to trains and planes ahead of time. They say it's a mark of insecurity. Maybe so, but I'm inclined to think it means only that there are some people who would rather be early than late. Neither a vice nor a virtue, and not particularly significant."

Lydia laughed. "Why did it take me so long to appreciate you?"

"You had to forgive me for being half responsible for the fact that you were born. You had to get over my not being a Brahmin, and, worse yet, having an embarrassing accent, and besides, there wasn't much to appreciate until after your father's death. I hadn't had the time or, more likely, taken the time to find out if I was a person."

Until after the death of Lydia's father, most people at Briley thought of his wife as the woman he had chosen to be his housekeeper and, incidentally, married. After all, before her marriage Helga Lyman had been first a maid, then a waitress, and, before either of those, a lady barber in Sweden.

When Henry Lyman died of a coronary at the unseemly age of fifty-eight, it was felt that his widow, who was ten years younger, would find the rest of her life an anticlimax. What in the world would the poor, retiring thing do with herself? And she had that embarrassing accent, too.

After a decent interval of mourning, six months, what Helga Lyman did do was enroll as a freshman at the college of which her husband had been president. Several members of the faculty were mortified, and so was her family, which consisted of her daughter Lydia.

If Helga Lyman was aware of that fact, she never mentioned it. She majored in European history, with a minor in speech. In less than a year the accent was gone, and in a little less than three, she received her Bachelor of Arts degree, *cum laude*. She wrote a Master's thesis on the life and works of Emanuel Swedenborg and continued in the graduate school, studying art appreciation, medieval history, and the Russian novel. She taught herself Russian at the age of fifty-eight.

And she traveled ("always alone, which everybody does anyway, but not everybody realizes it") part of every year. The rest she spent in the Colonial house, entertaining and listening to the troubles of a great many students, gardening, reading, and looking on the world and its inhabitants with a beady but amused eye.

"Besides," said her mother, "you were a seven-months baby, and they never have an easy time of it. I read the other day— I forget where—about a woman who was one, and she said, 'I've been looking for those two extra months of warmth ever since.'"

The two bearded boys screamed past again, in the opposite direction, and Lydia's mother said, "Every year the beards vary in length, cut, and, lately, in color. Mrs. Russell says that proves they're sick. I maintain it's just another sympton of the unending search."

"I just wish they bathed more," said Lydia, "but that may be a personal prejudice."

"People over forty never think the young take enough baths. It's only a question of habit. In his entire life Frederick the Great never had a bath, and he was a remarkably healthy man. However, I've always thought that's the reason Voltaire wrote him so many letters instead of going to see him."

Lydia rose. "I've got to get cracking. I've got all those last-minute things to do."

"Are you excited?"

"And a little scared."

The air was suddenly chill; the sun had disappeared behind an egg-shaped white cloud.

"Naturally. But you'll have a lovely time. Travel may not be the chief end in life, but it's away up there, and it comes as close to bringing back childhood—I don't mean second childhood, either—as anything I know. You start *looking* at things, and the colors are bright again and the landscapes are vivid and people exciting. I envy you."

"Sure you won't come with me?"

"Positive, although I'll regret missing Christopher's wedding. Give him all my love, and don't worry about Day. I'll look in on her every once in a while. Besides, Raph is a rock of a man."

"I hate good-byes," said Lydia.

In reply her mother said, "The year your father died, once the shock was over and the tears were ended, I discovered something really rather pleasant. I found out that I was a person, whole and complete. I think women always have some doubt about that, particularly if they've devoted themselves to a man.

"I haven't been much help to you these last months. I felt that you had to heal thyself. We all do, whether we're physicians or not. I've thought a lot about you, though, and about Simeon, and about marriage. I'm a great thinker, you know, not deep but a lot.

"It may well be that marriage is impossible. Some people say that domesticity is the enemy; others claim it's the daily erosion of two people living together. I don't know, but some marriages do last. Maybe it's because when love is gone, when affection is over, what's left is that the two people involved are used to each other, and it's too much trouble to get used to someone else.

"I don't think you and Simeon ever got used to each other. It just wasn't possible because Simeon, poor man, has in fifty years not made peace with himself. How could he make peace with anybody else?"

Lydia kissed her mother's cheek. "I'll miss you," she said.

"I'll see you in London in August," said her mother, "and we'll have lunch at the Savoy and go hog wild shopping at Harrod's. I may even buy myself a mini-skirt. Now, scat."

Chapter 6

A white Triumph was parked beside the front porch of Lydia's house. When she saw it, she was tempted to turn her aging Chevrolet around and race off in the opposite direction.

But she didn't; one doesn't. She sighed inwardly and turned into the drive, parking the Chevrolet behind the shiny Triumph. She spoke to the elderly stranger seated inside.

"Hello, Simeon."

He looked up from the book—Simeon always had a book in his hands; he would have looked naked without one—and said, "Ta." Somewhere, surely not at Magdalene College, Simeon had gotten the idea that "Ta" was the British way of saying hello. No one had ever told him he was wrong, or if they had, he wasn't listening, so, "Ta."

"I hope you haven't been waiting long," said Lydia, the first thing that came to mind.

"Not long."

After Simeon and Lydia were divorced, Sybil had said, "There'll come a day when you'll see Simeon and feel totally uninvolved."

That day has not yet come, thought Lydia. What I feel right now is nervous. My hands are trembling and the palms are moist, but on the other hand my throat is dry.

"Come in," she said, hoping her voice sounded hospitable. At such times you can't be sure.

She walked onto the porch and unlocked the front door. The clapboard house had been built in the garish style of the late 1921's. It was not grand, not remarkable, not even particularly comfortable, but Lydia had always liked it. The house and the small acreage on which it stood had been a wedding gift from her father.

As she stepped into the hallway, Lydia thought, Simeon is going to say, "How are things in the house at Pooh Corner?" He has been saying that with some regularity since the day we moved in. On that day he looked briefly at the house and said, "It's Pooh, pure Pooh, pure A. A. Milne, sheer lower-middle-class piffle."

"Don't you really like it?" She was a child bride, no question of that.

"It's ordinary, utterly ordinary, but it'll do for the nonce," Simeon had said. "We're going to build a house of our own and abandon Pooh to the ordinary people who live ordinary lives. Pooh, pooh."

But they were never able to build the house of their own, and what can you say about that except, "I'm sorry"?

"How are things in the house at Pooh Corner?" said Simeon.

"Fine. Just fine. Would you like a drink?"

"No, thanks." Simeon seated himself on the Queen Anne chair and started to teeter back and forth. For some twenty years, Lydia had been sure that he was going to break the legs, but he never had.

"I'm on the wagon," he said. "Congratulate me."

"I think that's wonderful."

"It isn't that I was a problem drinker. It's a matter of discipline. It does one good to give up something one has grown to depend on. I know that discipline isn't highly thought of these days, particularly by those who remember the corruption of the word as it was used by the dictators."

Simeon threw back his head in a gesture that Lydia had once thought of as defiant. As always, a lock of the now-white hair fell over his forehead. He wore it in a style that had once been affected by certain members of the United States Senate. It curled around the edges, and a student who felt he deserved a higher grade had once said that Simeon looked like a wilted chrysanthemum.

Simeon was saying, "And I haven't even had a sip of beer for three months."

"Do you feel a lot better?"

"To the contrary, I feel very much worse."

They laughed, and for a moment it was like the old days, when they had laughed a great deal. At the end of a relationship, when you are drawing up a bill of indictment against the partner, you tend to forget the good times. In the beginning Simeon and I did laugh at the same things.

"How about some coffee and a sandwich?"

"Just the coffee, thanks," said Simeon.

As Lydia started back to the living room with the coffee, she thought, Simeon will have moved the Buddha.

The Buddha was of green jade and had been brought back from Java by her father, and since he knew she loved it, he left it to her in his will.

She had placed it on the hall table, where it caught the light from a tiny stained-glass window. But Simeon had moved it out of sight, behind some books, where it had stayed until after their separation. Then Lydia once again put it on the hall table.

Lydia looked into the mirror in the passageway that led to the living room. Not bad, she thought. The beige suit was well cut, and it became her and was perfect for traveling.

There are two things I can be sure of, she thought; Simeon will not like the suit, and he will have moved the Buddha.

The Buddha was on the bookshelf behind *The Charterhouse of Parma*.

Simeon toasted her with the coffee, then, "That a new suit?"

"Uh-huh."

"It's nice, but don't you think it makes you a little heavy in the hip area?"

"As a matter of fact, I don't."

"You're looking in good health, anyway. A little extra weight becomes you. Frances Trollope, when she returned from Cincinnati in 1820, wrote, 'The women are without exception sadly undernourished in appearance.'"

Lydia wanted to say, "Mother Trollope certainly had a ready observation to fit every occasion." She did say, "What did you want to talk to me about, Simeon?"

"First, this," said Simeon.

Lydia untied the package, which was wrapped in silver paper, with gold string. Inside was a cashmere travel shawl in pastel shades of green and blue.

"It's beautiful," said Lydia. "Thank you."

"Penny picked it out," said Simeon, "and she brought it home on approval, but I thought it looked like you."

"It's lovely," said Lydia.

True, I have always associated travel rugs with little old ladies wearing lace at their faded throats, a stage I haven't quite reached yet. As Mother Trollope would be the first to point out, I am too well nourished, especially in the hip area. But from the vantage point of twenty-three, which Penny is, a lady of my years is doubtless considered someone ready to totter into the grave.

Oh, I know lots about Penny. What is this nonsense about the wife being the last to know? The minute Simeon's romance —I'm being Victorian; we could use more of that—with Penelope, long for Penny, began, the woods, the town, the gown, the supermarket, the superette, the meetings of the American Association of University Women, the League of Women Voters, and the congregation of the First Methodist Episcopal of Briley were jammed with volunteers who couldn't wait to tell me all.

"It's really none of my business, Mrs. Brady, but I felt, we being best friends and all, and I know if my husband were . . . I'd want some really good friend to do me the favor of . . ."

Many of these best friends I had never laid eyes on before, and if my luck holds out . . .

I was told Penny's age—in the beginning she was twenty-two —that she was a graduate student in English, was considered bright, and at Simeon's suggestion was writing a thesis on the novels of Willa Cather. I was informed that Penny was vaguely pretty, had red hair, a hollow giggle, and had been around some, quite some. Ask the Sigma Nus and the boys at the Phi Gam house.

Lydia had seen Penelope (Penny) once, on a street corner, waiting either for a streetcar or for Simeon. The red hair was true enough, but she was more than vaguely pretty; she was beautiful, and she had a sensual-looking body.

Lydia felt sure that Penelope had been named for the faithful wife of·Ulysses who, if Homer was to be believed, was so beset by wooers that to scare them off, she said that she couldn't have any truck with them until she'd finished weaving whatever it was. A sweater, socks, a muffler, a codpiece?

Then, also according to Homer, she unraveled every night what she'd done during the day. It went on for years like that.

Homer, thought Lydia, was a great man and a great writer, and since I am neither, who am I to doubt his word? It does seem to me, though, that Penelope's wooers weren't overly bright. Otherwise, they'd have noticed that she was a tediously slow weaver. And they could have offered to help, too. Two can weave faster than one.

Penelope, thought Lydia, and I mean Simeon's Penelope, the redhead over there—she can't be waiting for a streetcar; there aren't any in Briley—doesn't look to me like a weaver, not to mention an unweaver. Neither is easy, nor is constancy.

But I've got news for Penelope (Penny). She won't last. Not with Simeon. Doris didn't; Henrietta didn't, and neither did Georgiana nor Helen nor Betty. And so forth. They never last. Not with Simeon. They are all part of a sad, insistent search for love, from all members of all political parties, including cuddly Communists, from the wind in the trees, the sand on the beach, and every star in the sky.

In a sense, Penelope did last, though.

"I'm finishing the book," Simeon was saying. "I've written eight pages in the last three weeks."

Lydia looked at him, hoping that it was true, that after all the years, all the broken promise and promises, he was at last finishing the book on the Trollopes.

"That's wonderful," she said, knowing it was a lie.

She looked at her watch. "I've got to finish packing. What did you want to talk to me about?"

"You're still going to Portugal?"

"Still."

"And to Franco Spain?"

"Still."

"Do me just one favor. When you walk down the Avenida José Antonio in Madrid, kindly remember that it is named after a Fascist thug who alone was responsible for the deaths of tens of thousands of innocent people."

"I know that, but I can't bring back the innocent dead, and I want to see our son and the girl he's going to marry. What did you want to talk to me about?"

Simeon hesitated, and then, not exactly in reply, he said, "I've been thinking about the night I told you I wanted a divorce."

Lydia saw that Simeon believed what he was saying. That was the way he remembered it; maybe that was the way he had to remember it.

It had been an unfriendly night in November. The wind was menacing, and there was an occasional lackluster attempt at snow. It was Emily Brontë weather, inside the house and out.

Lydia and Simeon had—Lydia had, anyway—planned to go to a concert of the college glee club; they were singing Purcell.

"I'll be home at six," Simeon had said, "and if anything should happen, I'll call you, but nothing will happen. And I hope you're going to wear the basic black; we're sitting next to President Mumbles and his mentally underprivileged wife. She'll probably be in sackcloth and ashes."

"I shall try to dress well enough not to embarrass you, Simeon."

"She probably doesn't know the difference between Purcell and Richard Rodgers. See you at six."

After Lydia cooked dinner—chicken curry, for those of you who are sticklers for detail—she dressed for the concert. She chose the basic black, although it had been basic for quite some time, like its wearer. But if she had worn anything else, there'd have been a scene; there might be anyway, but why take a chance?

By the time Lydia had on her best with her face, it was five thirty, and she set the table.

At seven—she'd had a martini, and we all know what drinking alone leads to—she called Simeon's office; no answer. (Had she expected one?) She waited dinner until eight, no Simeon, no call, and so far no surprises. She turned off the oven; the curry was overcooked, and she found it inedible.

At eight thirty she changed from the basic black into a pink dressing gown and runover house slippers. (Aren't they always?) She played some Purcell on the piano.

Farewell, love, and Sylvia, too.
Long have I been unregarded,
Sighs and tears still unrewarded. [Was it ever thus?]

She read the afternoon paper; nobody anywhere was up to any good. What's got into people, anyway? She thumbed through *TV Guide;* nothing of any interest unless she stayed up until five thirty the following morning. They were showing a Norma Shearer movie she'd seen nine times when it first played at the Orpheum in Briley. She'd once known practically every line of dialogue by heart, but it was all gone except for one cherished speech. When asked if she loved Robert Montgomery, Miss Shearer replied, "I love him more than the earth, the sun, the sky, the moon, more than anything."

Lydia found herself laughing at the lovely, fraudulent lines, and then she found herself crying. After a while she asked herself the question to which, up to then, there had been no answer: "Is this all there is?"

But on that discomforting night in November—it had begun to snow—she answered it.

No, this is not all, not remotely. Somewhere beyond the vengeful wind there is sunshine; there are interesting sights unseen, fascinating people unmet, illuminating conversations unheard. I want to see some of these sights, meet some of these people, participate in some of these conversations. I want, from here on in, to arrange for my own punishment; I want out.

Selfish, you say? Perhaps. Harsh? Maybe, but then so was the night. If there had been a moon, if the wind had been less disquieting, if the falling snow had looked less secondhand, who knows what might have happened?

At a little before eleven, Lydia heard Simeon's uncertain step on the porch and heard him slam the front door of the house he had lived in for twenty-four years and hated. He walked with drunken dignity into the living room he despised, and, not looking at the woman he had married (how he felt about her we will never know), he said, "Am I late?"

To the idiotic question, Lydia made an idiotic reply. "It's eleven," she said, "hardly late for dinner, if we were in Spain, that is."

"Oh, it's going to be one of our sarcastic evenings."

"It's not going to be any kind of evening. Dinner's on the table if you want it. A little cold, of course."

"If you're interested, I'm late because—"

"I'm not interested."

"I'm late because—" There had been term papers to grade. He was working on the lecture he was going to deliver the following week at . . . And old Dr. Stewart had dropped in and bent his ear. Simeon felt sorry for the poor old basket. Three excuses when one would have done. Simeon had never been a good liar, which was, I expect, to his credit.

Simeon approached the bar as if it were an accomplice. "Want a drink?" he inquired of the wall. Then, since there was no reply, he said, "I think I'll have one. I started to telephone you (still to the wall), and then—"

Lydia wanted to say, "I can't save you, Simeon. I'm not a good enough swimmer to keep both of us afloat, not anymore. Can't you see how spent I am?"

What she did say, rather quietly, too, was, "I want a divorce, Simeon."

Simeon's surprise was genuine enough. "What's that supposed to mean?"

"I want a divorce. You can get it, or I will. Whichever you prefer."

"You'll play hell getting a divorce, I can tell you that. If you think you can blow up some silly campus gossip—"

Lydia started for the stairs. "Good night, Simeon," she said.

Simeon grabbed her arm, his nails digging into it; Lydia was grateful for the pain.

"On what grounds?" he shouted. "To get a divorce you have to have grounds."

On the grounds of boredom, thought Lydia, boredom with the Trollopes, Anthony and Frances, boredom with the breath that smells always of Scotch, boredom with the suits that reek of a strange perfume, boredom with the excuses for failure, boredom with the lies about infidelity, with the plausible reasons for work undone, for mistakes, for sin, for foolishness.

I want a divorce on the grounds that I need peace, not an isolated hour of it, not a stolen moment now and again. I want a peaceful life. I am too old to do battle. I am too tired for hatred.

I want a divorce on the grounds that there is more to life than this.

She said, "If you like, I'll get the divorce in Mexico, and I hope that you'll be gone from the house when I get back."

"That was always the trouble," said Simeon. "It was always your house, your land, your property, left to you by your father, the great windbag, the distinguished nonentity."

"It was always our house," said Lydia, "but beginning tonight it's mine."

"You never gave a tinker's damn for me," said Simeon.

Lydia started to say, "But I loved you completely."

She didn't, though. She realized that everyone sees the stage from a different angle, and where emotions are concerned, there is no exact truth. So she said again, "Good night, Simeon."

After she went to bed, the panic began.

That's about all. Two weeks after the divorce—uncontested, of course—Simeon married Penny. The wedding took place in the office of Justice of the Peace Clyde Johnson, a rather smelly old man who had long been in need of a new upper plate. Clyde is eighty-four.

Lydia was told several times that Clyde forgot a good half of what he was supposed to say, and since his eyesight was gone, he couldn't read the service. He had to improvise. Considering Clyde's age, he was said to have done well. What was surprising according to Norma Palmer, Clyde's secretary, who was the witness, was that the bridegroom was intoxicated. "Sim Brady was drunk as a lord," Norma said, or was said to have said. "He could hardly stand up straight, and if I'd been Clyde, I wouldn't of married them."

In addition, according to Norma, who told several people, who told Lydia, the bride giggled once in midceremony. The groom turned to her angrily and said, "Would it be asking too much if you'd keep quiet just this once?"

Under the circumstances, Norma couldn't help wondering if the thing was legal.

"What did you want to talk to me about?" Lydia asked again.

"It's about Day," said Simeon. "I saw her in New York yesterday."

"You must be mistaken. Ralph and Day have been in Dallas since Tuesday."

"I'm hardly mistaken about my own daughter. Day was walking on Fifth Avenue with Kevin Stewart. I shouted, but she and Kevin ducked into Sak's. Kevin's the one she should have married, of course."

"I want you to go now, Simeon," said Lydia, "and I don't want you to come back."

"The next time you'll beg me," he shouted, and he threw his empty cup in the fireplace, much the way he had the night of the reception for the new president.

Watching the dangerous child who had been her husband, the golden boy who was no longer golden, Lydia thought, I have with pain learned many things these last few months. I have learned that it is better to be alone in an empty room than alone in a room with someone. I have learned that I do not have to settle for second best, in people or in anything else; I have graduated, degree or no degree.

"Good-bye, Simeon," she said.

"You'll beg me on bended knee," he said. That was all, except for the final slamming of the door and the fact that the house shook a little.

They put out all those marriage manuals, thought Lydia, hundreds of them, and they are all filled with good advice to which nobody pays the slightest attention, although the books do often come in handy as doorstops.

My only advice, young lovers, and it's free, is this:

Never marry a child, unless you're one yourself, that is.

She returned the green Buddha to the library table. She put the green and blue travel rug on the bookshelf, behind *The Charterhouse of Parma.*

Chapter 7

As Lydia brought her bags downstairs, she thought, I don't want to be angry like this again, not ever. And she thought, Simeon couldn't possibly have seen Day in New York yesterday. Ralph and Day are in Dallas and will be until next Tuesday.

How like Simeon to plant doubts, to sow worries, to cultivate unease. Ralph and Day are fine. The last time I saw them, four nights ago, they were holding hands, rubbing, touching, and Day was saying, "Since we're getting rid of Mother by shipping her off to Europe, and since we're going off to Dallas, Texas, to bring them culture and enlightenment, I think we ought to celebrate by getting a little potted."

"*I'm* not getting rid of your mother," said Ralph. "*I* like her. For one thing, if it weren't for her, no you."

And his eyes followed Day's every movement.

Day and Ralph are fine. We said our good-byes Tuesday morning and they won't be back in New York for a week, and there is no reason in the world for me to worry or to waste money on a long-distance telephone call.

"There's a thirty-minute delay in calls to Dallas," said the long-distance operator, who was George Carson's wife; Lydia and George had gone to high school together. "I'll call you back, Mrs. Brady."

"Please do. I'm leaving in forty-five minutes."

"I saw in the paper. You're going all the way to Europe. Do have a good time."

After she put down the phone, Lydia mixed herself a drink, a strong one, and seated herself on the Queen Anne chair that her grandmother and Day's great-grandmother had taken all the way to the Philippines and back. She thought, Sybil, damn her, is right. I love both my children, and I have tried neither to show favoritism nor feel it, but I suppose I have loved Day more. She needed me more.

Christopher was born self-sufficient as well as blond, blue-eyed, and beautiful. And he learned very early that all he had to do to get what he wanted in life was to smile, which, naturally, he did most of the time. He never cried. What did he have to cry about?

"He's the most beautiful baby in the history of the world," his mother once commented, objectively, to Sybil.

"That takes in a lot of territory," said Sybil. "Who knows, for instance, what Michelangelo's David looked like at that age. And there is always the possibility that Christopher may not be overly bright. However, if he grows up that pretty, he won't have to have brains."

Day, who was born the following October on a rainy Wednesday afternoon, cried a great deal and was underweight and, as a baby, not pretty. But she had gray-blue eyes that looked directly into the place you lived and forgave you for any inadequacies noted there.

"She's going to be just like you," said Sybil. "She's going to *feel* everything."

And it was true, Day was a feeler. She was a lover, a people-lover and a principle-lover, a truster, a believer in elves and all manner of Druids and in true love.

From the beginning, there was never any doubt that Day would marry. As a little girl she didn't play with her dolls; she lived with them, warmed milk for them, sewed clothes for them, chose furniture for their houses and constantly rearranged it, gave comfort to them, and never punished them. Why should she?

"They're just as good as gold, all of them," she said.

Once, when Day was nine, Lydia came across a sheet of paper on which was written:

Things to do today

1. Be nice to Miss Applegate. Try to think how I would feel if I were old and ugly and smelled all over.

2. Read at least twenty pages of *Idylls of the King*.

3. Practice for at least two hours. *At least*.

4. Help mother cook one new thing.

5. Think about whether it is more important for a husband to be good-looking or to have a good disposition.

Day's decision about the last item we will put aside for the time being, but she never changed her mind about any of the other four.

She was always nice to smelly old women, derelict dogs, abandoned cats, hungry goats, chickenless hens, henless chickens, and all manner of people needing something, usually affection.

She continued to read, and she thought about and understood what she had read. She became a superb cook, for which Lydia, naturally, took full credit, although the fact that Day graduated *magna cum laude* from Cordon Bleu may have played a part.

She loved music and continued to practice, and by the time she was twelve had learned all that Lydia had to teach. When she was sixteen, the head of the school of music at Briley came to Lydia and said, "Day is going to be a superb pianist one of these days, if she continues to work, and I think she will. The question she'll have to face is whether she wants to go on and become a professional."

When Lydia mentioned the matter to Day and asked, "How would you like being a concert pianist?" Day said, "I'd loathe it. I have no intention of having a career, and I'm not going to apologize for putting *occupation: housewife* on my tax return."

At Wellesley, where Day was almost as good a student as she had been at Cordon Bleu, she met a number of girls who tried to persuade her to change her mind.

"When I say I want to get married, they look at me as if I weren't bright. They all want to be tycoonesses or famous ac-

tresses or write. I'm not of a marrying generation, and I gather
you weren't either. It was the generation in between that had
broods of children."

"How about you, broods?"

"No. I want a small family. Three or four. If you have more
than that, you can't love them in the right way."

"What's the right way?" asked Lydia.

"You should know," said her daughter.

From the time Day was fourteen there were always boys, and,
like Christopher's girls, they were remarkably similar. They
all talked a great deal, mostly about the arts. They were all
about to rewrite the Bible, take over the Philharmonic, make
a musical comedy out of *Lohengrin,* or they composed folk songs
and without any urging at all ran through their entire output,
accompanying themselves on the guitar. The folk singers were
always prolific, and you'd be amazed at how many had adenoidal
problems, among others.

Day never seemed to prefer one to the other. She treated them
warmly, laughed at their jokes (not easy), listened to their am-
bitions (tiring), and made each feel that he was destined for
greatness (simple).

They all, excepting one, seemed to Lydia insignificant, but
Day never asked her what she thought, and Lydia had learned
not to volunteer, not in this area. She did dislike Kevin Stewart,
though, more than all the rest put together. Let's face it; she
loathed him.

Does it surprise you that Simeon thought Kevin was charming, in every way an exemplary young man, and close to being
a genius?

In odd moments of time, Lydia prayed that Day would marry
well. And if it's Kevin, I'll murder him in cold blood, and any
jury in the land will award me a medal. All I'd have to do
would be to show them a picture of the little snot. A mercy killing if ever I saw one.

What did Day think of Kevin? Stick around.

The important thing here is that during spring vacation of

her senior year at Wellesley, Day called from the city, where she was staying with a friend, and said, "Are you and Sim still coming to the city tonight?"

Lydia at once recognized the excitement in her voice.

She said, "Unless Columbia University has banned discussion of the novels of Anthony Trollope, we are."

"Could you come and have drinks with me?"

"With pleasure. Is everything all right?"

"Superbly so. I want you to meet somebody special. He's an architect, and he's a genius. Everybody says so, and his name's Ralph Gunderson. We'll meet in the lobby of the Algonquin at six, and, Mother, I do hope you like him."

"I'm sure I will." There had been a great many geniuses in Day's past, but she had never before said that she hoped her mother would like them.

"It's probably not Day's idea that we meet," said Simeon. "It's probably his. He's probably hustling for his firm to get the commission for the Fine Arts Center."

"It seems a rather indirect way of getting a commission."

"Nonsense. His firm saw in the *Times* that I'm chairman of the building committee, and young Gunderson managed to get introduced to Day, which I would imagine is not difficult."

"About ready?"

"If I had a dollar for every time you've asked me that question, I could have given the money to build the Fine Arts Center myself," said Simeon.

He picked up his lecture notes, started for the door, and added, "I shall make it clear to young Lochinvar that this particular commission has nothing to do with his friendship with my daughter. I can handle these smooth young operators who seem to feel that if they *know* somebody, that's all there is to it."

Ralph Gunderson was six feet, five in height, and his body was in every way enormous—shoulders, feet, hands, even the features of his face, which looked as if it had been carved by a careless sculptor who had other things on his mind and had left before quite finishing the job.

His hair was the color of summer wheat, and even if he had taken the time and the trouble, it seemed unlikely that it would ever be tamed. The weathered skin of his face looked as if he had just come in from plowing the south forty. The suit he wore was double-breasted and the trousers were a little too long, while the sleeves of the jacket were somewhat too short.

When Simeon and Lydia came into the lobby of the Algonquin, Ralph stood up and almost knocked over Day's drink. He said that he was pleased to meet Lydia, and then he shook Simeon's hand, causing minor bruises and abrasions.

"I'm told you're an architect," said Simeon, nursing his hand, which he used frequently in his lectures, particularly when he got excited about the abominable actions of Sir Hugh Clavering.

"Yes, sir," said Ralph Gunderson.

"Where did you go to school?" asked Lydia, a question she placed on the same level as, "And what do you want to be when you grow up, little man?"

"Harvard, ma'am," said Ralph Gunderson.

"What kind of buildings do you do?" asked Simeon.

"Beautiful ones," said Ralph Gunderson.

Some time later Simeon said, "We're planning to build a new Fine Arts Center at Briley."

"Briley?" said Ralph.

"I told you, you jerk," said Day. "That's where Simeon teaches."

Simeon said, "I was wondering if your firm was among the bidders."

"I'm sure I couldn't say, sir," said Ralph. "Should we all have another drink?"

They ordered another round, and Simeon said, "I gather such a project wouldn't interest you personally."

"It might," said Ralph, "but only under impossible conditions."

Day looked at him the way Guinevere must have looked at

Lancelot when he first brought up the subject of the Holy Grail.

"Such as?" asked Simeon.

"Well, for instance, I'm sure there's a committee that has to approve the plans."

"Simeon is chairman of the committee," said Lydia helpfully.

"I didn't know," said Ralph.

"I told you, darling," said Day.

There was a moment of uneasy silence, and then Ralph said, "What do you teach, Mr. Brady?"

"He's head of the English department," said Day. "I told you, darling."

"You probably did. Well, sir, that's exactly my point. I'm sure you're an excellent teacher, but, if you'll excuse me, I don't see that a knowledge of literature in any way qualifies you to be chairman of a committee that passes on the complexities of the architecture of a Fine Arts Center."

"That's a very good observation," said Day.

Ralph Gunderson reached across the table and enclosed Day's hand in his.

He went on, "It's as if somebody had given three million dollars to your college library to buy the first editions of as many as possible of the best novels ever written, and I was appointed chairman of the committee to choose them. I'd be, excuse me, sir, out of my depth and make a great many errors, most of them foolish and some of them quite possibly fatal."

Lydia said, "Simeon and I had better get a move on. Dr. Brady is lecturing at Columbia tonight."

Simeon said, "I happen to know a little something about a few subjects beyond English literature. I imagine, Mr. Gunderson, if you took the trouble to look into the subject, you would find that the men of the Renaissance did not limit themselves to one subject. They were generally considered quite well-rounded men."

Ralph said, "Robert Frost used to say, 'Of what use is the well-rounded man, except for rolling?' "

"It's getting awfully late," said Lydia.

"I agree with Robert Frost," said Day.

"I gather there are few matters in the world about which you do not have strong opinions," said Simeon.

"That's not quite true," said Ralph. "Music, for instance, no opinion at all, except that I could listen to Day play the piano indefinitely. Or literature. I'm widely unread, no opinions. But on painting and sculpture and architecture, and I've studied all three, I have opinions."

"It's been awfully nice meeting you, Mr. Gunderson," said Lydia rising.

"I hope I didn't sound off too much," said Ralph, once more almost upsetting Day's drink.

"Don't apologize for expressing your opinion," said Day. "After all, Simeon is a member of the American Civil Liberties Union."

"It's very refreshing, getting other points of view," said Simeon, "especially from the young."

Lydia looked at Day and smiled, but Day was looking at Le Courboisier of the future.

Later, Lydia said to Simeon, "What do you think of him?"

"Fortunately he's not Day's type," said Simeon.

Ralph and Day were married a few days after Day was graduated from Wellesley. His parents came all the way from an 800-acre farm near Minneapolis. They were clearly awed by their son and didn't quite understand what he was up to, but they loved him and he loved them back.

Just before the ceremony, Lydia kissed Day and said, "You're going to be happy. I can tell."

"You'd think you were marrying him," said Day. "Do you think Simeon will really give me away, to Ralph, I mean?"

Irene Carson said, "We're ready on your call to Dallas, Mrs. Brady."

And then Ralph Gunderson's voice said, "How nice of you to call. You must be about ready to go to the airport."

"I am," said Lydia, and then she said, "How's Day?"

"She's fine. Buying up Neiman-Marcus, I guess. She'll be sorry she missed talking to you."

Had there been a pause, a change in the tone of voice, any nervousness? None.

"I'm sorry, too," said Lydia. "Did they like your drawings for the theater?"

"Yep. And now they all want me to build them castles, complete with moats, of course."

"Good. Get rich; you can support me in my old age, beginning tomorrow. Give my love to Day."

"I will. And have a good trip. We'll miss you."

As Lydia hung up the phone, a car was turning into the driveway, the taxi. She felt reassured. Day was all right. Of course. Simeon had been lying. Of course.

She looked around the room. Too late for good-byes, she thought. She walked into the hall and touched the green Buddha. It isn't a bad house, she thought. It is one in which two children have been raised with love and hope, a house in which I was happier than I had any right to be and more miserable than I deserved. But now there is no time for looking back; we are flying into the sunshine. From here on in, it's forward, march.

She turned on the porch light and opened the front door.

"Hello, Billy," she said. "I'm afraid I've got rather a lot of luggage."

Chapter 8

❧ Lydia saw no reason to doubt the reassuring statistics in the airline's advertisements. The chance of getting killed on a flight across the Atlantic was far less than the chance of breaking your neck in your very own bathtub in Briley. Or of being struck by lightning in the south forty. Or of getting run over by a laundry truck, and it was true that George O'Hare of Hare's Kwick Kwality Klean and Press was a bad driver.

As she walked into the Swissair terminal at Kennedy International, Lydia reminded herself of these facts. Moreover, she told herself, the Swiss have never cracked one up, or if they have, they have kept it a secret.

Furthermore, a woman ahead of her in the weighing-in line said, "You feel so safe with the Swiss." The woman said it two or three times, and the oftener she said it, the more terrified Lydia became. Why hadn't she gotten herself a nice cabin on the *Queen Mary?* What was her hurry, anyway? And was it too late to turn back?

She handed her passport to the pretty blond young man behind the counter, and the porter threw her bags on the scale. Her bags were four pounds overweight. Fortunately, she thought, they do not weigh the passengers, because there are a lot of very hefty American ladies on this flight, and as Simeon was kind enough to point out, I am myself a little heavy in the hip area. Frances Trollope would approve of me and, very likely, write a book about me. It was difficult to keep Mother Trollope from writing books, and there were no doubt other reasons why her son Anthony got up at five in the morning. If

I'd been Anthony, I would have. Or else I'd have given Mother Trollope forty whacks.

"You feel so safe with the Swiss," the woman in the lavender coat said again. Mother Trollope would have been ecstatic with *her* size.

The pretty young man gave Lydia her change and smiled. "It is a most clear night," he said.

As Lydia walked the last mile to the insubstantial, crash-prone plane, put together with old hairpins and rubber bands, she could see that the young man was perfectly right about the night. The moon was still full and orange; there were a great many stars, and the air was comfortably cool. On such a night, thought Lydia, love should be made. Eternal fealty should be sworn, and one should have faith in God and Swissair and feel safe in His and their hands.

Shortly after she seated herself next to a window, the crew walked through the plane, large and blond and competent-looking. They smiled at each other and at the passengers and at the pretty stewardesses and the handsome steward. The members of the crew all wore magnificent wristwatches, undoubtedly Swiss, and, thought Lydia, Swiss watches always keep perfect time, and Swiss planes always arrive on time and in one piece.

It is going to be a nifty flight, Lydia said to her ego and her id, and then she fastened her seat belt. The takeoff is the worst, she thought.

The takeoff could not have been smoother, and the stewardesses almost immediately started serving drinks, and the steward offered her a tray of canapés. The Swiss, thought Lydia, are like nice Germans, and if it were possible to feel safe in a flying coffin, I would feel safe with them.

The small, dark woman next to her said, "I'm Mrs. Dr. Callen from Dayton, and I've never traveled alone before, have you?"

Lydia shook her head, remembering:

"Pack for me, will you, darling? You're a wonderful packer . . . Did you remember to put in the flask? I'll bet you didn't. You never remember to put in the flask . . . my black tie? The last time you forgot, and do you remember what a time we had finding a black tie at the last minute in Paris?"

No, Mrs. Dr. Callen, I have never before traveled alone, but it has its compensations.

"I'm meeting the doctor in Lisbon; he's been attending a con-clave of surgeons in Glasgow. We've never been to Portugal. Have you?"

Lydia said no, she had not.

Sybil, who had been everywhere, had said, "On your way to the nuptials, stop off in southern Portugal, Armação de Pêra. The sun will shine every day; the ocean is beautiful and warm, and so are the people. The Arabs were in those parts a long time, and they left many souvenirs behind them, gentle souvenirs. And Mr. Bernardes at the hotel is divine. He and I—"

"You told me. I'm going for the sun."

"That's what I thought when I left, but—"

Mrs. Dr. Callen of Dayton continued. "They say it's just as nice and cheap, too, and the way things are going back home, socialized medicine and all, we have to count every penny, don't you?"

Lydia said that she did, and she thought, you feel so safe with the Swiss, and those little bumps are nothing to worry about. So I've read, and if it wasn't true, they'd sue.

"Don, that's our youngest son . . . Yale . . . Fred . . . the doctor . . . I wish I could sleep on a plane, but I never can. Too nervous, I guess. You?"

Lydia shook her head. She had never been able to sleep on a plane. Who nice can?

Later she was vaguely aware of being shaken, but she mum-bled something hostile and turned the other cheek. Probably a stewardess trying to give her dinner. They always do, the way nurses in hospitals wake you up to give you a sleeping pill.

But Lydia did not really wake until dawn, and she just had time to wash and do her face when the plane made an ef-fortless landing at the Lisbon airport.

It was a magic day, the air immaculate, the sun warm and bright. There were a number of smart-looking people in the airport restaurant, which was largely glass. Lydia sat sleepily at a table, from which she could see the bright green grass and the lazy palms and the blue sky with pink clouds.

She felt wonderfully relaxed and rested, not really quite awake, and since there wasn't time to go into Lisbon itself, she drank the strong, black coffee and listened happily to the announcements in three languages—flights to Rome, to Cairo, to Zurich, to Casablanca, to Istanbul, to the ends of the earth.

She imagined herself a character in one of those sophisticated movies in which handsome people are always fearlessly climbing in and out of indestructible planes.

The old life is behind me, she thought; it is April, a month of beginnings, and I am ready to begin. But what?

Since she couldn't think of a really good reason not to, she ordered a Scotch on the rocks, a large one. The last time she had had a drink in the morning was at Day's and Ralph's wedding.

As she spoke to the waiter, the man at the next table looked at her and smiled. He was a huge man, with broad shoulders and dark skin, almost-black hair worn a little too long for Lydia's taste.

Probably a European fortune hunter, she thought, and he thinks I'm one of those rich American widow ladies he's heard so much about. She did not smile back.

The man was very tanned, and nobody nice, thought Lydia, could be that tanned at this time of year. If I had smiled back, which I, of course, had no intention of doing, I might easily have ended up in one of those obscure South American republics, in a house of ill repute. Or am I a little long in the tooth for that?

The man turned away. (Which answers my question, much too long in the tooth.) He was in his late forties, had a tough face, an enormous crooked nose, large gray eyes, and the chin of someone used to getting his way. But not with this chicken, thought Lydia, not even if he wanted to, which he doesn't.

She sipped at the Scotch the waiter had brought her; Scotch can be very refreshing in the morning, and if they just had the right advertising campaign, it might even take the place of orange juice.

When her flight to Faro was announced, Lydia felt light-headed, but then, she thought, that's not unusual for a member of the jet set.

The dark man with the nose that had been broken smiled at her a second time as she started for her plane; it was rather a shy smile. He could, she thought, be one of those rich Greek shipowners. When I was a girl, the Greeks ran candy stores; now they own fleets of ships and are all as rich as Midas. But are they happy?

Lydia did not see the man again until she was seated on the plane. He stood in the aisle, looking massive. With a pronounced Midwestern accent he said, "May I sit next to you?"

You can't be rude to a fellow American far away from home and no doubt lonely.

"Of course," said Lydia. She couldn't help noticing that the man was not wearing a wedding ring.

Part Two

—THE INVINCIBLE SUMMER—

Chapter 9

❧ His name was Paul Julian; he was from Chicago. He had been in Portugal for some time, and he loved it.

"The Portuguese have never really fought anybody," he said. "When Brazil, their principal colony, said it wanted to be free, the Portuguese said, 'Are you absolutely *sure?*' The Brazilians, also a gentle people, said that they were. So the Portuguese said, 'Well, good luck, then.' And that was that."

He asked where Lydia was going, and when she said "Armação de Pêra," he told her that he knew it well.

"I have a place not far from there," he said. "Are you staying at the hotel?"

Lydia said that she was, and he said, "It's a beautiful place, and the hotel is magnificently run. The manager's a friend of mine. I'll see that he gives you the A-treatment."

"Are you in business in Portugal?" asked Lydia.

"No," said Paul Julian, and that was the end of that.

Most people would volunteer what they do, thought Lydia, but that is because most people feel about silence the way nature feels about a vacuum.

Paul Julian opened the elegant black dispatch case he was carrying, took out a copy of *Figaro*, and started to read.

A professor? There aren't too many nonprofessors around who can read French without moving their lips. But, somehow, I don't think so, and I am something of an expert on the subject of professors. Professors are almost always aware of the sound of their own voices, and at least two I have known well parsed every sentence before they spoke it.

Paul Julian has a pleasant voice, but he doesn't give the impression that he's practiced what he's saying. Thought about it, yes. A writer? I've known a few of those, too, and, unlike Molière's doctor, they seem to have been born knowing that they were speaking prose.

Lydia had often heard that you can tell a lot about a person by his hands, and she studied Paul Julian's hands for a while, surreptitiously, of course. They were large and brown and well cared for, which proves, thought Lydia, that he does not bite his fingernails and can afford manicures. And I doubt that he's a manual laborer.

Paul Julian was wearing a blue silk suit, the lapels of which were a little wide by the exacting standards of Brooks Brothers, but the suit was well cut and emphasized the feeling of physical power about him.

If I were a man, thought Lydia, I wouldn't want to get into a street fight with Paul Julian, any kind of fight, for that matter. He looks like a winner of battles of his own choosing and fought by his rules. He may like gentle people, but he doesn't look to me like a gentle man.

But then, "The gentle mind by gentle deeds is known/ For a man by nothing is so well betrayed/ As by his manners." I live in an age, thought Lydia, where good manners are often confused with homosexuality.

We continue with the mystery of Paul Julian, a man whose gender seems to be particularly well defined.

He is not a jiggler; no tapping of feet, no clasping and unclasping of hands. He seems to be relaxed, and that, too, is unusual in this part of this nervous century.

But what does he do for a living? How can a man who is true blue and a one hundred percent American be that tanned in mid-April? Maybe he's a spy of some kind. I've heard that Portugal is filled with them. They're thinking of forming a union.

The name Paul Julian is vaguely familiar, I think. Just vaguely, which could mean that he was written up in the newspapers. A wife murderer? An income-tax evader? Someone whose name I saw listed as "Wanted" in the Briley post office?

But surely a man sought after by the authorities wouldn't

be that relaxed. Unless inside he's all aflutter and has several bleeding ulcers.

To me he doesn't look like a bleeding-ulcer type, and while we're on the subject, I have to admit there is something sensual about him, and he has an air of vitality, which I have always found much more attractive than mere good looks.

He could be an actor, of course. Since my passion for John Garfield, I haven't really kept up on actors, but if he were an actor he'd have those gray temples touched up and his nose rebuilt. Besides, I've been sitting here a good three minutes, and he hasn't yet whipped a mirror out of his pocket. He's not an actor.

When the plane was airborne, Paul Julian looked up from *Figaro* and said, "I'm always glad when the takeoff is over."

"Do you hate flying, too?"

"I wouldn't say I hate it, but I prefer it when I'm at the controls."

"Are you a pilot?"

"I've flown a plane, largely for my own amusement," said Paul Julian, returning to the news of what the French were up to.

When the stewardess came around, Paul Julian said to Lydia, "Would you like a drink?"

"No, thank you," and to the stewardess, "I'd love some orange juice."

There was another moment of silence, and then Lydia, with what she was afraid might be described as birdlike brightness, said, "Are you from Chicago originally?"

"I was born in one of the more fashionable suburbs," said Paul Julian. "Gary, Indiana."

Again Lydia waited for more, and again there was no more. He could, she thought, be a member of a family that owns steel mills, but from the way he said "Gary, Indiana," I doubt it. Not bitter, but hardly benevolent either.

Although my experience with people who own steel mills is limited, I gather they find little wrong with the state of things

as they are in Gary. And I'll bet you dollars to escudos that Senhor Julian does. And now that you ask, I'll tell you another
thing. *He* didn't break his nose playing tennis, golf, or tiddly-
winks at the Gary, Indiana, country club. Moreover, while
he has no trouble with words of more than one syllable, the
accent is not one he picked up at Groton and Harvard.

Unfortunately, he is not one of those fellows who goes around
dictating his autobiography into the nearest open ear, although
my shell-like ear is certainly open.

The name, damn it, is familiar. Is he one of those usually
reliable sources they're always quoting in dispatches from Our
Nation's Capital?

"A magazine, senhora?" asked the stewardess.

Lydia nodded and chose a copy of *Elle*, the French fashion
magazine. More than one of us can decipher French. Mine may
be a wee bit rusty, but I can translate certain key words, like
t-a-n-t-e and *p-l-u-m-e*. Besides, in *Elle* there are a lot of pictures,
which are worth a thousand words anyway, particularly French
words.

The flight was short, and a little more than half an hour later,
the plane swept down over the blue Atlantic and the green
fields and made another perfect landing.

Paul Julian put his newspaper back in the dispatch case and
turned to Lydia. "My car's at the airport. Could I give you a
lift?"

"No, thank you," said Lydia. "The hotel is sending a car."

"I know the car, and I know José Carlos, the driver. Believe
me, you're safer with me."

"I don't want to put you to any trouble."

"You're not."

There are people who can cope with the complexities of luggage at airports and those who can't. Paul Julian could. His
Portuguese seemed to be excellent, and he seemed to know
everybody, and everybody knew him. There was a good deal of
grinning and bowing and singing, and within five minutes

Lydia's bags, looking somewhat the worse for the long journey, were in the red Alfa Romeo that belonged to Paul Julian. José Carlos and the car from the hotel had been dismissed.

A few minutes later they were in the narrow streets of Faro. They passed a great many young men in uniforms of one kind or another, most of them with a great deal of braid and in various bright colors.

Paul Julian said, "They say that one out of every two men under thirty is in uniform, and I wouldn't doubt it. But how can you take them seriously? They all design their own, and at the slightest provocation they break into *fado*. Do you know the *fado?*"

"I've heard it."

"I'll take you to a place where there's a woman who sings it better than anyplace in the world. When she sings it, it's a kind of sweet lament over the sadness of life. Unlike the Spanish *flamenco*, which is an angry complaint."

I like this man, thought Lydia. I like someone who prefers a sweet lament to an angry complaint. This is a nice man, and if I don't see him again, which I probably won't, I'm glad I met him.

But she knew she would see him again.

They were now in the open country on a narrow two-lane highway that was paved but not in good repair. There were no other cars, only an occasional burro and cart. The houses were all tiny, but they were all beautiful, pink and blue and yellow and white. The fields were startlingly green, and there were tiny new leaves on the fig and almond trees.

After a while Paul Julian drove the car around a sharp curve and stopped. There, far below, was the ocean, larger and wilder and more beautiful than anybody else's ocean anywhere. In the distance was a white ship, and there were many small fishing boats, most of them with red sails, some with blue.

Paul parked the car on a pink cliff that jutted out over the water. Lydia said nothing. At such moments, which are rare, what is there to say?

After a time, Paul started the engine of the car again, and he said, "As you will see, the view from my terrace is even more beautiful."

Senhor Ernesto Bernardes, the manager of the hotel, was a good-looking young man of about thirty, with a dark face, very white teeth, and eyes that had seen everything, twice. He had the manners of a Medici, one of the nice ones.

It was immediately apparent that while he recognized Lydia as the queen mother traveling incognito, he felt that Paul Julian would be unanimously elected president of the Parliament of Man as soon as man got around to setting one up.

Senhor Bernardes snapped his fingers, and instantly half a dozen small boys in green silk uniforms appeared from various places and started to take Lydia's luggage out of the Alfa. They all had enormous black eyes, brown skins, and the manners of elderly gentlemen.

"Are you stealing more of my money Friday night?" Senhor Bernardes asked Paul.

"Of course."

The *senhor* sighed.

"Senhor Julian has taught me poker," he said, "and in a few nights he will own the hotel."

He once more snapped his fingers, and then he went back into the hotel, followed by a minuscule army in green silk. Back home, thought Lydia, those boys would be in school learning important things like how to wreck their father's Cadillac, and during recess they would be playing games like Slash-the-Tire.

"I'd ask you to have dinner with me tonight," said Paul Julian, "but you'll probably want to take it easy. How about lunch tomorrow? At my place; I've got a wonderful cook."

"I'd love it."

"I'll pick you up at one," said Paul.

He started for the car, then turned and said, "I should tell you, I feel I already know you. I heard your husband lecture once, at the University of Chicago."

"Oh, did you?" said Lydia, and then she said, "Simeon is no

longer my husband," and then she said, "Did you enjoy the lecture?"

"Since he is no longer your husband," said Paul, "I can tell you that Simeon Brady struck me as a man who knew a great deal about trivial things."

"I hope you'll be comfortable here," said Senhor Bernardes, opening the door of Lydia's room.

There were two walls of glass that faced directly onto the ocean; a third opened onto a terrace, and the fourth was made of restful pink brick. The floor was green tile, and the furniture was new and comfortable-looking. The bed was huge, and beside it was a handsome table lamp with a frosted bulb that seemed to be large enough so that a lady suffering from near-sightedness, especially lately, could make out the small print. There was a separate dressing room, mostly mirrors, and a bath with the same green tiles as the floor.

"I may stay here forever," said Lydia.

"Do you know the Portuguese word *saudade?*" said Senhor Bernardes. "It means a sweet and sad remembrance of things past. I hope that you will stay a long time and that when you leave, you will feel *saudade.*"

"I'm sure I will," said Lydia, and she did.

"Dinner is at seven, until ten. But if you'd rather, you can have it here in your room."

Lydia tipped the six bellboys, and then she said, "I think I'll have it here."

Bernardes nodded. "Good. I shall send you a menu. And if there is anything else, please only to call."

He bowed. "You are fortunate to be a friend of Mr. Julian. He is much known by all of us here. He is a most good man."

"I don't really know him well."

"He has been here almost a year," said Bernardes, "and he has a villa of great exquisiteness. I believe he does no work. I asked him once, and he said, 'I occupy myself with counting the waves in the ocean.' I think he must be rich."

After a long, luxurious bath, Lydia opened the glass doors

and stood on the terrace, looking at the sea beating against the patient rocks that were not pale yellow. The beach was wide and clean and covered with soft brown sand and thousands of tiny orange and black pebbles.

It took me forty-two years to get here, she thought, but better late than never. I'm glad I finally made it, and I'm glad I've met a good man who is rich and who occupies himself with counting the waves in the ocean.

Then she went back into the room and lay down on the bed.

When she woke up the next morning, she discovered that if she hurried, she'd be able to make the last sitting at breakfast.

Chapter 10

❧ At breakfast Lydia met all but one of the other guests in the hotel. There was an American couple who were elderly and quiet and intent on keeping to themselves. A French couple, a middle aged man and an extremely pretty girl who, Lydia was at first sure, was his mistress. It turned out that the girl was his wife, and they had three children. There were four English businessmen who were buying up land in the neighborhood to build luxury hotels, and Lydia hated them. They want to make this beautiful village just like all the other resorts in the world, she thought. Leave it to the English. And then she thought, ah, no, I'm done with hating; it takes too much out of you. Besides, who am I to want to keep all this beauty to myself?

The man Lydia did not meet that first morning was of no discernible nationality. He was always alone and was about forty. He wore horn-rimmed glasses and was usually reading a book. He spoke to no one, not even the waiters, not even the tiny soldiers in green silk who stood in the lobby smiling and opening doors, their innocent eyes saying observe me; here I am.

Lydia called the man who was always alone the Silent Man, and she paid little attention to him, which was a mistake.

Here it is Thursday morning, she thought, and I am sitting on a pink cobblestone terrace just above the bluest ocean. There are yellow cliffs stretching far beyond the horizon to the right and to the left of me. The magenta sky is without a cloud, and I have nothing except euphoria on my mind and nothing at all in my hands, not even a mind-improving book.

And I don't care whether I deserve these many blessings. I have learned with pain—how else do you?—that you don't get what you deserve; you get what you get.

The young gardener, who was doing something or other to a cactus plant in the sand, raised his head and smiled at her.

Lydia smiled back. The boy was far too beautiful to be going around butchering cactus plants. And, unless I miss my guess, he is either going to be a Portuguese movie star or one of those gentle bullfighters who never kill anything.

He continued hacking away at the cactus and humming softly.

It would be awfully easy to get used to this, Lydia thought, and I may.

She leaned back in her chair and closed her eyes.

When she woke up, it was twelvethirty.

She asked herself a question, "Is there such a thing as Portuguese sleeping sickness? Because if there is, I've got a very bad case of it."

Then she answered herself. "No, but there is such a thing as peace of mind, and when you find it, you can usually sleep without the aid of a Seconal."

She dressed slowly and with care, finally deciding on a gray tricot that had come from Paris by way of the Sak's in White Plains. Simeon had, of course, not liked the tricot.

"It's nice, but you're not planning to wear it tonight, are you?"

"I was."

Silence.

"What's wrong with it?"

"There's nothing really *wrong* with it, but it seems a little informal for the occasion tonight."

"To go to the Mortons? You're joking."

"I thought you liked Ann and Harry?"

"I do, but I doubt that they're expecting me to show up in a Dior dinner dress. Particularly if we're going to have, as we have perhaps a thousand times before, some of Ann's good, old-

fashioned Hungarian goulash, for which she is so justly famous. Do you think that's all she knows how to cook? Harry can't
have gotten that fat just on goulash."

"It's a lovely dress, sweetie, but why don't you wear the blue
silk we got in Acapulco?"

Sweetie started upstairs to change into sackcloth and ashes,
and Simeon said, "I'll make the martinis."

But that, thought Lydia, was long ago and in a country far
from here. In Portugal people don't kill each other.

She unnecessarily adjusted a strand of hair, which until
recently had been brown, a drab brown, she always felt. But
then Mr. Kenneth came into her life with his alchemy, his elix-
irs and his incantations. Overnight, abracadabra, Lydia became
what Mr. Kenneth called a chestnut blonde.

"With your delicate coloring, which is so rare these days, you
should have been *born* a chestnut blonde."

In my case, a considerable improvement. God cannot be
everywhere, the sparrow situation being what it is, and that is
the reason we have the Mr. Kenneths of the world.

The fact is that for a grass widow going on forty-three, I am
not half bad. It took some time—I am a late developer—but I
have thinned down, and nothing has sagged much.

My legs are still shapely. They have often been favorably
commented on, particularly by young men who wanted to learn
how to talk the way Simeon talks, meaning fancy.

I know what they said about my legs because they told me.
I suppose they hoped I could teach them how to speak as if
they had their mouths full of hot mashed potatoes. Or maybe
they wanted me to talk to Simeon about their grades.

In any case, I do have good legs. As for my face, there
may be a few born troublemakers who would find the nose a
trifle too long and the chin the slightest bit too sharp, but I do
have these nice high cheekbones, the result of having chosen a
Lyman as a father. High cheekbones run in the Lyman family,
as do the blue eyes.

"Your eyes were almost—*almost*, mind you—the first thing

I noticed. Turquoise blue; that's rare in eyes. And yours had something else. They looked as if they expected a lot of surprises. Pleasant ones."

Lydia took a last look at herself in the mirror.

"All right," she said. "Snow White is still the fairest in the land, but for my age and weight, I'll do."

Then the telephone rang. Paul was waiting for her in the lobby.

He stopped the car at the edge of a winding gravel drive. The villa, which was white and immaculate, stood at the crest of a hill that was slightly higher than any of the others. There were expanses of luxurious and freshly cut lawn on either side.

"I would have guessed you lived in a house like this," said Lydia.

As they proceeded up the drive, which was lined on both sides with almond trees, Paul said, "I made up my mind some time ago that I no longer wanted to be in houses where people are at war with each other."

He looked at her quickly. "I've thought that, but I never said it before. Maybe it sounds a little pretentious."

"Not to me," said Lydia.

They stood for a moment in the hallway, which was two stories high and had white walls with immense windows that looked out toward the sea. There was a delicate stairwell carved out of a reddish wood Lydia did not recognize, a long table with a parqueted top, two handsome Portuguese leather chairs, and on one wall a large abstraction the color of a winter sunset. The only other object in the room—it caught the light from every window—was an exquisite small statue of a happy satyr that had been sculpted in gold.

"Some people think it's a Cellini," said Paul. "I don't, but it's beautiful, which is what matters. Would you like the grand tour first?"

The rooms of the villa were all large, and so were the windows, from each of which was a different view—a hill, a tree of unusual shape, a glimpse of the ocean, sometimes only a warm yellow rock.

The furniture was of no particular period, but Lydia felt that each piece had been chosen with an eye to its comfort and an appreciation of its beauty. Everything fitted together, as beautiful things always do.

There were not many paintings, one or two to a room, and none was by an artist that Lydia recognized, but each had character and was pleasing to the eye.

And there were books, all of which looked read.

"This is where I spend most of my time," said Paul.

The room was the smallest in the villa; it had a Louis XV desk, two black leather chairs, a white Kashmir rug on which were a series of bluebirds in endless flight, and a small filing cabinet. There was a photograph of a dark, pretty girl of twelve or so on top of the desk.

At eye level on the white wall facing the desk was a small Renoir, a family all pink and blue and joyous, having a picnic by a lazy river.

Lydia looked at the picture for a long time.

"It's lovely," she said, and, standing closer, "a wonderful reproduction, too."

Paul smiled, and Lydia said, "It is a reproduction, isn't it?" knowing now that it wasn't.

"Renoir's practically my favorite painter. I guess he is my favorite," she said. "Have you read his son's biography of him?"

Paul pointed to the desk, and there, of course, was Jean Renoir's loving portrait of his father, bound in leather.

"Do you believe that part at the end, where about an hour before he died he said, 'I think I am just beginning to understand'? Or was that just something his son made up?"

"I believe it. Renoir was a happy man. That's why he painted such happy paintings."

"I guess it was the time, 'those innocent Sunday afternoons.' Somebody called them that. Now, no more innocence. No more happy men. At least, I don't know any."

"Maybe you haven't been looking," said Paul.

"What a pretty girl," Lydia said of the photograph on the desk.

"Isn't she?" said Paul.

Chapter 11

❧ They had lunch on the lawn, under an almond tree the branches of which were shaped like a bird in flight.

Fernando, who served it, had large dark eyes that looked hopefully out at the world from under graying arched eyebrows. Lydia saw at once that he was fond of Paul. Later she was to discover that Fernando was capable of the fiercest loyalty, and no questions asked, not even the price.

The food was superb—huge clams with bacon, loin of pork with a sweet and sour sauce, green salad, orange cake, Portuguese cheese made of ewe's milk, and a great deal of wine. She and Paul had each had two martinis before lunch, too.

Paul leaned toward her. His head touched hers, and he said, "You're staying for months, of course, years maybe, decades."

"I'm staying for a week. I'm meeting my son in Madrid and his fiancée. And I'm staying for the wedding, that's in May."

"The last thing a son needs when he's getting married is a mother. And as for the girl, she probably has a mother of her own to contend with."

Lydia indicated to Fernando that she would have just a soupçon more of the red.

"On Monday," said Paul, "when Ernesto Bernardes said that an American lady was arriving on Wednesday, alone, I said, 'In that case, we shall postpone our poker and our conversations until after she has gone. I shall be conspicuously absent during the American lady's stay.'

"Ernesto asked why, and I described to him what I was sure you'd be like. First, *that* voice—querulous, unmodulated, unceasing."

Lydia, who had always prided herself on her voice, said, "I shall never speak again. I shall enter one of those orders in which absolute silence is required."

Paul smiled and said, "I told Ernesto that in addition you would have *that* look, a look of a woman denied something she is convinced she deserved—angry, pinched, disapproving. A look of permanent dissatisfaction. In addition to eyes, small and too close together. And a permanently closed mind with the key thrown away."

"My eyes are a little close together," said Lydia. "Under the circumstances, I'm surprised you spoke to me."

"I was surprised myself. That's why I was so wary. You looked intelligent and shy, which is a fine quality in a woman. But there were several unanswered questions. Were you a compulsive talker? I've known a few, one very well, but let's not go into that.

"On the plane I figured if you could maintain reasonable silence until we got to Faro, there might be some hope for our becoming friends.

"But the real test was when you first looked at the ocean. I could see that you liked it, but you didn't *ooh* and *ah* over it. I'm not much for the oohers and ahers."

"Have you known many?"

"One is more than enough," said Paul. "I had one further fear. When I picked you up this afternoon, would you be wearing pants? I know some people call them slacks, but I don't."

"I never wear them," said Lydia, who had brought only two pairs. How do you get rid of two pairs of slacks? A private burning on the beach?

"Of course you don't, and you don't rouge your cheeks or paint preposterous eyebrows in the middle of your forehead. And your hair is untampered with."

Lydia concentrated on the redness of the wine. I see no reason to get into a discussion of Mr. Kenneth or the story of how I became a chestnut blonde. That can wait until the publication of my autobiography, which will be posthumous.

"A liqueur, madame?" Fernando was asking.

"Dear me, no," said Lydia.

"The chartreuse is great," said Paul. "I was looking forward . . . but if you don't have any, I cannot and will not. Drinking alone is a sure sign of alcoholism."

"Just a little," Lydia said to Fernando.

"Yellow chartreuse is no good at all," said Paul. "Only the green, and don't let them tell you otherwise."

"I certainly won't," said Lydia.

Paul lifted his glass. "I haven't had so much to drink in the middle of the day for years, and I'm enjoying every minute of it."

"So am I."

After Fernando went back into the villa, Paul leaned across the table and kissed her on the lips. Lydia felt something she had not felt for sometime, something she may never have felt before.

"This is not according to my plan," said Paul, "but thank you."

"Sometimes in the morning," Paul was saying, "when I get out of bed—Fernando doesn't come in until noon—I have to turn on the radio to be sure there's somebody else in the world."

"Do you do that, too?" said Lydia. "I thought I was the only one."

They were walking along the endless beach, and the sea was sweeping softly against the cliffs, in which there were millions of tiny white shells. It was as if nobody had ever been there before and never would be again.

Lydia thought of a prayer she had said as a child when she was happy. "Please, God, keep it always like this." She said it now, to herself. "I am not a praying woman, God, but, please, keep it always like this. Or, since nothing is forever, keep it like this for as long as possible, and I won't complain again, not for the rest of my life. I promise."

Aloud she said, "Do you have a bad time? I mean a time of day or night, and it doesn't matter how good or bad the rest has been, when, maybe just for a minute, you're filled with despair."

"Of course. Everybody does. Mine's in the late afternoon, just after sunset, just before you have to turn on the lights for the first time. Because for me, turning on the lights separates the afternoon from the evening. I'm all right later, but at that moment—huh-uh. When's yours?"

"It's funny," said Lydia, "but mine's the same. Isn't that a funny coincidence?"

"I think it's rather nice, and we're both Taurus. And speaking of coincidences, have you—you're probably too young—but have you ever heard my favorite song, 'Show Me the Way to Get Out of This World'?"

" 'Cause that's where everything is,' " sang Lydia, and they started laughing.

"You can't go in a week," said Paul. "I won't allow it, and if you should be foolish enough to try, Ernesto Bernardes will call the police, and they'll impound your luggage. And if you try to protest, you'll be thrown into a dungeon. This isn't a police state for nothing."

"Oh, my darling," said Lydia, and she was surprised to find that there were tears in her eyes.

Paul took her in his arms, and after a time he said, "I told you, none of this is according to my plan. I'd made up my mind. No one person would ever again be the whole world or even any substantial part of it. Not whom shall I love but whom shall I not love."

He took her hand in his, and they started back to the white villa on the green hill.

"I'm not much for promises," he said, "but I make you one. I shall try never to hurt you. I looked at you this afternoon when you walked out of the elevator at the hotel, and I thought you were the most vulnerable person I'd ever seen."

"We have that in common, too," said Lydia.

They were silent on the way back to the hotel, and as Paul stopped the car in the drive, he said, "Tonight we'll go to the *fado* place. All right?"

"All right."

"I'll pick you up at nine."

One of the small boys had opened the door of the car. As Lydia got out, Paul said, "Thank you for not asking questions."

There were three dozen yellow roses with very long stems in Lydia's room. The maids put them in vases, and in the late afternoon sunlight, the roses covered everything with a golden haze.

Chapter 12

❧ The woman who sang was tiny, small-boned, and with delicate, dark features. She was perhaps fifty, and her face, like her bearing, was proud. It was melancholy but without self-pity. She was still beautiful, and, more important, had what Lydia had always found the most attractive quality of all, vitality. Call it life.

She wore a black dress and had a black shawl over her head; she stood erect in front of two young men—Paul had said they were her sons—who played quiet Portuguese guitars. She sang softly, and although Lydia could not understand the words, she felt she knew what they were about. That life is sad, sometimes almost unbearably so. But it is always interesting, and even in the most painful moments, you must turn the page; you must find out what happens next. The purpose of life is to live.

Lydia felt as she had when she first heard Rubinstein play; she must have been twenty. When she saw Laurette Taylor in *The Glass Menagerie*. When she heard John Gielgud read the *Ages of Man*. When she happened on *Pride and Prejudice*. When—oh, well, there had been perhaps a dozen such times in her life, none of them recently.

I have of late been afraid to feel, she thought. I was living in terror. I had closed down the factory, padlocked the gates, barred the windows, manned the machine guns, and chased away all would-be visitors, most of them friendly.

It was a long winter, she thought, and there were times— not many—when I came close to reaching for the sleeping pills in the bottle by the bed.

But I didn't. I waited for April, and I am grateful for whatever it is in my genes or my psyche that makes me once more want to turn the page. Who says you never get a second chance? You get a hundred. What you have to do is recognize them and take them.

Paul was looking at her, and she squeezed his dark hand and smiled. I like this man, she thought. I don't know who he is, but I know what he is.

"You know what your trouble is, don't you?"

"I have a few hunches, but do tell me what my trouble is, Simeon, and I'm glad it's only one."

"Your trouble is, you're always making gods out of people, and since they're not gods, they're always letting you down."

Sybil: "You're such a truster. You always expect the best of everybody. I always expect the worst, and ninety-nine times out of a hundred . . ."

Christopher: "I'm not sure I trust you to be all alone in Portugal. Don't buy the bridge across the Tagus; it belongs to Dr. Salazar. And don't get into any card games."

And Sybil: "When someone says he loves you, don't just start purring. Ask yourself why he said it."

When the song ended, there was not much applause; it would have been like applauding in church. The woman bowed, without smiling, and then she came to the table where Paul and Lydia were sitting.

Paul stood up, took the woman's hands in his, and kissed them.

"You're an artist," he said. "This is Mrs. Brady. May we buy you a drink?"

"*Muit obrigado*, no."

She looked at Lydia and smiled; it was a smile that included all of her face.

"I am glad Senhor di Cavalcanti has a friend," she said. "He comes here always alone, and he is too handsome and too *gentil* to be alone. I would marry him myself, except for the business of having a husband."

She kissed him on the cheek and went into the kitchen.

Paul ordered two more glasses of port, and then he said, "Go ahead. Ask me why she called me Di Cavalcanti."

"I agree with the *senhora*," said Lydia. "You are *gentil* and you are handsome."

"My name was Paulo di Cavalcanti, but I discovered that for a young man on the make in Chicago, that was too hard to pronounce. So I changed it. Paul Julian has such a nice Anglo-Saxon sound, and the only trouble is, I don't have a nice Anglo-Saxon face.

"My father was born in a village just over the hill. If you'd like, I'll take you there someday."

"I'd like, maybe tomorrow," said Lydia.

"It's very poor. People fish for sardines, and sometimes they make a living, and sometimes they don't. When he was eighteen, my father came to Gary. I don't think he thought the streets would be paved with gold, but he did think the United States was the promised land. It turned out not to be, and on Memorial Day in 1937, in front of a onetime dime-a-dance hall called Sam's Place, that sweet failure of a man was shot to death by a member of the Chicago police force.

"That may have been the day—I was nineteen—that his son decided two things: that he wanted to be a millionaire and that he was someday going to be mayor of Chicago."

They drove slowly through the narrow, winding roads. There were no other cars, and the burros were bedded down for the night. On either side of the road the white farmhouses shone in the bright moonlight. There was the sound of a gentle breeze among the almond and fig trees and of the lazy, distant surf.

As they got close to the villa on the hill, Paul said, "Will you come in for a nightcap?"

Lydia hesitated only a moment. "I'd love to, thanks."

They took their drinks to the terrace. Paul had put a Haydn mass on the record player; it was pure and clean, like the night. Below were the lights of a few fishing boats and from nearby the reassuring beam from a lighthouse.

"You must come for the sunset," said Paul. "It's a hundred times bigger than anyplace else in the world, and they say if you listen very carefully, you can hear it drop into the sea. I haven't yet, but I'm an optimist by nature, and I keep listening."

They were silent for a time, and then Paul said, "I never got to be mayor of Chicago, but I did make a lot of money, and then one hot July evening two years ago, I came home, late and tired, as always. The house was empty, and eighteen rooms are a lot of emptiness.

"I mixed myself a drink and sat down in a living room that was twenty by forty and furnished with odds and ends of unbeautiful things, each of which had cost a king's ransom, a seventeenth-century king, not one of those unseated, hungry kings that hang around Lisbon.

"Among my friends there had been much dying that year, one with the agony of cancer, the rest of heart attacks, of failure, of liquor, of overwork and underliving.

"I sat there alone in the darkness and asked myself a question most of my friends had never gotten around to asking: 'What the hell am I doing here? I want to read a book; I want to listen to some music; I want to look at some paintings. I want to find out the secret of me, if any.'

"That's almost all. My wife is really a very nice woman. She talks too much, but that's hardly a sin against the Holy Ghost. We simply wanted different things, and who's to say who was right?

"I asked her to come with me, but she wouldn't, and I was glad. She won't give me a divorce; she probably never will. You should know that.

"And you should know that I've been in jail twice, once justly, and that I'm considered a very unsavory character by a great many people and a simple pariah by others.

"I consider myself quite a decent fellow, but it took some time to come to that conclusion, forty-eight years. I try never to be deliberately unkind to anyone. I don't always succeed.

"Today I found out something that pleased me very much.

I found out that I can love. Still. Not everyone can, you know."

Lydia rose, and over the sound of the sea and the Haydn mass she said, "Sometime you must tell me why people think you're unsavory, but not now. Now let's go upstairs."

Later, as they lay together in the serene room, listening to the eternal ocean and to the erratic beat of their hearts, Lydia said, "I never enjoyed it before."

She kissed Paul and rubbed the soft, dark hair.

"And I always thought it was my fault," she said.

For a long time they were in each other's arms, at peace with each other and with the world. That by itself is rare enough, but they knew it, which is rarer still.

Chapter 13

❀ Paul was snoring ever so slightly when Lydia woke up, and she stayed in the bed beside him for a while. She looked at him, but not for long. Sleep is, after all, a private matter.

She looked at the broken nose. On closer examination it appeared to have been broken more than once, and not too carefully set. He is not a handsome man, she thought, but I like what is written in his face. It is a lived-in face, it has been suffered in, and it has felt joy. It is a man's face, and most of the male faces I have encountered have been those of members of the Little League in their forties.

Paul Julian is a manly man (I hate the word *virile*). Let us not go into the reasons, but there are not too many manly men these days. And if you're a womanly woman, which I like to think I am, you are grateful for the happy accident by which you met one. And I am, very grateful.

She got up quietly.

There was a woman's dressing gown in the closet, blue and well made, and a pair of woman's house slippers. They had not been worn often but were not brand new, either. I am clearly not the first of Paul Julian's female guests to stay the night, thought Lydia, and, naturally, I can't help wondering who the others were. Curiosity may have killed the cat, but if you're a woman, it's good for the liver. I'll never ask, though, she thought, and she never did. We each have our secrets, and it's better that way.

There was a new toothbrush in the bathroom. Paul Julian was awfully confident that I was going to stay, thought Lydia, and for a moment she resented the fact, and then she was glad.

She was pleased to see that he was a man who squeezed the toothpaste tube from the bottom.

The kitchen was enormous, and there was a stainless-steel electric stove and a large refrigerator. There were fresh eggs, and Lydia decided to make pancakes.

As she squeezed the orange juice, she thought, I know you're not supposed to say so, but I enjoy cooking.

Look, keep it to yourself, buster. The fact that I enjoy cooking, don't hate the town I grew up in, and am fond of my mother, if all that were reported to the F.B.I., they'd probably throw me in solitary for life. Or else they'd figure that, like Leo Tolstoy, I had a screw loose somewhere. I've got very little to say in defense of my mental stability, judge, but I'll tell you this: Leo once went for four years without changing his socks, and I can prove that I rinse mine out every night in one of those sudsy detergents that keep your hands smooth and unwrinkled until you're a hundred and two. Or they fall off.

All right, then. I plead guilty to enjoying slaving over a hot stove, but I don't care to talk too much about it. I'm not one of your *chatty* gourmets—"And the sweet basil must be chopped very, very fine, and the truffles *must* be from Provence. You can get them at this divine little shop. I'll give you the address, and just mention my name. . . . Sauce Béarnaise must be made of plover's eggs. We have them flown in by chartered plane from Guernsey, and . . . She served rosé with the filet of sole. I thought I'd die laughing, and I said to Hermie . . . I wouldn't give this recipe for quiche Lorraine to just anybody. Jebediah and I got it personally from the chef of Louis XVI when we were at Versailles."

Cooking for one is not for me, though. It's nice to have a man in the house when you're cooking. It's nice when you go to bed at night and when you get up in the morning. It's nice.

There was a radio on the work table. But I don't have to turn it on. I know there's somebody else in the world.

She found herself humming. I am in love, she thought. I love and am loved, and I am enhanced by it and enlarged by it. A little late, you say. I couldn't agree less, sorry. At twenty-two you feel it's no more than your due; at forty-two it's an unexpected and delightful surprise.

It won't last, you say; nothing is forever. Don't be too sure. At forty-two, having suffered some few disappointments in the past, you may just have learned how precious it is. And how fragile. You must handle fragile things tenderly.

And if it doesn't last, I'll settle for yesterday and today, and I should like to point out that the weather forecast for tomorrow is promising.

I am a happy woman who is loved by a happy man, and if I'd brought my paints along, I'd whip you up a Renoir, all pink and blue and innocent. But in the meantime, I'll settle for pancake batter.

At the end of breakfast, which they ate on the small cobblestone porch overlooking the ubiquitous green lawn, Paul said, "Your pancakes are better than Fernando's, but how is your octopus soup?"

He leaned across the table and touched her.

"I notice that when you're in love, a lot of touching goes on," he said. "I guess that's to make sure the other person is still there. Shall we go look at the ancestral estates?"

The village in which Paul's father had been born and spent the first eighteen years of his life was small. It consisted of a single street built at the edge of a tranquil beach. There were a few small fishing boats. Several old men sat on the sand, looking out at the sea, and a group of small boys were playing *futbal* in the sand.

Everyone knew Paul. The old men solemnly shook his hand. He kicked the ball with the boys for a while, and half a dozen small girls waved at him from the sidewalk and said, "Goodbye, good-bye," which they thought meant "Hello." The girls and the women wore checked skirts under which were numerous petticoats.

It was a calm day, a peaceful day. Inside and out, thought Lydia.

The house in which Paul's father had been born had three small rooms: a kitchen in which there was an open fireplace, a bedroom with four beds packed close together, and a minuscule parlor with a round table and four straight-back chairs. Several crucifixes hung on the whitewashed walls; there were bright, exotic flowers in boxes at the windows and on each side of the front steps. Everything was scrubbed and shining.

The woman who lived there alone had no teeth, but she had a smile of great beauty. When they left, Paul pressed something into her hand, and she blessed him.

"Five years ago," said Paul, "her husband and two sons went fishing in the morning and never came back. We are building a rocket to the moon, but we haven't yet made it possible for men to go fishing and survive."

They continued down the unhurried street, and he said, "My mother was like that. She was a mountain of a woman, a ninety-eight-pound mountain. After my father died, we were so poor that lots of times there wasn't enough to eat. I know that's not unique, then or now, but in those days there was all that lovely Roosevelt relief money available, and I felt we ought to get some of it. Never. The welfare people used to come to our house, and they'd look around—my mother was what now would no doubt be called pathologically neat—and they'd say, 'But you don't *need* relief.'

"The neighbors used to say you could eat off my mother's floors. True enough, but I always wanted to know, eat *what?*"

"Is kissing on the street against the law in Portugal?" asked Lydia.

"Not to my knowledge, but bikinis are. You don't wear a bikini, do you?"

"I bathe in a Mother Hubbard," said Lydia, kissing him. "I've been told I'm a little heavy around the hips," she added. "What's your considered judgment?"

"You're beautiful around the hips and above the hips and below the hips, and whoever said that you aren't should be sued for defamation of character. You are beautiful, you know."

"I'm more beautiful today at this time than I was yesterday at this time," said Lydia.

At the hotel when she changed into her bathing suit, Lydia noticed that her passport was on top of the dressing table. She was sure, pretty sure, anyway, that she'd left it in the right-hand drawer. But I must be wrong, she thought. I was more than a little giddy when I dressed last night. She looked through the case in which she kept her private papers. Nothing was missing, and so she dismissed the matter from her mind.

She and Paul spent the afternoon on the beach. Sometimes they swam, and sometimes they sat on the brown sand, soaking up the sun. They talked about the two of them separately and together, and about their remarkable childhoods and adulthoods, and the miracle of their meeting, and other miracles, major and minor.

Sometimes they were silent. Paul Julian was not a man undone by silence or by his thoughts.

Toward sunset, as the yellow cliffs turned pink, Paul said, "Could I interest you in another swim?"

"Not on your life. When I turn into a vegetable, I turn into a vegetable, and while you may have heard that I am a poisonous mushroom, it's not true. I'm a carrot gone slightly soft."

Paul raced into the surf and threw his brown body against an impatient wave, and Lydia wondered who had hurt him and why. Had there been several someones or only one? Whoever it was, it hurt a lot and for a long time, and then she thought, but that doesn't make him unique. Not in this place and this time. And don't get me started on *my* operation.

Besides, she thought, the hurting time is over, for both of us. Although it is still only April, the invincible summer has begun.

In the evening they had drinks with Ernesto Bernardes in the bar at the hotel. He could tell that they were lovers, and although he was too well-mannered to mention it, the idea delighted him. He spoke of Sybil.

"I thought," he said, "that she was the saddest woman I ever saw, and the most lonely."

It's true, thought Lydia, although she had never really articulated the idea in her mind. Sybil is lonely, and she is sad. She is in constant search for love in the beds of strangers. And who knows, it might just be there in the brownstone on East 81st Street, with the shy and lonely man she married to purge herself of poverty. There are many kinds of poverty, though; the soul sometimes gets hungry, too.

"You are staying longer than you planned, I hope," Ernesto said to Lydia.

"I'd love to, but I can't. My son is getting married in Madrid, and I am going to meet his fiancée."

"Is it customary in the United States for the mother to pass judgment on the bride?" asked Ernesto. "Here, such is the custom, and my mother never approves of the girls I wish to marry, and I never approve of the girls she wants me to marry. And so I remain a bachelor, which is often pleasant."

"Mrs. Brady will be staying for some time," said Paul. "I'll persuade her."

"Good," said Ernesto. "I shall take you to the pilgrimage of Our Lady of Piety in Loulé. It is most beautiful."

At dinner Paul said, "Next week I have to go to Paris for a day or so. We'll stay at the Ritz."

"Next week I'm going to Madrid," said Lydia.

"Christopher struck me as a young man quite capable of handling his own affairs," said Paul.

"Sure. You had a nice long chat with my son, and he said, 'Mr. Julian, sir, I am a young man quite capable of handling my own affairs, and when you see my mother, I hope you'll tell her so.' "

"Not exactly," said Paul, "but I was in Madrid last month, and I went to the embassy on business. A good-looking young man named Christopher Brady helped me out, and he had blue eyes that are remarkably like his mother's. I liked him. He was polite and competent and *interested*. The last is rare.

"I said to myself at the time, 'This young man, the very model of a public servant in the American foreign service, must have a wonderful mother, and if I possibly can, I'm going to arrange to meet her.'"

"But you didn't tell me," said Lydia.

"You didn't ask."

"How did he look?"

"Here we go. Do you think he's eating regularly? Is he working too hard? Is he going to get promoted? We will now have a whole series of mother questions."

And they did. Paul answered them rather well, too, considering the fact that he had spent no more than a casual fifteen minutes with Christopher Brady, boy diplomat. What Paul didn't know, he made up, which is often the best way.

They had coffee in the lounge, and, among many other things, Lydia said, "I'm so afraid I won't like Candice."

"I hope you do," said Paul, "but if you don't, it won't really matter much. You're not marrying her."

"But suppose I don't and Christopher asks me what I think?"

"He won't ask you what you think; he'll tell you what you think. Besides, you have to remember that the girl you'll see isn't the girl Christopher sees and loves. Am I right? As usual?"

In reply, Lydia said, "It's so odd, your having met both Christopher and Simeon."

"Not particularly, and I didn't *meet* Simeon. He only talked at me, me and several hundred other people. He convinced me of one thing. I would have gone to any lengths to avoid spending an evening with any member of the Trollope family.

"And now, if I could, I'll take you back to the house, and first, we'll listen to some music. How do you feel about Casals playing Bach?"

"Warm," said Lydia, "about Casals playing Bach I have a very warm feeling."

Lydia did not notice that the Silent Man was sitting in the lobby of the hotel, reading a copy of the international edition of *Life* magazine; Paul did, however.

Chapter 14

✿ Lydia decided to stay another week, and when she called Christopher, he seemed to accept the idea of another week of separation from his mother with no great pain.

He said she sounded wonderful, and Lydia said that she was and, feeling deceitful, added that she had met some nice Americans. Nothing wrong with a certain amount of deceit. Heaven save us from the truth-tellers.

She and Paul didn't see any other Americans, nice or otherwise, or any Portuguese except, on occasion, Ernesto and Fernando. They were a peaceful island of two.

The time passed quietly. They swam, they read, they listened to music. In the evenings they sometimes went to a tavern in a nearby village and drank Portuguese beer. Or they would walk through the silent streets or stand on the seawall and watch a bright ship in the distance or the waves or each other.

Once they went to an American movie in Faro.

"I warn you," said Paul, "going to a movie in Portugal isn't an evening's entertainment; it's a career."

Half an hour after the advertised time for the movie, the bar was still doing a flourishing business, and the theater was filled with happy groups eating six-course dinners out of brown paper bags.

When the lights finally did go down, the theater smelled of port wine, garlic, fish, babies, and the bodies of people who were not convinced that cleanliness is next to godliness.

First, there were a great many garish advertisements for foolish things, and then a long newsreel proving beyond doubt that although Lydia hadn't read a newspaper since leaving

Briley, she hadn't missed a thing, except *Peanuts*. After which, there was another long intermission, and the bar was once again crowded. Those who had digested their dinners started in on midnight snacks.

Lydia said, "It's a career all right, and I'm about ready for the gold watch for my fifty years of faithful service."

"This is only the first intermission," said Paul.

Eventually the feature did start, but before the end of the second reel and the beginning of the second intermission, Lydia said, "This may be a body blow to the movie industry, but I wish to announce my retirement."

When they were outside, Paul said, "You have to remember that a lot of these people only go to a movie about once a year, and it's a real event in their lives. They like to have it take a long time."

"Once a year is far too often to spend a lifetime at the movies," said Lydia.

"Besides, there's almost no television."

"Some people have all the luck. By the way, what was that movie about and who was in it?"

"I was about to ask you," said Paul.

But most of the time they talked. Every sentence began a new voyage of discovery. Who says the age of adventure is over?

About Paul's nose:

"I was quite a violent young man. The first time it was broken I was defending the chastity of the young lady who turned out to have entertained almost the entire personnel of our Pacific Fleet. I was thrown in the brig, where I spent an educational few months. The second time it was over a matter of principle, and the other fellow went to the hospital. I went to jail, assault and battery."

"What was the principle?"

"The more port you drink, the better for the Portuguese economy," said Paul, pouring her some.

He mentioned his wife only once; her name was Fran.

"A great many people said I married her for her money, and

it's true that her family had more than mine. Her father was a master plumber."

Once he said of his daughter, whose photograph was on the Louis XV desk in his study, "There are all those books about children who think their parents can't be theirs. What about all the parents who, observing their children, wonder if there wasn't some kind of mix-up at the hospital?"

And, "I was born disenchanted and knowing that, despite the Reverend Donne and Mr. Hemingway, every man is an island, and we are all filled with selfish, aggressive appetites and destructive impulses, and we must curb them as much as possible. But to deny them is foolish and likely dangerous."

"I couldn't agree more," said Lydia, who up to that moment would have fought to the death anyone expressing such heresy.

On the ninth day they gave Fernando the evening off, and Lydia cooked dinner. Filets of beef, thick and aged and beautiful. Lydia had bought them herself, at a butcher shop in Faro. She had thought some of taking along the butcher's assistant, who had eyes made of black velvet and skin of a slightly lighter shade. He was beautiful and competent and serious and anxious to please.

My grandfather, thought Lydia, spent a good ten years of his life agitating for the abolition of child labor, and rightly so.

But somewhere along the affluent way, something went wrong. I give you an evening at home with the American Mother of the Year, any year, and her All-American son, aged eleven, known to his Moms as Junior, to his acquaintances as Fatso.

"You mean I've got to walk two whole blocks to pick up a lousy quart of milk? I'm *tired.*"

"Of course you are, dear. Looking at television all day does tire you out. I'll go. Mummy needs the exercise."

"Yah. Well, don't slam the door when you get back. I'll be looking at *Petticoat Junction,* and bring me a carton of Hershey Bars and a couple quarts of tutti-frutti."

After dinner that night she and Paul played dominoes, which is almost as popular in Portugal as *futbal.* Lydia didn't feel she was quite up to the latter, but with dominoes she could keep part of her mind occupied with other matters, contentment, for instance.

After ten the telephone rang.

"It's Ernesto," said Paul. "There's a transatlantic call for you. Do you want it transferred here?"

It took a minute for Lydia to reply. Something has happened to Day, she thought, something awful. Day is dead. And then she thought, no, Day isn't dead. It's my mother. I sensed I shouldn't leave, and that last day, I knew it. But I didn't turn back. Intent on my own selfish pursuits, I . . .

"Have it transferred here."

When the phone rang a second time, Lydia picked it up, and an unfamiliar voice said, "Mrs. Brady? Briley New York calling Mrs. Simeon Brady."

"Lydia?" The voice was old and faraway.

"Hello, Mother. Are you all right?"

"Hello, dear." The voice wavered.

"What's wrong, Mother?"

"I didn't know whether to call you or cable, but I was afraid you would see it in the paper. Now you must promise—"

"Darling, please tell me what it is."

"It isn't really that important, in a way, to you, I mean, anymore. But I said to Sybil, I called Sybil . . ."

It's Simeon, thought Lydia; Simeon has killed himself.

"He died right away. The doctor says there was no pain at all."

"How?"

"He shot himself. No one seems to know why. He just went out in the garage and shot himself."

"I'm sorry," said Lydia.

"I hesitated about calling you, but, as I say, I talked to Sybil. She would have, but, after all, I'm your mother."

Lydia was aware, with pain, that her mother's fine, sharp mind was not as fine or as sharp as it had been. Sadder still, her mother knew it, too.

"I'm talking too much. I'm a garrulous old woman. Now you're not to think of coming home."

"No, Mother, I won't come home."

"He's going to be cremated tomorrow. There's to be no service. His—the girl—she says he didn't want a service. Is that right? Did he?"

"No, he didn't want a service."

"Now you're not to feel that it had anything to do with you, because it didn't. Everybody says, whether it's true or not, that he and the girl were having trouble, and there were other things. At the college. I won't repeat them on the phone. Just remember it has nothing to do with you."

"I'll remember."

"Are you having a good time?" said the faraway, uncertain voice.

"I'm having a fine time."

"I'll write to you in Madrid, and I'll see you in London, and now I guess I'd better hang up. Garrulity, transatlantic, costs money. Give my love to Christopher and the girl."

"I will. Thank you for calling, dear, and good-bye."

Lydia put down the phone. She told Paul what had happened, and he gave her a brandy and sat in the menacing dusk beside her, holding her hand.

I am glad, she thought, that death came quickly and that there was no pain. Simeon was not good with pain. But then, who is?

I am glad, she thought, that Simeon has at last escaped the guilt of the books unfinished, of the promises unkept, of the furtive infidelity, of the waste of himself.

I'm sorry. That's all? After twenty-four years of mornings, of noons, and of nights, more nights than anything else, some of them endless, only *I'm sorry.* Not quite all. I am also relieved. Life for Simeon was no longer an adventure; it was an agony, and I could do nothing to relieve it. I tried, I tried hard, I tried always. But did I try hard enough?

After a time she began to sob, and Paul held her in his arms.

Later, when the first rays of the innocent sun gleamed on the distant water, Lydia said, "I failed him. If I hadn't failed him, he'd still be alive."

"From what you've told me," said Paul, "I'd say he was doomed, and one's duty to the doomed is not to interfere."

Lydia started to cry again, and Paul said, "You didn't fail him. He failed himself."

"I want to go back to the hotel now," said Lydia.

"Please don't. Please stay here. I'll give you a sleeping pill, tuck you into bed, and stay with you until you fall asleep, and while you're asleep, I'll be down here, thinking about you."

"I want to go back to the hotel," Lydia said again, her voice rising.

"Are you sure?"

"Quite sure."

"I'll take you, then," said Paul.

He drove slowly through the placid hills, through the waking villages, past the untroubled fields of oats and barley.

Once he said, "I know how you feel. You're suffering a kind of shock."

"You haven't the faintest notion how I feel," said Lydia.

She saw his hands tighten on the wheel. She said, "I'm going to Madrid in the morning."

"You can do that if you'd like," said Paul, "and if you like, you can suffer the anguish of synthetic guilt and be childishly self-indulgent and cheaply sentimental. I think you're too good for that."

"You haven't any idea what I think, either," said Lydia. "You never have."

"The founding fathers were remarkable men," said Paul, "but they were wrong about one of the inalienable rights. It's not the pursuit of happiness. It's the search for misery. People seek it out like homing pigeons, and once they find it, they gratefully lie down and wallow in it."

"You're jim-dandy at analyzing people," said Lydia. "All you need is a couch."

"I need you very much, and I think you need me, now more

than ever. I love you as completely as it's possible for me to love anyone, and I think you love me. Since it's the first time that's happened to either of us, and surely the last, I think we ought to cherish it and hang onto it."

"Don't worry about me. These American lady tourists that you pretend to despise, there'll be another along next week, just as I'm sure there was the week before I came."

"You're a hard hitter," said Paul, "right in the gut."

He stopped the car in front of the hotel, and a small boy once again held open the door and looked up at Lydia hopefully. It wasn't a tip he had in mind; it was a smile of recognition.

But as she got out of the car, Lydia looked the other way.

"Please let me stay with you," said Paul, "please."

Lydia started, half-running, up the sidewalk to the hotel.

"I'll call you at four," a distant, unfamiliar voice called after her.

But at four in the afternoon, Lydia was at the airport in Lisbon. She sat in the bar, where ten days before she had first seen Paul's wistful smile.

She thought, Simeon is dead, but he has once again arranged to punish me, and then she thought, no, not this time. This time I managed it all by myself, no one to blame but the undersigned.

She thought, Paul has just called the hotel, or maybe he's just gone to the hotel and found out that while Ernesto was in the village—I'm sure he told Ernesto to keep an eye on me—I checked out.

Paul's probably back at the peaceful white villa on the green hill, she thought.

"It's so beautifully furnished," she had said. "Who did it?"

"I did it," said Paul. "I thought I was doing it for me, but it turns out it was for us."

I could call him right now, and at eight I could be on a plane back to Faro, and he could meet me at the airport.

But at eight she was on a jet on its way to Madrid.

Maybe Sybil is right. An oak leaf is perfectly designed; it's the shape of the human heart that needs improvement.

Chapter 15

❧ When she got to Madrid, Lydia took a taxi from the airport to the Ritz. It was the first hotel that came to mind.

Fortunately, a room was available, large and bright and cheerful. From the window was a view of the handsome obelisk in the Plaza de Lealtad, and a little farther away was the Prado, looking proud and pink. Red azaleas were blooming everywhere, and in the air was the sweet aroma of the *acia* trees.

Simeon would have liked Madrid, thought Lydia; he had read widely in Spanish literature.

" 'No one is worth more than anyone else,' " he would say. "That's from Quixote, and I may be one of the few living non-Spaniards who has read it from cover to cover.

> For the poor without a penny
> Four houses are always open,
> The hospital and the prison,
> The church and the burial ground.

"I don't know who wrote that, and they're wrong about the hospital, but I'll tell you this: Privilege is the enemy of progress. That's vintage Simeon Brady."

Simeon never outgrew the simple, believing thirties, thought Lydia; he never stopped thinking that the world was not good enough. For that, maybe not to the head of the class, but I should think a passing mark.

And in the summing up, some attention must be paid to his mother. Not to blame her, that's too easy, but she is part of the portrait, a dark part. Simeon said of her, "That awful woman who bore me, after which, for the rest of her life, she bored me."

Simeon's mother, a would-be Southern lady with a dissatisfied face, small, clawlike hands that were never still, and a voice that was never silent.

A few days before her son's wedding she said to Lydia, "It's your business, in a manner of speaking, but that Sybil Lee, the one you're thinking of having for a bridesmaid. She may call herself a Lee, but I can smell one of the chosen people a mile away, and if you ask me—"

"I haven't asked you, Mrs. Brady, and I have no such intention."

"Then I guess Mr. Brady and I will not be on hand for the wedding of our only begotten son."

"Simeon's father will be perfectly welcome," said Lydia.

Later she said to Simeon, "I just can't compromise on that."

"I most sincerely hope not," he said.

For that, thought Lydia, a star of gold.

Lydia bathed, washing away the dirt of the day and as many of the cares as she could get at. Then she redid her face, put on a dressing gown, and called Christopher. The news of his father's death had already come over the ticker tape at the embassy.

Christopher's voice revealed no emotion. He had always been able to cope with the unexpected, whether good or bad.

"I'm glad you're here," he said. "I'll be at the hotel in half an hour."

While waiting, Lydia mixed herself a drink.

Christopher and Henry Lyman had spent a great deal of time in a male world that Lydia couldn't possibly have invaded, and they talked endlessly.

Lydia once asked, "What in the world do you and your grandfather talk about?"

Christopher—say he was eleven—thought a long moment, and then he gave a considered answer.

"Things," he said. No wonder he went into the foreign service.

When Christopher was fourteen, his grandfather had a coronary and for a month was unable to speak. Then he quietly died.

Lydia went alone to Christopher's school to tell him.

Christopher said, "I'm glad. He was such a good talker, and when I saw him the last two times, it wasn't really him at all. He's better off dead."

"If you want to cry, nobody would mind," said Lydia.

"I don't want to cry."

No, Christopher was not a crier. Moreover, he had been a boy whose hair was never mussed; he never had to be reminded to wash. His nails were always clean and neatly trimmed, his clothes always in order, his shoes forever shined.

At times, quite a few times, Lydia wished that Christopher would skin a knee so that she could bandage it and kiss it and make it well. In other words, she wanted Christopher to be the kind of boy she had in mind rather than the kind of boy he was.

Lydia thought of the time he announced that he wanted to go into the foreign service.

"That would be wonderful," she had said, "and if you don't change your mind, I don't see why you shouldn't be very good at it."

Simeon said, "You'll probably turn out to be an actor. You were very damn good in that school play. What was it called?"

"I won't change my mind, Mother," said Christopher.

"I'm sorry I'm late," said Christopher, "but in Madrid, even Franco can't make the traffic run on time."

He kissed her, declined a drink, and seated himself on the Hepplewhite window seat that was covered with yellow silk.

I'd forgotten just how handsome he is, thought Lydia. You almost feel as if you ought to turn away for a moment; it's too much.

She looked at the blond, open face, at the innocent blue eyes, at the long, curling lashes, at the smile that had gotten him so much and saved him so much, and she thought, Simeon never looked like that, not even in the golden days.

And she thought, to be that good-looking is not easy. A great many people must have wanted him very much. To have resisted their no doubt enticing blandishments—and I think Christopher has—took strength of character and singleness of purpose.

"I called your hotel in Armação de Pêra," he said. "They said you'd checked out and hadn't left a forwarding address, but I had a hunch you'd be coming to Madrid. I called Day, too. She'd already heard, and she's okay. So, from the look of you, are you. You look the way you used to in the middle of the summer on the Cape."

"If the light happens to be kind, I do," said Lydia, and then she said, "I was a little shaken when I heard about Simeon."

"I was, too, a little. Candice saw it on the ticker. She told me. I didn't have much time to think about it, but when I did, all I could think was, poor old Sim, he was a good man, but he just wasn't up to much.

Lydia didn't answer. How can you? Honor thy father. That's a commandment, but I'm not God. Besides, honor, respect, esteem, those you earn. And if Simeon didn't, it's a pity, but no more than that. You can get from people only what they're willing to give.

"Your father was proud of you," she said.

"I'm sure he thought he was," said Christopher.

He paused a moment. Then he said, "Could I ask you a question? You don't have to answer it, but it's something Day and I used to talk about. Why did you marry him? You're so much stronger than he was."

Lydia looked at her son's loved, well-made head, and she said, "I didn't think that until quite recently. I always thought he was the strong one."

After a while she said, "Why did I marry him? Do you ever know for sure? Sybil once said, and God knows she's an expert, 'Never knock the beginning of a relationship. You both may have started it to stay alive.'

"For me your father was like a bottomless wishing well. I

kept pitching in bright pennies, hoping I'd get his approval, but I never did, and one day, not too long ago, either, I realized I never would.

"I realized something else, something you've probably known all along about yourself, that it was my approval of me that I had to worry about and work on. I have, too, and sometimes for as long as fifteen minutes at a stretch I'm quite happy with me."

"There are a couple of things I've always liked about you," said Christopher. "One is that you never gave Day and me an easy answer."

"There are one or two things I've always liked about you. But what about this evening? Am I going to meet Candice?"

"I'm sorry. The British are having a cocktail party, and we have to go. The honor of the republic depends on it. Could we have lunch tomorrow?"

"The three of us. You and Candice and I, here at the hotel at one."

"Great. She's looking forward to meeting you. You'll like her." Ah, there, Mr. Julian. *"He won't ask you what you think; he'll tell you what you think."*

"By the way," said Lydia, under the circumstances quite casually, she felt, "I've met someone who knows you, a man named Paul Julian."

Her son was not a man Lydia would have dreamed of playing poker with, not to mention the fact that even as a child he always beat her at Old Maid.

"Oh," said Christopher.

"He spoke well of you."

"That's always nice to hear."

"Any day now you're going to be Secretary of State," said Lydia.

"Under Secretary, perhaps," said Christopher.

He kissed his mother and went off to uphold the honor of the republic at a cocktail party.

Lydia called room service and ordered an omelette, a green salad, and because she felt she somehow deserved it, half a bottle of white wine. The meal was served with a great deal of pomp and circumstance, and if there is anything that helps the digestion, it is pomp and circumstance.

Afterward she placed a call for Paul, but there was no answer. I hurt him today, she thought. I hurt him because I wanted to hurt me, and he was the nearest target. I hope that he'll be able to forgive me, and I'll do my best to forgive myself.

Then she went to bed, and she thought, I never loved Simeon completely. Maybe I shouldn't have married a man I didn't love completely, virtues and vices, good and bad, strength and weakness, in sickness, in health.

But under the circumstances I did the best I could, and so, I am sure, did Simeon, a good man who just wasn't up to much.

Chapter 16

❧ The next morning Lydia woke up early, feeling rested, and after breakfast she called the beauty parlor. Although she didn't know how to say "the works" in Spanish, she apparently got the message across, because for almost two hours she was curled, beaten, rubbed, soaked, dried out, and anointed with sweet-smelling oils.

She decided to wear the severe black that had seen better days, but then so had its wearer, and a string of pearls that had once belonged to her grandmother. I hope, she thought, that Candice likes me and likes the dress. As Christopher says, I am bound to like Candice.

She tried to call Paul again; still no answer. So she decided to go to the Prado. She spent the rest of the morning looking at the exquisite portraits of what was surely the ugliest royal family in the history of the world.

Then she went back to the hotel to meet the long-legged girl her son was going to marry. I hope, she thought, that Candice isn't going to want to get into a discussion of Marcel Proust, although I am something of an expert on the Oz books and could go on for hours about the Bobbsey twins.

"This is Candice," said Christopher.

"Pleased to meet you, I'm sure," said Candice. She was perhaps a foot shorter than Christopher, who was a little under six feet, and her legs were thick-ankled and stubby. The seams of her stockings were not straight.

"I told Chris I wasn't sure I was dressed for the Ritz," Candice was saying.

"You look lovely, Candice," said Lydia, and she smiled the

way actresses do in those movies in which there are a great many nuns.

The dress was avocado green, and while it was probably expensive, it needed pressing, and Candice had covered her face with a thick coating of white pancake. It was a pleasant face, a little long for beauty, and she had wide, light brown eyes, but her long brown hair was pulled into an angry swirl at the nape of her neck. Her mouth was blood red, and there were two tiny eyebrows painted somewhere near the middle of her forehead, giving her a look of eternal surprise. I wonder, thought Lydia, why Candice has gone to so much trouble to make herself unattractive.

Lydia continued her mother superior smile, although she realized she'd never get a part in one of the nun movies. They were always playing baseball, and Lydia's batting average wasn't that good.

"I'm told the food is good here," said Christopher, "and since I have this crazy, rich American mother who is picking up the tab—you are picking up the tab, aren't you?—let's give it a whirl."

Candice said, "Lots of these places, my father says, when they see you coming they just hike up the prices until they're sky high if they see you're an American."

During lunch, Candice more than held up her end of the conversation.

She spoke of her hometown, Missoula, Montana. "It's one of the most truly sophisticated small cities in the entire United States. By comparison, New York is strictly from Hicksville. The university is in Missoula, you know, and Albert Toynbee —he's the historian—comes there all the time, and Auden— he's the poet—and Lennie Bernstein."

"The conductor?" asked Lydia, wishing she hadn't.

She saw, without pleasure, that Christopher was looking at Candice as if she were delivering the Gettysburg Address as well as the Sermon on the Mount.

"I can't wait for you and Chris to meet my father and

mother," Candice was saying. "My father's in wallpaper, and he's got these three stores. He's a former state commander of the American Legion, twice, and they wanted him to run for Congress, but he wouldn't. It was written up in all the papers, including in Wyoming. He said, 'I prefer to serve in Missoula.'"

"He sounds as if he'd be a splendid Congressman," said Lydia. She was not at that moment happy with herself. I am, she thought, acting like the kind of mother I despise. And I must remember what Paul said, the girl I am looking at and listening to is not the girl Christopher sees and loves. What's more, Candice is probably terrified of me and thus is not at her best. And I must remember that I was not invited to Atlantic City for the Miss America gala when I was Candice's age. Nor, as I recall, were any of my remarks included in one of those volumes of the world's great conversations.

As Candice continued, Lydia kept all of those things in mind; it did no good at all.

"What are you two having for dessert?" she asked.

"I don't think we'll have any dessert, will we, Chris?" said Candice. "My Uncle Chalmer—he's an M.D.—says if we stayed off desserts . . ."

"We won't have any dessert," Lydia said to the waiter.

"Anyway, Uncle Chal—we call him Chal—he says you can't start too young watching your diet. The body starts deteriorating at twenty-six, in some cases even earlier, and Uncle Chal says if you wait till you get older, like forty or so, it's too late."

Lydia called for the check, and Candice commented, "We've got this famous place, Richey's Café and Barbecue, and people come from all over. You can get a whole barbecued chicken dinner for two and a half, and they don't allow tipping."

Lydia found herself giving the waiter far more than she had had in mind earlier.

"I guess we'd better be getting back to the office," said Christopher.

"Certainly enjoyed . . ." said Candice.

Lydia said that she had, too.

"How about you and I having dinner tonight?" Christopher asked his mother.

"I'd like that, but won't Candice come, too?"

Candice answered for her fiancé. She said, "I said no, the two of you haven't had a chance for a good chin-chin, and I don't want to be a buttinsky. Besides, Chris and I have just been on this mad whirl, every night something, and I haven't had time to do my hair or anything."

"That's sweet of you, Candice," said Lydia.

"I'll see you at eight," said Christopher.

Candice added, *"Mucho gracias* for the luncheon, Mother Brady."

Christopher gave Mother Brady a quick peck on the cheek. "I knew you two would hit it off," he said.

In the endless afternoon, Lydia walked through the crowded Puerta del Sol, seeing and hearing nothing; she could have been in Poughkeepsie. She kept asking herself various questions or, more accurately, one question phrased in various ways: Why Candice?

Toward evening, not having come close to an answer, she sank into a seat at a sidewalk café across the street from the hotel.

She sat there for quite some time. She was surrounded by a number of smart-looking Spanish women whose black hair was piled high on their proud heads. A few girls were elaborately paying no attention to a handful of boys with long legs and noses, and there were several men discussing what appeared to be the most serious business, another Inquisition, perhaps.

There were, of course, the Americans, the girls in their simple, smart dresses, and the boys in their beards. And the old and well-to-do, the men with false teeth and the women with blue hair, all trying desperately to see everything before they died and wishing they could enjoy it more.

Lydia snuffed out the second cigarette and called for the bill, and then a voice said, "You look well at a sidewalk café in Madrid on an April afternoon, but you look lonely."

She looked up, and there he was, huge and brown and comforting, his dark eyes filled with pleasure and love.

He lifted her out of the chair, put his arms around her, and kissed her. The Spanish ladies looked startled, the elderly Americans looked envious, the younger ones looked approving, and one boy with an especially obtrusive head of hair applauded.

"I plan never to let you go again," said Paul.

Chapter 17

They were astounded at how much had happened to each of them in the little more than twenty-four hours they had been separated. Lydia decided that Paul hadn't changed much physically, a little paler, perhaps.

"I called you last night," she said, thinking of the blue dressing gown and the slippers in Paul's closet.

"Last night I played poker with Ernesto, lost for the first time in weeks, got demonstrably drunk, and decided I'd never see you again."

"And I called you again this morning."

"This morning, having the kind of hangover I haven't had since the morning after I was sprung from the Navy, I got a plane to Lisbon and then another one to come here. I was in no condition for the hazards of air travel, but I had to do it. It's the first time I've ever come after anybody."

"Have many people come after you?" asked Lydia. She felt the question was well phrased but possibly somewhat familiar.

Paul seemed not to have heard.

They discussed what they were going to do. They'd go to Toledo, of course, but not on a weekend.

Paul said, "Thousands of tourists, mostly Germans. You wonder who's back home planning the wars, but on a weekday you go to El Greco's house, which is so calm that after a while you think maybe you could paint as well as he did. Then you go outside, and everybody looks like the people in his pictures." Seville, naturally. Granada, to be sure. Valencia. "It's the most beautiful." Barcelona. "Madrid is metropolitan. Barcelona is cosmopolitan, which is more interesting."

"And there are other countries; we don't have to spend all our time in Spain."

"But are we going to *have* time?" said Lydia.

"Of course we're going to have time. We're both going to live well into the twenty-first century."

They watched an American woman of fifty or so, who was a little drunk and was sitting at a table alone, paying too much attention to one of the handsome waiters.

"Poor thing," said Lydia. "She's lonely."

Paul then delivered another part of his orientation lecture on American women abroad, which is somewhat repetitious, but the peroration goes like this: "While her husband was alive, she was one of those who spoke in soft whispers; butter wouldn't melt. All she wanted to do was make sure that she had acres of diamonds and minks and sables and two Cadillacs for each of the babies. Then the poor husband died of overwork, and off she went to see the world. Here she is, cluttering up the landscape. Widows like that are our biggest export. No wonder we're not universally loved.

"And there isn't one of those widows who ever took the trouble to learn how to please a man, particularly in bed. And don't say I'm a woman hater, because I'm not. I'm a hater of non-women."

When the woman's husband, a large domineering man who looked as if he might be an important Rotarian and was even drunker than his wife, appeared, Paul said, "I was speaking theoretically."

A little later a regal man wearing a white *djellaba* trimmed in gold seated himself next to them. Lydia was sure he was an Arabian prince.

"Either that or there's a Shriner's convention in town," said Paul. "Let's go."

They walked along the Gran Vía, which was crowded with people going nowhere in particular and enjoying every minute of it. There was a feeling of expectancy, as if something utterly delightful were about to happen. It's the people you go to Madrid to see, the people and the Prado.

"I met Candice," said Lydia.

"And you didn't like her."

"I wouldn't say that," said Lydia, and she described the luncheon in some detail. She felt her objectivity deserved a citation of some kind.

"You didn't like her at all," said Paul.

"The worst of it is," said Lydia, "Christopher seemed to think we got along fine."

Paul sighed. "It won't be easy, but at dinner tonight, why don't you try to perpetuate that myth? There's a lot to be said for myths; that's why they're so popular. And while you're at it, why don't you give some thought to what Christopher is going to think of me."

"He'll like you," said Lydia rather loudly, since she didn't for a minute believe it.

"Is one to see you later tonight?"

"I should certainly hope so. Where are you staying?"

"At the Ritz, of course."

They walked slowly back to the hotel, arm in arm, and Lydia thought, now I know why there are 382 quotations on the subject of love in *Bartlett's,* and I've read them all, and none of them got it right. I wonder if it shows.

She and Christopher had dinner at the Commodore, which was elegant and, to Lydia, somewhat intimidating. The last time she had eaten at a restaurant with her son, it had been at a Stouffer's in New York, and he had had some difficulty in deciding between a banana split and a double fudge sundae with nuts. No longer so. He ordered the garlic soup, roast pig, and fruit soufflé with commendable ease and carried on a long conversation with the wine stewards about the red and the white.

It was not until they were eating the soufflé that Christopher said, "I have to confess I was a little nervous at lunch. You can never be absolutely sure how two people are going to get along. How about some Tío Pepe?"

"I'd love some," said Lydia, and she added what she had known all along she would say, "Candice is a nice girl."

"She was so afraid you wouldn't like her," said Christopher. "She's very bright, don't you think?"

"Very."

"When I first got here, she'd already been in Madrid about six months, and I didn't notice her at all for the longest time. I was a little uneasy myself. You know, each new post, it's like going to a new school when you're a kid.

"One night I was working late, until after midnight, and on the way out, I saw that the light in the library was on. So I went in to turn it off, and there was Candice. She was reading a big book by Sumner Welles on American foreign policy. It turned out she came to the library three or four times a week.

"So I took her out for a drink, and we talked until it was almost time to go back to work. That's how it started.

"All the other girls I used to go out with, they always had it made. Candice doesn't, and she's full of surprises."

There you are, thought Lydia. My son is in love with a girl who is full of surprises, and since he has outgrown fudge sundaes with nuts and become an expert on vintage wines, I should guess he is quite up to picking out the girl he wants to marry.

"I have great faith in you," said Lydia, "and such high hopes, but most of all, I want you to be happy."

"I've got a pretty good start," said Christopher, "a good deal of it thanks to you."

In the taxi on the way back to the hotel, Lydia said, "You remember my mentioning Paul Julian, the man I met in Armação de Pêra?"

Her son nodded; whatever he was thinking was top secret.

"He's in Madrid; he got here this afternoon."

Since there was no reply, Lydia went on. "I don't know much about him, but he seems like a nice man."

"If you like him, that's the main thing, I should think," said Christopher. Live and let live, love and let love.

At the hotel Christopher said, "Most people wear a protective coat of armor; you don't. I doubt that one comes in your size."

He kissed her and said good night.

Lydia woke once during the night. The huge, comforting shadow of Paul was beside her, and she thought, Paul is my protective coat of armor, and she thought, he will keep me from all harm. He will try, in any case.

Which is what happened.

Chapter 18

❧ A few days later, with Paul's help, Lydia found an apartment in a residential hotel, not grand, quite shabby-genteel, in fact, but comfortable, and there was the privacy afforded by the fact that there were several rooms, privacy from self. Lydia did not like to spend the night in the same room in which she had to spend a good part of the day, no matter how large or elegant the room might be. The kitchen was large, and in the living room was a piano in good tune and a fireplace.

When the superintendent asked how long she was taking it for, Lydia hesitated a moment and looked at Paul, then said, "For a month at least."

"I should think," said Paul, "easily a month."

He kept his suite at the Ritz, and he went there every morning after breakfast.

Lydia's neighborhood was quiet, with broad boulevards and splendid plazas. At night the plazas were proudly lighted, like the paintings at the Prado, and the streets were crowded with shy, untouching lovers, and hopeful young men in groups, and anxious girls in other groups. Large families, usually with babes in arms, sat in the small cafés, happy and complete.

But Lydia liked the neighborhood best when she went shopping in the early mornings. The lines of solemn schoolboys in black caps and blue smocks, carrying austere briefcases. The immaculate milkmen in horse-drawn carts that were as white as virgin snow. And the street sweepers, making do despite the fact that the Spanish have not yet invented the broom.

On the day we are concerned with here, Lydia went out while Paul was still asleep. Before she left the apartment, she, as usual, took a final look at him, at the broad arm thrown, childlike, across his eyes to shut out the morning light. Even in sleep there was something comforting about him. He was a man one could depend on, and she did. Sybil had once said that a woman without a man was only half alive, but it depends on the man, thought Lydia.

Lydia and the butcher got along well, maybe because she could now count up to ten in Spanish and say words like *biftec* and *cordero* and *pavo* and *pato,* and she pointed a good deal. As a result of these accomplishments, the butcher charged her only about a third more than his Spanish customers and perhaps a quarter less than the other Americans who lived and shopped in the neighborhood. Besides, his assistant, who had red cheeks and green eyes, was in love with her, and she returned the passion. She didn't think Paul would mind, although the boy was eleven years old if he was a day. In my country, she thought, the bright ones are planning expeditions to the outer planets. In Spain and Portugal they seem to become butcher's assistants, and in the long run . . .

She had invited Christopher and Candice for dinner that evening. They hadn't met Paul, and although the rest of the evening might be a disaster, she wanted the dinner to be perfect.

She decided on chicken, which is always dependable, unlike veal, which is capricious.

At the vegetable store she picked out the mushrooms, which were huge and beautiful, some of the sweet Spanish onions, lettuce, which was greener than lettuce had any right to be, and artichokes.

It was a magic morning, more like mid-June than late April. The sky was bright and cloudless, the sun dark yellow, the air pure and refreshing.

On the way back she stopped to watch while an old man with Pinocchio's nose sold a gigantic egg-shaped balloon to a little girl with a face the color of a ripe olive and a smile that had never known disappointment.

I am feeling full of beans and optimism, thought Lydia. I am feeling cherished and needing and needed, and since, in forty-two years and seven months and some days, I have rarely felt any of these, I want to remember exactly how it is. If there are dark times ahead, I'll need some few bright memories.

As she passed the tiny bar around the corner from the hotel, a woman sitting on one of the yellow chairs spoke to her.

"Aren't you Mrs. Simeon Brady?" she asked.

Lydia said that she was, and the woman stood up. She was tall and had a faded girl's face that had been lovely. Now there were lines of displeasure about the somewhat beakish nose and a furtive look in the dismayed dark eyes. She was dressed in a handsome suit made of dark blue silk, and she had kept her figure; Lydia guessed her to be forty-five.

"You won't remember me," the woman said, "but we met once at a dinner party at Vassar. Later your husband spoke. I'm Mrs. George Emerson. Won't you sit down for a minute?"

"That's kind of you," said Lydia, "but I'm afraid I can't." She indicated the packages she was carrying.

"Oh, please," said the woman. "Just for a minute. My husband and I have been here for a week, and I haven't talked to any Americans except the kind who go on those awful organized tours. You know the kind."

"Well, just for a minute," said Lydia.

She sat down, put her packages on another of the yellow chairs, and ordered a mineral water.

The woman was, she said, from San Francisco. Her husband was retired, from what she didn't say. She loved the Spanish and Spain; she was lonely.

She had adored Simeon Brady; she'd never forget his talk. Was he with Lydia?

Lydia, who had no intention of going into details, said no, he was not. Was Lydia alone, then? Lydia said that she was.

"You must call us. We're at the Fenix. Maybe we could have dinner some evening."

Lydia smiled without commitment. The women talked a

little longer, and Lydia thanked her for the drink, excused herself, and walked on.

"I'm sure we'll meet again," the woman's voice called after her. "I'm just sure of it."

Lydia did not look back. There was, she felt, something elusively familiar about the woman's face, just what, she wasn't sure. It was ordinary enough, heaven knows, and maybe that was the secret of the vagrant memory. Or maybe it was simply a brief exchange of greetings in an evening at Vassar College. The woman was not someone Lydia would then or now have chosen to see again.

She thought no more about the incident for some time

That afternoon, while Lydia prepared the dinner, Paul went downtown, and when he came back, he brought two bottles of champagne.

"How would you feel about going to Paris in the morning?" he asked.

"Are you serious?"

"Perfectly. I managed to put it off for a few days, but tomorrow is D-Day." He filled a bucket with ice and put in one of the bottles of champagne; he put the other in the refrigerator.

"I have to see my lawyer. The Spanish are an admirable people, but they are understandably bored by the intricacies of the law. The French, on the other hand, are fascinated. And so I have a French lawyer, and I've got to see him. Come with me."

"How long are you staying?"

"If you don't come with me, I think I can make it in one day. I'd go tomorrow morning and come back the next. If you go, we'll stay as long as you like."

"I don't think I'll come," said Lydia. "I'm not exactly a member of the jet set—my, how I hate those words—and here I'll putter around and maybe go to the Prado, and tomorrow night I'll have supper alone and think of how absolutely marvelous it's going to be when you walk in the door."

"You're sure?"

"I'll miss you, but I'm sure. There isn't anything wrong, is there?"

"A detail," he said, "a detail that has to be attended to."

The dinner went well. The food was good, and the champagne did what champagne is supposed to do. Christopher and Paul got along from the start. They talked about bullfighting, about *flamenco* and *cante,* and about the rebellious mood of the Spanish students and the clergy. Candice was for the most part silent, although she several times said that the food was wonderful.

Afterward she volunteered to help Lydia clear the table and rinse and stack the dishes.

Paul and Christopher took a bottle of Tío Pepe to the small terrace that overlooked the courtyard.

As Lydia and Candice worked, Candice commented on the apartment; she said that it was lovely.

"Of course, a rented place is never quite the same," she went on. "I keep saying to Chris that we'll just be wanderers, no roots or anything like that, and I don't like the idea of bringing up children among so many foreigners, but under the circumstances, it being the career he has chosen to pursue . . ."

Whither thou goest, thought Lydia, but she said nothing.

Candice said that Paul Julian was such an interesting man, and she wondered aloud what he did for a living.

"I think he's taking a long vacation," said Lydia.

"It seems so peculiar, a man in the prime of life like that," said Candice. "My father always says if he had to retire, he thinks he'd just curl up his toes and die."

Lydia gave special attention to a stubborn spot on one of the plates, and Candice said, "We really haven't had a chance to talk, have we?"

Lydia didn't answer, although it seemed to her that Candice had had ample chance, more than.

"I wonder if I could come see you, say, tomorrow afternoon?" said Candice.

"Fine," said Lydia. "How about coming for tea or drinks, around five?"

"There won't be anybody else here, will there?" said Candice, inclining her head toward the terrace.

"I'll be alone."

"Goody," said Candice. She looked at the terrace conspiratorially, and then she said, "Don't tell Chris."

Lydia was tempted to say that she didn't like keeping secrets from her son and that it seemed odd that his fiancée should, but she didn't. She only nodded; she was becoming an expert nodder.

"You and Mr. Julian are awfully good friends, aren't you?" said Candice.

Lydia felt the color rise to her face, and she saw that her hands were unsteady.

She said, "I'll see you tomorrow at five."

"I'll bet you're just like Christopher in a lot of ways," said Candice. "I keep telling him, a lot of people you meet, you can't trust them as far as you can throw them."

"Thank you for helping me with the dishes, Candice," said Lydia.

At eleven Christopher finished his Tío Pepe, rose, and said, "It's time for the slaves of Uncle Sam to say good night."

Candice also stood up, a little unsteady from the Scotch before dinner, the champagne, and the brandy.

"It's just been the nicest time ever," she said. "And it certainly was interesting meeting you, Mr. Julian."

Christopher smiled and shook Paul's hand. "Good night, sir," he said.

He kissed his mother on the forehead and said, "Thank you, ma'am." Then, so softly that only she could hear, he said, "I like Paul."

"Good night and *mucho gracias,*" said Candice.

Lydia and Paul sat on the terrace, talking until very late. The houses were dark, and once in a while a car passed, or a motorbike, but the streets were empty and the family bars had closed. Madrid is at its best in the early evening; at shortly after midnight even the Puerta del Sol is nearly deserted.

"I was right about Christopher," said Paul. "He's an extraordinarily nice young man, and he has good manners, not all of which he learned at school. I like good manners. Whatever happened to them, do you suppose? They're gone. Like old-fashioned reticence, like last winter's snow.

"He's bright, too, but more than that, he's perceptive. Perception and intelligence are not the same thing."

"He liked you, too," said Lydia.

"I'm glad. I think Christopher is going to be an important man someday. He has opinions of his own, and while he expresses them with discretion, he expresses them. If there are many like him in the service, the republic may survive after all."

"Candice was as quiet as a mouse," said Lydia, cleverly, she thought.

"Which means, what did I think of Candice?"

"Not at all. If you want to tell me, fine and dandy, but I wouldn't think of asking."

Their eyes met, and Paul laughed and reached over and took her hand.

"You're a wonderful woman," he said. "You're intelligent and a magnificent cook, and you play the piano beautifully, and so on, and so on. The list of your achievements is nearly limitless; you are without any guile at all."

"That hardly sounds like a compliment."

"Well, it is, and treasure it. I have no opinion of Candice. She's young, she's unformed, she dresses badly, she makes up her face like a circus clown. She's ill at ease and without grace. But those, most of them, anyway, are the faults of youth and will be outgrown."

"When I was her age," said Lydia, "I was the gracious mother of two children. I was adorable, mature, witty, wonderful and wise. Well, at least I knew what to do with my hands."

"It's true that Candice didn't go to the proper schools. You'd have preferred one of those dependable Wellesley girls for Christopher, or Vassar or Smith or Sarah Lawrence or Bennington."

"That's absolutely not true. You make me sound like a snob." She yawned ostentatiously. "I'm really very tired."

"You are a snob," said Paul. "Most of us are, but you have to be snobbish about the right things. It shouldn't be a matter of the schools people go to or how much money their parents have. It's the stuff people are made out of. I don't know enough about Candice to judge that. I think you want me to say that she's the girl we marry when we are lieutenants and regret when we are majors."

"I don't want anything of the kind," said Lydia, trying to rise. "It's really late, and you have a plane to catch in the morning."

Paul did not release her hand. He said, "If we have a quarrel, and I hope we won't, it's going to be over something that concerns us and only us, not even something as important as your son Christopher. Now stay here. Don't move. I'm going to get us some cold milk."

While he was in the kitchen, Lydia wiped the unwelcome tears from her eyes.

Sometime later—the night sky was already blue, and the distant trucks could be heard starting their distant journeys—he said, "One of the bitterest truths, I imagine, is that we cannot transmit our experiences to our children, and we can spare them nothing. We can only hope that they are lucky."

Lydia's eyes were closed, and her head was resting on Paul's shoulder.

Paul said, "Nothing is irrevocable, not even, I suppose, an unfortunate marriage. Besides, some of those who have married as second lieutenants have gone on to high places, including, I'm told, the White House."

And his cool breath brushing her forehead, he said, "You're not to get up in the morning. You're to sleep, and in the evening I'll call you from Paris, and you're to remember that I'll miss you. Inordinately, I believe the word is."

At nine Lydia was aware of Paul's getting out of bed, ever so quietly; he was a thoughtful man.

After he went to the bathroom, she got up quickly, did a few essential things to her face, none of which helped in the slightest, and went to make breakfast.

As she worked, she thought of something Sybil had said in one of Sybil's more positive moments, which were many:

"It isn't that women want to emasculate men. It's that women can now do everything a man can, and this tends to rob them of their masculinity."

Lydia had not answered. One of the reasons their friendship had endured was that Lydia didn't have to comment on Sybil's nonsense. A good deal of the time she didn't even listen.

But now, she thought, there are quite a few things women can do that men can't. And one of them is to make breakfast when a man is going off to a hostile land where the natives are not at all friendly, like France."

"I knew you'd get up," said Paul. "I knew that no matter what I said, you'd drag yourself out of bed and make coffee for me. Eggs and bacon I wasn't so sure of, but thanks."

When he finished breakfast, he said, "Come with me. Put on a dress; we'll buy the rest in Paris. Come on. I can finagle you a seat on the plane."

"Nope. We've agreed. You're going to be busy, and I'm going to spend the day looking at paintings of contented dwarfs."

Paul kissed her one final time.

He said, "My mother used to tell me, 'If you have it good when you're young, you'll have it bad when you're old. And if you have it bad when you're young, you'll have it good when you're old.' You and I will have a magnificent old age."

"Hurry back, darling."

"I left my various telephone numbers in the bedroom. If anything should happen, anything at all, call me. I'll be on the next plane."

She heard his step on the marble stair, a light step for so large a man, an eager step. She thought of running after him. Wait. I'll go. I'll go just as I am. I've waited too long for this to miss a minute of it now.

She didn't, of course. One never can, not if one is over twenty. And in a way that's a pity.

Chapter 19

❦ After Paul left, Lydia tried to sleep, first closing the windows of the bedroom (not a breath of air), then opening them (too noisy). She lowered the shades, raised them, lowered them again. She tried putting a pillow over her head. Then she threw the pillow across the room, knocking over a nineteenth-century tree of life that she and Paul had found on a street off the Puerta del Sol. The tree of life broke into several thousand pieces, and as Lydia swept them into a wastebasket, she cut her hand. Twice. Talk about your symbolism.

She tried a hot bath to soothe her, but in the beginning the water was too hot, and then it was too cold. She spoke severely to the discomforting water. If you can't depend on the comforts of a hot bath, what is there?

She drank several cups of coffee, black and hot, but the coffee tasted of ashes.

Around eleven, the bellboy, the nice ugly one who was always studying, brought her a letter from her mother. The letter, which had been written before Simeon's death, described the green meadows beyond her mother's house and said that the lilacs were in bloom and the dogwood and the rhododendron. The letter said that her mother loved her and missed her.

Lydia put the infuriating letter aside. She tried not to think of Paul, who by this time was probably halfway to Paris.

"Absence not long enough to root out quite, all love increases love at second sight," she said aloud, and she said, "Where does that come from, anyway, and who said it, and who cares, and I don't believe a word of it."

"*Si, señora,*" said one of the maids.

Lydia dressed and took a taxi to the Retiro. She found the grass too blatant, the box hedges too prim, the roses in questionable taste. Besides which, she was surrounded by people screaming at each other in several foreign languages, including English.

She considered going to the Prado but changed her mind. This was not a day on which even Velazquez could put her at ease.

On the way back to the apartment, the taxi driver drove a block out of the way. She spoke harshly to him and reduced his tip from five pesetas to three.

I am certainly behaving maturely today, she thought, like a mature fishwife, and it's just as well Paul isn't here because when I'm in a mood like this, nothing and nobody are safe. Not the most innocent bystander, not tables, chairs, cups, saucers, spoons, not cows jumping over the moon. Take to the storm cellars, fellows, here comes Typhoon Lydia, spreading disaster every which way.

On the other hand, she thought, if Paul were here, I wouldn't be feeling this way. Would I?

At the apartment she tried writing a letter to Sybil, but there was too much to say, or not enough, all or nothing, and there wasn't time for all, and anyway, she'd be seeing Sybil in less than two weeks.

She picked up an American novel that she had bought on the Gran Vía a few days before. It was about a cloying group of California children at a summer camp, and there was all kinds of fancy carrying-on between campers of both sexes as well as between the counselors. Most of the carrying-on was out of doors and in the nude, but nobody got poison ivy, developed a cold, or was caught.

California is an odd state, thought Lydia, and unless I turn into an orange, I have no intention of going there, even for a short visit.

She put the book aside and made herself some more coffee; it still tasted ashy. She put a Montoya on the record player; Montoya had lost his touch, and his guitar was out of tune.

I am, she thought, in a city I have always wanted to be in. I love and am loved; everything in life is proceeding with tranquillity. What's wrong?

Nothing is wrong; that's what's wrong.

At a little after three, the studious bellboy brought an enormous white box from a florist. Inside were thousands of white violets and a card that said, "You know, and always. Paul."

Lydia put the violets in several small bowls, and then, feeling better, she took another bath. This time the water was exactly right. Could the plumbing system have been changed since morning?

By the time the doorbell rang, she was wearing a freshly ironed dress that matched the violets, and she was feeling relaxed and quite human again.

"Hello there, Mother Brady," said Candice. She was once more wearing the avocado-colored dress, but it had not been pressed. Maybe she doesn't have an iron, thought Lydia. Candice had on a little more makeup than usual.

"Would you like a drink?" asked Lydia.

"I guess a little drinky wouldn't hurt me," said Candice.

Lydia mixed a potent Scotch with not much water and two small ice cubes for Candice and another one of the same strength for herself.

"Is he here?" asked Candice.

"He?"

"Thanks. Oh, you know."

Lydia sipped her drink in silence.

"Mr. Julian, I mean."

"I'm quite alone," said Lydia.

"You must get awfully lonesome, Mother Brady."

"Not particularly," said Lydia, wondering why she had never liked the word *lonesome*. Lonely, yes, lonesome, no.

"Do you have a maid?" asked Candice.

"There are three girls who come in for a little while every day," said Lydia, defensively adding, "They work for the hotel."

"Three," said the judge. "My goodness, in a little dinky place like this."

"It's part of the hotel service," said Lydia, feeling she wasn't doing much of a job pleading her own defense. It might be better to throw herself on the mercy of the court.

"My mother says she doesn't know what she'd do all day if she didn't have her house and garden to take care of."

Lydia drank. Candice had apparently not noticed that despite the warm late afternoon, her future mother-in-law was shivering.

"Of course, she's younger," said Candice.

Lydia tried to ignore a nerve that was quivering in the small of her back, no doubt a sign of approaching decay.

"She's an Eastern Star," Candice went on, "and she's been every point of the star once, and now she's being groomed for Worthy Matron."

You won't get a word out of me on that one, Can, thought Lydia, although truth to tell, a few inquiries do occur to me. Just how worthy is a matron? And how does one go about grooming one? With a curry comb? And wouldn't you think that someone who has been every point in the star once would be able to pass muster without additional grooming?

"You're not a sister, I take it," said Candice.

Lydia, wondering if there was a Madrid branch of Alcoholics Anonymous, took a gigantic swallow of her drink, coughed, and said, "No, I'm an only child."

Candice placed a munificent smile on her blood-red lips and said, "I can't wait to write that to my mother. Sisters are what you call the girls in the Star. My father's a Mason. He's going to be a sixty-fourth degree."

It sounds like a pretty stiff sentence to me, thought Lydia. She said, "I believe you mentioned that your father was in the American Legion, but I didn't realize he was a Mason, too. Is he by any chance an Odd Fellow?"

"He was asked, but he declined. He says it's better to do a few things well than to scatter your shots."

"I certainly agree with your father there," said Lydia. "Would you like another drink, Candice?"

"No, thank you, Mother Brady. One's my limit until after dark, and Chris and I have agreed that he's not going to have anything after dinner from here on in. It takes too much out of you the next morning."

To be sure, thought Lydia, "Chris (*sic*) and I have agreed that he's . . ." In other words, even before the wedding, Chris is being reshaped, redesigned, brought up to date, dried out, drained. Not only of alcohol, but unless I miss my guess, which in these areas I seldom do, of the juices of life. Of independence.

"Are you having another one, Mother Brady?"

At least, thought Mother Brady. And she said what had occurred to her once or twice before. "Candice, dear, it's silly of me, but I wonder if you'd mind not calling me Mother Brady?"

It wasn't easy to tell what went on beneath all that makeup, but Lydia had a feeling that Candice had been reached.

"It's not really important," said Lydia. "I guess it's just that Mother Brady makes me feel older than I want to feel."

"I'm sure I didn't mean to offend," said Candice.

"You didn't."

"What would I call you, then?"

"Why don't you just call me Lydia?"

"You're sure people won't think it's fresh?"

"No, dear," said Lydia, and because of her noteworthy forbearance she did not add, I should think the last thing in the world people will ever think is that you're fresh.

Half an hour later, after Candice had filled Lydia in on the history of the Masonic orders and the state of Montana, with a lengthy refresher course on Missoula, she got to what Lydia took to be the purpose of her visit.

"I expect Mr. Julian is in Paris?" said Candice.

"I expect so."

"I expect he's on business."

"I expect."

"What kind of business is he in, anyway? Chris says he didn't say."

"Candice," said Lydia, as patiently as she was able, "I don't inquire too closely into matters like that. My friends tell me what they want to tell me, and I leave it at that. I find that's the best way."

"That's what Chris says, but I tell him if the government didn't look into things, I don't like to think where we'd be."

"I'm not a government," said Lydia, not raising her voice. She went to the record player and put on Segovia playing Bach; she turned it low.

"A small town," Candice was saying.

"I beg your pardon. What was it you were saying about a small town?"

"I was remarking that the foreign service is just like a small town, everybody knowing everybody else, and they certainly do talk, and one little bit of gossip, and your career is in jeopardy."

For the second time in two days, Lydia felt a flush on her face. This time it was partly alcohol, only a small part, though.

Lydia heard herself saying, "Candice, are you trying to tell me that there's been talk about Paul Julian and me?"

"I didn't say that."

"Then don't, please, because I'm too old and too tired to pay attention to gossip. Or to the people who report it. Are you sure you won't have another drink?"

Candice rose abruptly. "I gather you're going right on having your pleasure, and you don't care what happens to Chris's career." She slammed the door behind her.

I didn't do it well, thought Lydia. If I'd tried harder, been more understanding, if I'd been kinder . . . no, that's not true. Nothing, no words, no deeds, no amount of patience on my part can alter the fact that Candice and I are natural-born enemies, and if hostilities hadn't broken out today, it would have been tomorrow or next week.

And, she thought, the house in Missoula where Candice

grew up must be a barren house, barren of love, of beauty, of good manners, of all the things that make life agreeable. And I'm sorry for that. I'm sorry for Candice, but I don't want her to marry my son. She is made of inferior stuff.

When Paul called, his voice was faint but cheerful. He was back at his hotel, would have dinner in his room, go to bed early, and be in Madrid in the morning.

"Are you all right?" he asked.

"I'm wonderful," said Lydia, "beyond the fact that I miss you."

Chapter 20

It was nine in the morning, two hours before Paul was due, but when the doorbell rang, Lydia was sure it was he. He'd caught an earlier plane.

She looked at herself in the hall mirror, fiddled with a strand or two of the chestnut-blond hair (any day now, she'd have to find herself a Spanish Mr. Kenneth), moistened her lips, and opened the door.

"You've heard about bad pennies," said Day.

She was standing in a shaft of sunlight in the otherwise dark hallway. The hopeful gray-blue eyes were streaked with red. She had been crying, and she looked as if she hadn't slept for some time.

"Before you ask," said Day, "Ralph and I have called it quits."

"Oh, no," said Lydia. The words escaped her lips like an involuntary sigh. A moment passed, then she kissed her daughter on the forehead and said, "Come in."

Day walked into the hallway, put the handsome overnight case on a chair, and said, "I called Christopher from the airport. He gave me the address."

She looked approvingly at the apartment.

"Nice," she said. "Sort of what I would have expected. Somewhat somber, but I'm told the Spanish are a somber people. Very elegant."

"The elegance is a little frayed," said Lydia, "and although three maids convene in it for a few minutes every day, it could stand a good, thorough cleaning, and the plumbing is temperamental."

"You're so American," said Day, seating herself on one of the overstuffed chairs. "You're just not happy unless you're in a Hilton hotel."

"I'm a creature who likes creature comforts," said Lydia. "Is that against the law now? I haven't been following what Congress has been up to since I left."

Day smiled. "I knew you'd cheer me up. Could I please have a Bloody Mary?"

"You can. Is one allowed to ask what happened between you and Ralph?"

"I'll tell you all about it," said Day, "but please to remember, I'm twenty-three years old."

"That is not something I'm likely to forget."

"And you're not to hover, and you're not to make a tragedy out of it, because it isn't."

"Are those orders or just friendly advice?" said Lydia.

"I'm sorry, I didn't mean to be snippy. I just don't want you to think it's more important than it is."

Important enough, thought Lydia, to bring more tears to Day's eyes.

Three ounces of vodka, no, make it four, Ralph and I have called it quits, six ounces tomato juice, it's not more important than it is, a dash of bitters, and you're not to hover, and ocean-fuls of ice. No tears, though, because they taste of salt, and this is the age of the cool. And easy does it. Put aside feeling, forget concern, eradicate love, and in the name of Winken, Blinken, and God, have the caring gland removed. At once. It's a simple operation, as painless as modern dentistry, and it leaves only a temporary emptiness, like an extraction.

And while you're up, how about getting me a giant economy size of euthanasia, special this week, only one to a customer.

As she started back to the living room, Lydia thought, I had it all figured out, indexed, annotated, signed, sealed, delivered. Day made a happy marriage, Day is safe, Day is secure, Day is sheltered from all storms. Well, I was wrong, as usual. I was wrong, it sometimes seems, as always.

"Delicious," said Day. "Thanks."

She drank, not looking at her mother. She picked up a magazine, put it down again, walked to the record player, chose a record, asked, "May I?" and without waiting for an answer, she put the record on; it was a gypsy guitarist playing *flamenco*. She walked to the window and looked out.

Day is extraordinarily well put together, thought Lydia, and although I know it's not the fashion just now, she has the figure of a girl, not an effeminate boy. The whiteness of her skin is a gift of God (heredity, if you prefer, genes), and the same is true of her generous mouth, her straight nose, her broad forehead, and the fine brown hair that even on this morning of her despair she has taken the trouble to comb. I take some credit for the slender legs and trim ankles, and I am happy to note that her stockings are straight.

"Such a beautiful street," said Day, "and all those beautiful little boys on their way to school. But they don't laugh. Why don't they laugh? But then, what is there to laugh about?"

Day finished the Bloody Mary and once more seated herself on the overstuffed chair. She said, "It would be easier if I hated Ralph, but I don't. I'd even love him if he'd let me, but he won't. He's already got one love, and it takes all of him.

"I didn't realize when we got married that Ralph was committing bigamy. He was already married to the noble profession of architecture.

"That became what you might call obvious on the first night of what is laughingly referred to as our honeymoon. We were in this sensational motel on the beach in Puerto Rico, and the surf was beating romantically away outside the open window. I put some music-to-make-love-by record on the phonograph, and then I went to the dressing room and dribbled L'Amour perfume all over me and put on my laciest nightie and rings on my fingers and bells on my toes.

"When I came out of the dressing room, Ralph was sitting at a desk, drawing. I tiptoed over and kissed him on the ear and elsewhere, and when he actually noticed, he looked up and said, 'Honey, why don't you go to bed? I'll be along in a minute.'

"He got to bed at eight the next morning, and he fell asleep at once. He'd been working on the plans for a museum for a small college in Quebec, and I couldn't compete with that or with the theater in Dallas or the art gallery in Indianapolis. Or, or, or."

She looked at Lydia hopefully, and Lydia thought, Watch your step on this one, dear heart, because there are treacherous rocks ahead, and be particularly mindful of the treacherous shoals to the starboard, left. What she said was, "The last time I saw the two of you, it seemed to me Ralph couldn't take his eyes off you."

"Oh, sure," said Day, "when he's not working, it's all hearts and flowers, but when he is, I just simply don't exist."

One might wonder, thought Lydia, how Mrs. Shakespeare occupied herself when her husband was writing the third act of *Henry IV, Part II*? Or that even more difficult period when he was at work on the sonnets? And how did Mrs. Bach make out when Johann Sebastian was composing the Tocatta and Fugue in E minor? And was there a Mrs. Goya around when Francisco y Lucientes was painting the Crucifixion?

"Dallas was the worst," said Day. "I should never have gone. Ralph was always with the billionaires who were putting up the money for the theater. Or else he was speaking at a banquet or at some university. When I'd ask if he wanted me to go along, he'd say, 'I'm afraid you'd just be bored. Why don't you take in a movie or something?'

"I spent practically every night at the movies, and one night, right there in line ahead of me was Kevin Stewart."

Lydia felt a sudden, sad stirring of her heart. I believe, she thought, that I can take it from here.

The reader will recall Kevin Stewart and the few words recorded about him earlier. You will also remember that Lydia, to understate the case, was not fond of him and that Simeon had been.

A few words about him would appear to be necessary:

Kevin Stewart was a short, compact boy with dark hair that was always in need of a shampoo, dark eyes that should have been attractive but were dull, perfect teeth that probably would have shown off well in a smile, but he never smiled. And Kevin's nails forever needed attention, his shoes wanted shining and a fresh pair of laces, and the skimpy levis that he wore needed laundering, as did his green shirts. Or was it only one shirt? He didn't wear socks, and his ankles were invariably filthy.

Had Lydia been forced to choose a gift for Kevin—luckily, she never did—she'd have been torn between a nail file, a scrub brush, or a new shirt, preferably black. He no doubt could have used a razor, too, since he always wore yesterday's shave, or last week's.

Kevin's parents lived near Greenwich—very proper Greenwich is, lots of cooks and maids and butlers in those parts, lots of bleeding ulcers, lots of acrimony. His father, whom Kevin didn't like (naturally), was a successful builder of bridges. His mother—this is Kevin speaking:

"She hasn't had a thought in her head for thirty years. The dinner conversation is a thing to behold. 'We're having Beef Stroganoff for dinner, Herschel; you've always liked Beef Stroganoff.' 'I do like Beef Stroganoff, Lucky. I always have.' 'That's what I told Carmela this morning. She asked what I wanted for dinner, and I said, "Let's have Beef Stroganoff, Carmela. Mr. Stewart has always like Beef Stroganoff." 'You're right there, Lucky, I've always liked Beef Stroganoff.' "

I'm sorry, Lydia had thought, I don't like young men who mock their parents. I know it's all the rage, it's as American as blueberry pie, but I still don't like it. I don't care much for beef Stroganoff, either.

Kevin was a writer. At least, he talked a good deal about writing, and he spoke often and unfavorably of a great many other writers, living and dead:

"Beyond that brittle and superficial appraisal of an infinitesimal part of the society of her day, what has Jane Austin got?"

Lydia, who could think of one or two other qualities that Jane Austin had—wit, for one, wisdom, for another—decided against mentioning them.

In addition to the several dozen plays that Kevin was about to dash off, he was any day now going to type up a novel about the problems of his generation, which were, as he was sure Lydia would be the first to admit, unique.

He said, "My generation never believed in anything. You at least were a Communist."

Lydia started to deny the allegation, but then she realized that the burning of witches was over, at least temporarily, and she gave Kevin what she hoped was an enigmatic smile.

"I knew you'd agree with me," he said.

"Kevin was in Dallas for the opening of his play," Day was saying. "They were trying it out at one of the little theaters, and he took me to see it. That was all, absolutely all, but when I told Ralph, he was furious, and he told me I couldn't see Kevin again. Well, we had a big fight. I am not his chattel, after all, and the next morning I packed my bag and went off to New York with Kevin."

"Did you say you were twenty-three?" said Lydia. "At this moment it's hard to believe it."

Day was not going to cry, but she was hurting.

"The least I expected was a little sympathy."

"Go on," said Lydia. "I'm all ears."

"Well, Ralph came back to New York a couple days later, and we sort of kissed and made up, and for a while everything was peaches and cream, and then Ralph got involved with an art gallery he's designing for Indianapolis, and he'd go to work in the morning and stay at the office for as long as two or three days at a stretch. He just sleeps in a chair and forgets to call. I told you, when he's involved, he's on another planet.

"So night before last—I can't sit at home alone all the time— I asked Kevin to come up for dinner, and naturally, that was the night Ralph came home."

"Naturally," said Lydia.

"He really gave Kevin a beating; he could have killed him. Kevin isn't strong, you know."

"I'm sorry I missed the beating," said Lydia, "but if anybody'd asked me, one of the third things I'd have said about Kevin is that he's not strong."

"If you're going to be like that, I'm not going to tell you."

"I can more or less guess the rest, but I'd love to hear your version."

"Well, Ralph called me a lot of names, and he said if I ever saw Kevin again, he'd kill us both, and I think he would, too. But I'm not his slave."

"Or his chattel," said Lydia, "but unless I am greatly mistaken, you are his wife."

Day was paying no attention to that one. She was looking at a discoloration on the gold wallpaper; it was in the shape of a dinosaur.

"Anyway"—her voice much softer now—"what I did was, I packed my bag, and I went to the airport and bought a ticket, and here I am."

"Home to mother, only mother is in Madrid, Spain. There are times when I wish there were some way of uninventing the airplane. What was it they said your I.Q. was at Wellesley? One hundred and forty? There must have been some mistake."

"Oh, Mother, you never take anything seriously, do you?"

"I'll come to that in a minute, but I do want to apologize. In advance. I was going to say that you're acting like a thirteen-year-old, but that just isn't true. Too many bright thirteen-year-olds around. A ten-year-old, maybe."

Day was crying once again, and Lydia said, "I'm taking it as seriously as I've ever taken anything in my life, because I love you and I'm fond of Ralph, and I want you to be happy."

Lydia put Day in the guest room, and for a time she sat on the edge of the bed.

"I need time to sort myself out," said Day. "I can stay, can't I?"

"We'll see."

Lydia told Day about Paul, and Day said, "I think I knew from the way you looked. I knew something great had happened to you. Do you think he'll like me?"

"I wouldn't be a bit surprised."

They spoke of Simeon, and Day, who had been somewhat closer to her father than Christopher, said, "There was such a sadness about him. Sometimes I just looked at him and burst into tears. I saw you trying to reach him, but you never did. I don't think anybody ever reached him."

Later she said, "One of the things about Kevin that appeals to me, I suppose, is that he has the same sadness. The play in Dallas wasn't much good. Kevin doesn't have much talent, but he suffers just as much as if he were—oh, I don't know. John Keats, maybe. That's why he has to have somebody to hold onto. Does that make any sense?"

When she could manage, Lydia said, "Yes, that makes sense."

"What's Christopher's intended like?"

"Candice is fine," said Lydia. White lies are better than black truths, aren't they? I'm sure I read that somewhere. In the Bible?

"We'll have such fun, the six of us."

"I can count five," said Lydia. "Who's the sixth?"

"Oh, didn't I tell you? Kevin's coming over as soon as he can argue the money out of his father."

"Go to sleep now," said Lydia.

While she was waiting for Paul, Lydia sat in the kitchen, drinking coffee. I was one of those modern mothers, she thought, sweet reasonableness all the way along. I never raised my voice in anger. I read my Jung, my Adler, my Spock. I admonished, I cautioned, I explained. I was tender, I was loving, I was kind.

There were, to be sure, some few rules. For one, until Day went off to college, she was, except on the most special occasions, to be home by midnight.

"Why midnight, for heaven's sake? If it's some silly thing like sex you're worried about, that can happen at high noon as well as at one in the morning."

"I'm aware of that," Lydia had said, "and the why is simplicity itself. I said so; that's why."

"What you don't seem to realize is that the age of repression is over. Queen Victoria is no longer with us."

"In school I was quite good in history," said Lydia, "and although the idea may shock you, I think there's a lot to be said for suppression, particularly where sex is concerned."

"The idea may shock you, but so do I," Day had said.

And, somewhat earlier:

"Can I go to the movies tonight?"

"Of course not. You've been twice already this week."

"But it's James Dean."

One's ever-alert, facile mind slips back to a time when a bright lass who will not be identified but who was often mistaken for Flossie Bobbsey said, in somewhat similar context, "But it's John Garfield."

Looking at Day's protruding lower lip, Lydia had thought, to me James Dean looks like everybody; I can't tell him apart. But then, she thought, in my Flossie Bobbsey days, there were probably senile individuals around who couldn't tell John Garfield apart, either, probably got him confused with Gregory Peck, the fools. I know they're two different people; I've seen them together in the same flick.

She said, "I know it's James Dean, darling, and I'm sure his King Lear—it is King Lear, isn't it?—is well worth a visit, but we've agreed. Two movies a week."

"But this is special, and if I miss this, I'll regret it for the rest of my life."

"For the rest of the evening, anyway. Have you set the table?"

And, "It's a slumber party at the Johnsons'."

"For both boys and girls?"

"Well, sure. What do you think?"

"I think you won't be allowed to go, and I see no reason for either of us saying anything more."

"But Mr. and Mrs. Johnson will be there."

Fred and Sabrina Johnson will both be loaded by seven o'clock tonight, and by eleven they won't be able to see each other, let alone a group of fourteen-year-old boys and girls slumbering. My, I'm behind the times.

"Please?" said Day.

"I like your lower lip that way; it really is becoming. I'd keep it like that all the time if I were you."

But all that was some time ago, thought Lydia, at a time when Day's tears were over simpler pains—a broken date, a quarrel with a best friend, the tribulations of Heidi, the trials of Oliver Twist, the untimely deaths of Heloise and Abelard, who were two parakeets, the disappearance of Hector, an unstable cat, the mercy killing of Tinker Bell, a blind and suffering mongrel.

The wound is deeper now, and the stake somewhat more important, but there are no rules, not one. I cannot order my daughter to make a good marriage. I cannot insist that she realize that for all his success, all his seeming completeness, all his dedication to his profession—and maybe Ralph is a genius—there will be many times of failure and anguish, and at such moments he will need the woman he loves, and I happen to think that woman is Day.

Day is still playing house, still administering to the needs of ailing dolls, of vagrant dogs, and of careless, inconsequential young men who will be forever careless and inconsequential. Administering to the less obvious but I should think more interesting and surely more important needs of a man of consequence—and Ralph is—will not be easy. But if Day is to save herself from a life of almost certain misery, she must try to do it.

You can say I didn't do so well in my own marriage. True, true. I cannot deny it. But surely I learned a little something from my mistakes. Why else all these scar tissues, inside and out?

And while we're on the subject of men of consequence—and

what an archaic, lovely word that is—I was once involved with a fellow who reminds me (in retrospect, of course) quite a lot of Ralph Gunderson.

Neil Gordon was a golden boy, no Adonis but pleasant-looking, and he was Phi Beta Kappa in his junior year, All-American (the only one Briley ever produced), debater, president of the senior class, chairman of the junior prom committee, moderator of the philosophy club discussions, editor of the yearbook, captain of the swimming team. You name it.

Sybil, always available with the irrefutable, said at the time, "Don't get involved with Neil Gordon. These campus heroes never come to much. In later life the gold invariably turns to dross."

Sybil's apt remark wasn't the only reason I didn't marry Neil; the other was that he didn't ask me.

I beg your pardon? What happened to Neil? Oh, yes. He is now a member of the Supreme Court of the United States.

Lydia remembered Day's diary: "Think about whether it is more important for a husband to be good-looking or to have a good disposition." She remembered the way Day had looked at Ralph the first evening at the Algonquin and the way he had looked back; she thought of Kevin Stewart.

Then she did two things. She called the airlines office and said, "I want to reserve a seat for one on the morning flight to New York tomorrow morning. Coach. The name is Gunderson. Mrs. Ralph Gunderson."

After that she sent a cablegram to Ralph, giving him the number of the flight.

Chapter 21

❧ An hour later Paul rang the bell, and when Lydia opened the door, she once more felt that alien joy she had known for the first time since meeting him. She'd known happiness before. She'd been glad and pleased with herself and other people. She felt herself fortunate, lucky, and blessed. She'd experienced pleasure, satisfaction, and contentment, but joy was a new emotion, large and rare and precious.

Later, Lydia was to remember that Paul looked tired that morning, but at the moment all she saw was the rocklike quality of him, the seeming indestructibility, the alert, delighted eyes, and the adored, imperfect nose.

After they said to each other what they said at such times, Paul handed her the package he was carrying. He was a giver of gifts—"because it's evening," "because we're alive and together," "because it gives me pleasure."

Inside was a tiny painting of matchless beauty—a tawny beach on which was stretched a single fishing net, an endlessly peaceful ocean, and on the blue horizon an inviting white cottage. The canvas was signed by Louis Boudin. Once in Portugal, Lydia had said, "When I am old and rich, I'm going to spend all my money on a Boudin, and then I don't care if I do have to go off to the old ladies' home."

"Thank you," said Lydia.

Another nice thing about Paul's gifts was that you didn't have to do what Lydia called "the Christmas act"—Jiminy crickets, Aunt Lucretia, this flannel chest warmer is just what I wanted. And what a lovely gangrene color.

Paul never said the familiar things: Do you *really* like it? If it isn't what you want, you can always return it. He knew that it was what you wanted and that you liked it because he had taken the trouble to find out.

"How was the trip?" asked Lydia.

"Lonely. Now I want to hear a second-by-second description of everything that's happened to you since I left."

"My time was filled with incident. Empires have fallen, thrones have tottered, and there've been one or two private executions."

She told him about Candice's visit, and he said, "Don't judge her too harshly. She'll get over being young."

"I've tried being fair," said Lydia.

"Try liking her," said Paul.

Since there was no answer to that, not immediately, anyway, Lydia described the arrival of Day, what Day had said, and about the call to the airlines and the cable to Ralph. "I'm not at all sure that I did the right thing."

"You did what you thought was right; that's the best you can do. What about tonight? Should I take you and Day out to dinner and one of the *flamenco* places?"

Lydia had given the matter of the evening some thought and had decided that to allow Day an evening on the town would seem to be a reward. The best thing, she felt, would be for Day and her to have dinner alone, spend the evening in the apartment, and in the morning she'd take Day to the airport and put her on the plane.

She explained her decision to Paul, and he said, "I hate not seeing you for another night, but we have quite a few nights ahead of us. And I think you're perfectly right. Don't change your mind."

He kissed her then and said, "What I keep forgetting about you is that you have common sense, and there's about as much of that around as there are unicorns."

"You don't think it's cruel?"

"Not if you want to save her from disaster. I do think we ought to meet, though. Why don't we have drinks right here?"

Day was wonderful. She was wearing a handsome blue and turquoise yellow paisley. Her eyes were clear, and the puffiness in her face was gone. She was rested and relaxed, and her attitude toward Paul was that of an adult young lady pleased to meet a friend of her mother's, nothing more. She admired the Boudin, and the three of them discussed what the artist had learned from Corot and his influence on Monet. They talked about Charles De Gaulle and why he was not an easy man to love.

"To have the French personality is a handicap in popularity contests all by itself," said Day, "but to confuse your identity with that of God and Joan of Arc—impossible."

They talked about Salazar and his influence on Portugal.

"He's a mathematician," said Paul. "Has there ever been a lovable mathematician?"

"Mother isn't sure what four and four are," said Day. "That's why she's so nice."

"Who needs to?" said Lydia. "You can always ask somebody, and when you do, they're always so delighted they can tell you."

She was thinking, My daughter is a bright girl. In matters of the head she has a clear, logical, functioning mind. In matters of emotion, she is still not quite ready for preschool. Emotionally, she still wants a chocolate frosted, a banana split, and a strawberry sundae all at the same time. But that isn't at all unusual. They haven't come up with a pill for that particular ailment, and you'd think they would. The common cold is a cinch by comparison.

As Paul left, Day said, "I have a hunch we're going to be seeing a lot of each other."

Paul said it had been a pleasure, and he said good-bye to Lydia, not kissing her. I like proper people, thought Lydia, one in particular. Will propriety ever came back, do you suppose? And what about a sense of obligation, of duty? And the sacredness of a man's word? My, I am being archaic today.

Day finished her vodka tonic and said, "I'm going to have another. How about you?"

"No, thanks," said Lydia.

"I like Paul," said Day. "There's something very substantial about him, and he's so assured, which is comfortable to be around. He adores you; you can tell. He thinks you're the greatest invention since cream cheese."

She put on a record, did a caricature *flamenco* for a few minutes, and said, "I'm so glad I came, really glad. I told you we'd have a ball. The first place I want to go is Toledo, no Granada, I think. If you agree, of course.

"I'll bet Paul will lay on a limousine and a chauffeur. He is rich, isn't he? Of course he's rich. How else can you afford a Boudin. You know, if worst comes to worst, you could hock that and exist very prettily for quite some time."

She danced around her mother. *"Olé, olé,"* she sang, and she said, "Poor old Ralph. I didn't tell him where I was going or anything. He'll be in a real snit. He won't know quite what's wrong. He'll just know something is missing, and maybe he'll think it's me, or maybe he'll think it's this month's edition of *Progressive Architecture.*"

If Lydia had doubted her decision, she no longer did; she started toward the kitchen. "What would you like for dinner?"

"Isn't Paul taking us to dinner? How come?"

"I asked him not to," said Lydia.

"You're kidding. My first night in Madrid and we're having dinner in this dump, alone? Oh, and remind me, in about an hour I've got to call Kevin and see if he's got the money from his Pops."

She came to her mother and bussed her on the cheek. "I know you want to have a long, serious talk, but not tonight. Pretty please. Tonight we go out."

Lydia said, "I've got steak and lamb chops. Which would you rather have?"

Day did a few more steps of *flamenco,* then, "Well, if Paul isn't going to take us out, I will. Where would you like to go?"

Lydia hesitated, then in a voice she had seldom and perhaps never used with her daughter she said, "Neither of us is going anywhere."

Day laughed, not with amusement. "You can stay here if you want to be silly," she said, "but I'm not going to."

She started toward the guest room.

"While you were sleeping," said Lydia, "I did something I've never done before and hope I won't have to do again. I went through your purse and took out all the money, twenty-six dollars and eighty-five cents and the pesetas I imagine you got at the airport, four dollars' worth. It's at the desk. When you're back in New York, I'll send it to you."

"What a rotten thing to do," said Day. She was frightened now, and her voice trembled. She went to the bar and started making another drink. After a few minutes she said, "I assume there's some explanation for this, but you needn't send the money to New York. I'll be here some little time, and when Kevin joins me, he'll have plenty. I'm going to call him right now."

She started for the phone, and Lydia said, "I've told the operator not to accept any calls from you, local or international."

Day put down the phone, and Lydia told her about the airplane reservations and about the cablegram to Ralph.

Two elusive tears appeared in Day's eyes and ran down her cheeks. "There must be some reason for this," she said, "but I simply fail to understand it."

"There is," said Lydia. "I'm saving your life. You won't agree now, but I think you will later and be grateful for it."

Day giggled, somewhat hysterically. "This is straight out of the Middle Ages. Nobody in the world would believe it."

Without replying, Lydia went to the kitchen and started peeling the potatoes for dinner. She heard Day running toward the bedroom; then she ran through the living room and into the hall.

Without looking up or raising her voice, Lydia said, "I've told Señor Hernandes to stop you at the door. If you try to leave, they'll bring you back here, and I'll lock you in your room until it's time to put you on the plane in the morning."

Day went back into the living room; there was the sound of another drink being made.

Minutes passed, then she came into the kitchen, her face once more swollen, her eyes again red. Her manner, however, was all sweetness and reasonableness; her voice was that of a nurse speaking to the senile or the incurable. "I'm sure you think what you're doing is right. We have different points of view. I've brought you a drink. It will do you good."

"Thank you," said Lydia. "Are you sure you don't want something to eat?"

Day smiled gallantly, and this time in her voice there was more than a little vibrato. 'Under the circumstances, I doubt that I'll be exactly ravenous." She shook her head in the manner of one refusing a final meal before the unjust execution— Mata Hari, Marie Antoinette?—"just nothing at all, thanks."

"I think I'll have a small steak," said Lydia.

Day seated herself on a kitchen stool. She leaned toward her mother rather in the way she had leaned forward during the "quality of mercy" speech when she had played Portia at Wellesley and said, "There's one thing you ought to know before we continue this madness. Ever since that first night in Dallas, Kevin and I have been sleeping together."

Lydia first lighted the oven. "I knew that from the minute you said that you and Kevin went to see his play and that that was all, absolutely all. Unnecessary details like that invariably reveal the inept liar."

She could see that while Day thought Mother Carey was in her dotage, Day had to admit the old girl wasn't so dumb after all.

"You weren't shocked?"

"The breaking of the seventh commandment hasn't shocked me much since at the age of sixteen I happened on *Madame Bovary*. It's like all those plays about perversion. No shock, just boredom. The people who engage my interest and, forgive me, my compassion, are the ones who don't break the commandments, or try not to. And while the perverse have their

place in the scheme of things and are no doubt as good as the un-
perverse, I refuse to admit they are invariably better."

Day rose and with the dignity of the badly shaken and the
almost drunk walked to the living room and could be heard
making herself another drink.

While Lydia set the table for herself, Day sat in a chair
with her back to her mother. She had a book in front of her,
but Lydia doubted if she was reading much of it.

"I think you're going through change of life," Day said.
"That's the only possible explanation."

As Lydia ate she found the steak, though tender, almost impossible to swallow. The salad was galling, and her mashed
potatoes were, for the first time in years, lumpy. She ate them,
though; better than hemlock anytime.

Lydia finished the steak, and she saw that Day was sitting
in the chair next to her. The look on Day's face this time was
that of the seeker after knowledge.

"You just don't begin to understand the physical attraction
I felt for Kevin, do you?"

"Once, maybe," said Lydia, discovering that if you swallow
fast you can even get down a piece of gristle. "More than once,
no. In the first place, I'm practically certain that Kevin must
be incredibly inept in bed and probably downright dull. (She
could see she had struck pay dirt there.) I certainly feel any
physical contact with him, even shaking his hand, is, to put it
kindly, untidy. Has Kevin washed his ankles lately? And how
about those nails?"

Day said, "I used to think you were intelligent," and a moment later she added, "What you will never in a million years
understand is that Kevin is revolting against that scrubbed, up-
per-class Greenwich conformity of his parents."

"I'll make a mental note of that," said Lydia. "Now I know
why Kevin acts and smells like an untrained goat. I'm sure
I'll be able to work it into a conversation sometime. It's a
pity, though, that his Mommy and Poppy weren't filthy, so he
could revolt against that."

"Ha, ha, ha," said Day.

*   *   *

Although the evening seemed to have more hours then evenings usually do, it did continue, and other words were said in other places.

"You could even put me on the plane, but I won't stay on."

"I'll tell the stewards to see that you don't get off. The ones on Iberia Air Lines are very hefty boys. Unless you mean you intend jumping off in the middle of the Atlantic, and you don't swim that well."

A half-suppressed sob. "You mean you'd really humiliate me publicly?"

"You bet I do," said Lydia.

A few sniffles, half-sobs, and Camille-like coughs later, Day said, "The minute Kevin gets the money, we'll come straight back."

"I hope not, but if you're foolish enough to come to Madrid, stay out of sight, because if I see you, I'll do exactly what I'm doing now to you, and if I have the misfortune to see Kevin, I'll have him up before a firing squad before you can say Francisco Franco. Things like that are easy in Spain."

Since there was no reply, Lydia returned to the book she was reading but not making much sense out of. A few minutes later she yawned loudly and said, "I'm going to bed."

As she started toward the living room she added, "I'd advise you to go to bed, too, because we'll have to start to the airport early."

Day, sobbing yet again, said, "I'll hate you for this for the rest of my life."

"I sincerely hope not," said Lydia, "because as you surely know, I love you. I respect you, too, and I hope not to see you make a mess of your life with a worthless boy."

Day walked to the edge of the terrace and looked over. "I won't be alive in the morning," she said.

"Good night, darling," said Lydia.

After Lydia went to bed, Day put on the record player as loud as she was able. She danced, stamping the floor angrily. She sang, screaming out incomprehensible words. She could be heard to make drinks. She could be heard in the kitchen, breaking dishes. She could be heard to throw something in the courtyard, and whatever it was broke. She could be heard to sob, shout, and scream, and then she could be heard to go to bed.

A few minutes later, Lydia tiptoed past the door of the guest room; Day, fully dressed, was lying halfway across the bed, sleeping soundly. Lydia quietly took off her shoes and slipped off her skirt and sweater. She put Day under the covers and opened the window.

As she was leaving the room, Day woke up for a minute and said, "Please don't make me go."

"Good night, baby," said Lydia.

Then she called Paul and told him what had happened.

"Every so often," he said, "we all ought to be put in a play-room fully equipped with noisemaking toys, and we ought to be left there until we get as much as possible of the childishness out of our systems."

"I may be driving her straight back into the limp, unsavory arms of Kevin," said Lydia.

"Never make the same decision twice," said Paul.

And he added, "Day looked to me like a girl destined some-day to develop common sense, perhaps not as much as her mother, but nevertheless."

Later, Christopher, whose profession was, after all, diplomacy, said to give Day his best, and he and Candice would be sorry to have missed her.

The next morning, Day was once more fresh and rested-look-ing; Lydia was neither.

"I acted stupidly last night," said Day, "and I'm sorry. I guess we were both overwrought."

She walked to the window and looked out at the shining morning. "It's another day, and on a morning like this, who could feel anything but magnificent?"

"I've put your breakfast on the table," said Lydia, "and now I've got to get dressed."

"You really mean it, don't you?"

"I really mean it."

"You never understood me at all," said Day, "not once, not even a little bit. Christopher was always your favorite."

Lydia looked at her daughter with amazement. Was that actually what Day thought? Could she possibly? Or was it one of those chance, hurting remarks that always seem to be available, just below the surface of our consciousness, when we want them.

"That's not true," said Lydia; then she stopped. After twenty-three years, Day either knew or she didn't. It was too late to start over. It always is.

Day was silent all the way to the airport and in the terminal. After the flight was announced, Lydia said, "May I kiss you good-bye?"

Day, not answering, walked toward the other waiting passengers and then onto the plane; she did not look back.

Watching the plane lift into the air, Lydia felt neither triumph nor jubilation. She felt tired and used up and uncertain. She cried all the way back to the city.

Chapter 22

Paul was waiting for Lydia when she got back from the airport. He knew what her mood would be; he always did.

Such sensitivity to the mood of another is rare. But Paul had it, and not only with Lydia. In his youth, in that eager dash from the slums of South Chicago to the baronial estate on Lake Shore Drive, Paul had not only had to run faster and think faster than anybody else, he had had to listen with his inner ear to the temper of those along the way. Which were the honest men and which had fraud in their hearts, which were the truth tellers, which the liars.

And so that morning in Madrid, Paul first kissed Lydia and then he gave her a present, a marble Fabergé egg the color of an emerald.

He had bought it in Paris to give to her on her birthday, but, clearly, today was when she needed it. Now there was to be no introspection today, no wondering if what she had done was right or wrong. For in areas where the heart is concerned, how do you ever know? At such times there is no catechism. It is best only to hope and if one has a God or gods, to pray.

And indeed, except for an incident late in the afternoon and another around midnight, it was a good day. The weather was perfect. The sun shone, and the air was tender, and grateful Madrilenians surged joyfully through the streets. Madrid, they say, is nine months of hell and three months of winter. Thus, every pleasant day must be taken advantage of. Tomorrow it will rain, or a chilling wind will sweep down from the Sierra, but today is *fiesta*, the kind not listed on the calendar. The unexpected dividends are always best.

Lydia and Paul went, first, to the royal palace, to the dusky rooms in which long-faced infantas played silent, lonely games. There was a rocking horse with a broken leg, a giant top without a spring, a life-size doll with a missing arm, one slightly smaller that was without a head, and a third whose body looked as if it had been mutilated by an angry revolutionary.

They looked at the long, graceful staircase, the steps of which are slabs of black and white marble, at the halls hung with good tapestries, the great mirrors in which anxious queens had given themselves a final look before entering the immense ballroom, the throne made of polished silver, with two silver lions on guard on either side.

Paul told her of the uneasy royal families who had lived in the palace—the queen who fell in love with a handsome corporal, the king who translated Dickens into Spanish, the not-very-bright one who in his entire life had only one suit of clothes and who filled its pockets with toys and a tiny prayer book, the one who had a coat of armor cast for his greyhound.

Afterward they walked through the gardens with the placid lake, the silent umbrella palms, and the dark, serious young men practicing to be bullfighters.

They had *sangria* in the outdoor restaurant facing the statue of Philip IV on his favorite horse. The statue had been designed the Velázquez, and it flattered the king.

"We've been invited to a party," said Paul. "The hostess is an Italian duchess. There'll be a lot of deposed royalty there. How do you feel about royalty?"

"I loved the Red Queen in *Alice*," said Lydia, "although I felt she carried head-chopping to excess, and I'm fond of the present Queen of England. She always makes me think of several members of the ladies' garden club back home. I always have the feeling that if asked, she could go on for hours about her hybrid rhododendrons.

"But I've never actually met any royalty except when I was a tiny tot. Queen Marie of Rumania came to Briley once to lecture, and she stayed overnight at our house. The next morning my mother asked the queen how she'd slept, and Marie complained that the mattress was hard. Later, much later, Eleanor Roosevelt spent the night on the same mattress, and she said she'd had a wonderful night's sleep. Since then I haven't been much for royalty."

"Fine," said Paul. "We won't go to the party. When we're together, other people are always an intrusion."

On the lake two boys and a girl in a canoe were laughing quietly, and a great orange bird flew from one plane tree to another.

Lydia looked at Paul. She could see that his mind was faraway, but that won't last, she thought. He'll be back. Of that I'm sure. My Orphan Annie days are behind me, and about time, too. The market is glutted with middle-aged foundlings.

I wonder if Day ever felt this way with Ralph, with Kevin. Does Christopher feel this way when he is with Candice? I certainly do hope so, because, dear friends, this calmness of mind, this evenness of temper is what it's all about. Why didn't somebody tell me?

Later, as she and Paul walked down the bright green slopes of the royal garden, Lydia said, "You haven't told me a thing about Paris."

"Paris is a greatly overrated city," said Paul, "and at this time of year, every day is like a rainy Monday. The suicide rate is astronomical."

It was then that Lydia felt a sudden unease, and, although the sun was still high in the sky, a chill.

Paul must have felt them, too, because he said, "I told you I'm an optimist by nature, and I'm a man of faith, even when there is no evidence to support it."

Chapter 23

✤ After they left the palace grounds, they walked for a time in silence. The streets were nearly deserted; it was *siesta*, and there were only the somehow melancholy tourists. Lydia wondered what they had expected and not found. The fountain of youth? El Dorado? A city of gold? A bluebird?

"I wouldn't want to stay in Europe," said Paul. "I mean live here, would you?"

Lydia shook her head. Nor anywhere else, she thought, without you.

"I don't like the expatriates," Paul went on, rather urgently. "In the twenties, maybe it was all right, but now, the ones I've met, they seem dispossessed."

They went on, past the unfinished cathedral, past the statues of departed kings, past deserted parks.

And then Paul said, once more with a kind of urgency, "If it were possible, would you marry me?"

"Yes, darling, I would," said Lydia.

She had prepared the answer to that particular question sometime before.

Paul squeezed her hand, and he said, "I'm not much of a bargain, God knows, but I'd try to make you happy."

Lydia didn't say that he already had; he knew that. You always do.

A moment later he said, "It won't be easy, but nothing I've ever really wanted has been impossible. How about you?"

"Never," said Lydia, which was not quite true, but right then it seemed to be.

Paul excused himself; he had to go downtown. He'd meet her back at the hotel at six.

Lydia watched him cross the street, walking, as he always did, with a sure, almost defiant stride, ignoring the cars and the people. As he got into the taxi he waved at her, and she waved back thinking, who said there are no more heroes?

She remembered something he had said to her sometime earlier: "I realized three, no, four crucial things at a very early age. One, I was not God. Two, that when other people were in panic, and most people are most of the time, all I had to say was, 'Don't worry. I'll take care of it.' By the next morning, whatever it was that had panicked them had usually taken care of itself. Three, that there's never enough information about anything to make a decision. So you make it anyway, and, right or wrong, never look back. And, finally—I'm nearing the end of the lecture—I was never afraid to fail. That last is the cancer that eats away at people, the fear of failure."

What's this nonsense about there being no more giants in the earth? Or am I prejudiced?

When Lydia got back to the hotel, Señor Hernandes, who was behind the desk in the outer lobby, said that a lady was waiting to see her. No, the lady had not given her name.

Lydia wondered if Sybil had arrived ahead of schedule, but decided not. Sybil would have telephoned or cabled.

The woman sitting on the Barcelona chair near the elevator was the one Lydia had talked to on the street a few days before. Mrs. Emerson, Mrs. George Emerson of San Francisco.

She was once more expensively dressed, this time in a chartreuse silk with neat rows of black roses. On the floor beside her was a handsome bag of Moroccan leather.

When she saw Lydia, she rose and smiled, but there was no welcome in the smile. Her hands were tightly clenched at her sides. Lydia had the feeling that if the woman released them, the hands might involve themselves in heaven knows what pursuits of their own. There was a sense of restlessness about the woman, almost of violence that was, with great difficulty, being suppressed.

But perhaps, thought Lydia, it is only nervousness. We can't all be serene.

"I wonder if we could talk for a few minutes," the woman said.

"I'm terribly sorry," said Lydia, "but I'm afraid I'm already late for an appointment."

The woman, her manner vaguely menacing now, said, "I believe you'd find it worth your while."

Lydia looked behind her; she was glad to see that Señor Hernandes was still behind the desk.

"I'm sorry, Mrs. Emerson," she said, "but I'm afraid I'm late for an appointment as it is."

"My name isn't Emerson," the woman said, "and I'm not from San Francisco. I'm from Chicago. I'm Paul Julian's wife."

Lydia stood motionless for a moment; she looked at the woman—she could not think of her as Paul's wife—at the uneasy eyes, at the clenched hands, at the thin, tight mouth, and she said, surprised at the unruffled sound of her own voice, "I'll give you fifteen minutes."

"I think you'll discover that you're no longer calling the tune," said the woman. Her voice had an edge of hysteria now.

The woman examined the apartment with the critical eye of a prospective tenant.

"Not much of a love nest," she said. "It looks just like the photographs."

Lydia said nothing, but she thought, of course there are photographs, and there are tape recordings, and there have been interviews with bellboys and maids and with Señor Hernandes. There have been innuendos and leers and lies. Specialists in the unsavory are abundantly available for a crumpled bill, a few escudos, a peseta or so.

"Aren't you going to ask what photographs?" said the woman.

She had given her hands their freedom, and they were clenching and unclenching themselves with the regularity of a metronome.

"You have exactly twelve and a half minutes," said Lydia.

"Don't try to rush me," said the woman. "We won't get anyplace at all if you try to rush me. I'll come to what I have to say in my own good time, and you'll sit there and listen."

Lydia removed her watch from her wrist. Holding it in her right hand, she said, "Twelve minutes."

"I'm in charge now," said the woman. "I've got all the chips."

She put the bag on the floor and seated herself on the sofa. She examined Lydia as if taking her measurement for a shroud.

"You're not at all what I'd have expected," she said.

She paused, again waiting for a question, but Lydia, examining her watch, said, "Eleven."

"How many other homes have you broken up?" the woman asked. She seemed now to be addressing a jury, and there was no question at all that she was going to ask for the death penalty. Preferably by burning at the stake.

I have never seen this woman before, thought Lydia, and yet I have seen her everywhere before. There is no place in her heart for love, no place in her mind for thought, no place in her body for tenderness, and her soul, if any, is shriveled and as hard as a stone.

"I suppose Paul has told you what happened in Paris," the prosecuting attorney continued. "Or has he? Probably not, and even if he has, don't believe a word of it. Paul is a pathological liar."

"Nine minutes," said Lydia.

"Paul's lawyer made me a generous offer, but I won't accept it, not even if he were to give me every cent to his name."

Lydia walked to the front door of the apartment and opened it.

"I'll see to it that neither of you ever draws a peaceful breath as long as you live," said the woman. "I'll arrange it so that you'll be ashamed to show your faces in public."

She said more, a good deal more, but the rest, with one exception, was repetitious. The exception was, "How are your son and daughter going to feel about all the notoriety?"

After the woman left, Lydia found herself trembling.

You can say, she thought, that the woman is frightened, that she's afraid of being alone, of growing old, of death. But that does not excuse the murder in her heart. Attila the Hun, I am told, came from a broken home.

Paul had said that his wife was really a nice woman. I'm afraid, thought Lydia, that that is our first disagreement.

She undressed almost immediately and took a very long shower.

Chapter 24

❧ By the time Paul got to the apartment that evening, Lydia hadn't made up her mind whether or not to tell him about her visitor of the afternoon. But the minute she saw him, she decided against it. His face was already gray with fatigue and worry.

When she absolutely had to tell him, she would. But why now? Why mess up today when you can as easily mess up next Tuesday? And who knows, next Tuesday may never come. That's cowardice? It most certainly is. But there's a lot to be said for us cowards. Not only do we live longer, we're much nicer people. Quieter, for one thing. Heroes are forever telling you how brave they are, or else they're demonstrating it: "So I took out my sword, and I went so, and I . . . oops. Terribly sorry, old bean, but you've still got one arm." Ever hear of a coward starting a war? And who keeps the insurance rates up? Not us cowards.

Paul handed her a cablegram.

"It just got here. Hernandes gave it to me."

Lydia was never quite able to rid herself of the notion that no cablegram was a good cablegram, but, nevertheless, making use of her stiffest upper lip, she tore the lethal thing open and read the message through twice. Then, finding herself still possessed of a voice, she read it to Paul.

"Day arrived, safe, sound, sleepy; she sends you her love and so, of course, do I. Letter follows. Ralph."

Paul handed her a martini, and he said, "I won't tell you I told you so, largely because I didn't tell you so, but I'm glad.

Now why don't you get dressed in your gladdest glad rags? I'll take you to the Sambra."

The Sambra has the best *flamenco* singing and dancing in the world. The star that night was a woman of about forty with a beautifully ugly face. Her body was broad but not fat, and she danced with grace and precision. Her legs were those of a ballerina.

When she danced, the clapping of the other performers became more frenzied; the *olés* were more uninhibited, and the audience joined in, too. It was as if the entire room had been charged with electricty.

The dance ended abruptly, and it was a moment before the applause began, but when it did, it was thunderous. The madame—Lydia and Paul had called her that from the beginning —neither bowed nor smiled. She was great and knew it. Why give thanks for something she had earned?

She left the stage abruptly and didn't return, even though the applause and the *olés* continued for some time.

Lydia saw that Paul had left her again; his color was high, and his eyes were angry. He rose abruptly.

"Excuse me," he said.

He strode to a table next to the wall. Lydia had not been aware of it, but the man she had first seen in Armação de Pêra was there, the one she had called the Silent Man. He was wearing the same horn-rimmed glasses, the same dark sack suit, the same look of hostile indifference.

When he saw Paul coming toward him, he got up and stood tensely beside the table as if he weren't sure whether to expect a hit or an embrace. Neither happened. Paul said a few harsh words to the man. The man said something back, and Paul turned angrily away.

Paul returned to the table where Lydia was sitting.

After a time he said, "Our friend there is a detective. He tells me he's just a cog in the wheel. He's just taking orders, just making a living."

He paused for a moment, then added, "The world is filled with the minor functionaries of evil."

They both watched as the Silent Man paid his check and left.

"I told you once I would try never to hurt you," said Paul, "and that should go equally for other people who will try to do it to get at me."

"You will find," said Lydia, "that in many ways I am quite a grown-up girl, able to cope with the outrageous slings and arrows. I've had lots of practice."

"I also told you," said Paul, "that while I find myself a decent enough fellow, there are those who think I'm a scoundrel or worse. You'll have to judge."

"I already have," said Lydia.

Paul talked that night more than he ever had before or would again. He talked until the Sambra closed, and he continued as he and Lydia had coffee in all-night cafés and as they walked through the uncrowded streets, the deserted squares, and dark boulevards.

It must not, however, be supposed that Paul told Lydia all of what follows during that long night in Madrid. Some of it came earlier, during those calm days and nights they spent in the white villa in southern Portugal, and a good deal came later, in the days and weeks that are to come.

The saga of Paulo di Cavalcanti (one of the picture magazines called it that) is placed here, with a proper beginning, middle, and end for the convenience of the reader. He probably has trouble enough trying to create some order in his own life without having to worry about whether what Paul said in Madrid comes before or after what he told Lydia in Malaga or Paris.

Paul didn't especially like talking about himself, either; to the contrary, he liked it less than most of us. At one point in his life he consulted an analyst, three afternoons a week for nearly six months.

The young priest—his seminary had been Johns Hopkins —was thirty-two. His hands were pudgy and slightly moist, and his nails were bitten.

On the final afternoon Paul said, "I won't be back on Wednesday."

"Ah, we've exposed a raw nerve."

"No, Father, I'm bored with talking about myself, and your interpretation of my dreams isn't half as interesting as my own."

"But we were getting so near to an understanding of the conflict within you caused by—"

"So long," said Paul, shaking the insecure hand. I, he thought, should be analyzing *him*.

In what he told Lydia, Paul no doubt managed, perhaps unconsciously, to put himself in the most appealing light. As has been observed earlier in this narrative, where human affairs are concerned, there in no exact truth.

One wonders what his wife Fran would have to say about the cataclysmic night we're coming to or how Paul's daughter would describe the last good-bye. And what did that aging banker really say when Paul walked into his Jacobean office wearing a double-breasted suit that came with two pairs of pants and a free necktie, any tie in the store, eleven dollars and ninety-eight cents?

But let us begin.

First, and don't discount the importance of it, there is that tiny house—three rooms and an outside toilet—in Gary, where there was sometimes no food, but the floors were immaculate. Hunger is a powerful drive, maybe the most powerful, and the Depression had a terrifying effect on an entire generation. A friend of Paul's once said that he couldn't really like anybody who didn't know what it is like to be willing and able to work but be unable to find a job.

Now, like the Second World War, the Depression is being sweetened and softened and sentimentalized. Shortly it will be proper material for a musical comedy or a television series. Canned laughter every thirty seconds.

Most of the boys in the neighborhood where Paulo di Cavalcanti grew up were Italian, and many of them became Communists. At that time in that place, to be a member of the party
was to belong to the establishment. Other boys got to be cops;
a few were gangsters. As you know, Paul made it to Lake Shore
Drive. In terms of miles that isn't far, say twenty, but in other
ways it's half a world away.

Paulo loved his father. He saw in him that sweetness of spirit
that Paul felt must have motivated Sacco and Vanzetti at an
earlier time. José di Cavalcanti had the simple belief that the
world could be improved and that he must try to help with the
improvement. He was a romantic who, as you know, got in the
way of a policeman's bullet on Memorial Day in 1937. After his
death the Communists tried to claim him as one of their own,
but he never was. He was an optimistic majority of one.

Paulo's mother was a realist. It's root hog or die; the Lord
helps them that help themselves; men are not gods, and we
must, therefore, be wary of them.

"I was never a world tinkerer," said Paul. "I always felt
that there are those who win and those who lose, the ins versus
the outs. I wanted to win. When people asked me what I
planned to be when I grew up, I said, 'a multimillionaire.' Any
other questions?"

Shortly after his eighth birthday, he got his first job. Please,
no visions of Oliver Twist. Before going to school, he delivered
copies of the *Chicago Tribune* to some of the more stately
homes and mansions of Gary.

Later he had other jobs. One was sweeping out a neighborhood saloon that in the early mornings smelled of stale beer
and of still-smoldering cigars, and there were echoes of the
voices of defeated old men repeating to themselves and to each
other why and where everything went wrong.

And he decorated the windows of the haberdashery that had
those eleven-dollar-ninety-eight-cent suits and free neckties.

So far no surprises, very Horatio Alger.

What made Paul unique was that at fourteen he was no

longer delivering newspapers. He was circulation manager for all of Gary, and twenty boys were working for him.

At the end of three years in the saloon he had bought a fourth interest in it. He was then seventeen, still not old enough to buy a drink, and it was against the law for a minor to be in the liquor business, but enforcement of the law was casual.

After four years in the haberdashery, the owner decided to sell. When Paulo found out, he bathed, in a washtub, if you want the truth. He shaved twice, dressed himself in the suit we've described, and knotted a free necktie around his neck. Was the necktie made of hemp?

Then he took the El to downtown Chicago and walked into one of the largest and soundest banks on Michigan Boulevard. He was glib of tongue and a handsome boy, and the secretary of the president, a maiden lady in her fifties, let him into the old man's office. Sex has opened a great many doors.

The president was an elderly man whose white hair looked blue in certain lights. Paulo introduced himself, and then he said, or remembers saying, "I've come to get a loan of five thousand dollars. I want to buy a clothing store in Gary."

The old man smiled gently. He was a gentle man and would probably never have been president of the bank if his father hadn't been one of the founders. There wasn't a ruthless bone in his body.

He said, "How old are you?"

"Seventeen."

"Son, you've got more chutzpah than the whole staff of this institution put together, but at seventeen your signature on a note wouldn't be binding."

"I know that," said Paulo. "You'd have to have faith in me. My word is good, and I'm ambitious."

"No doubt about the last and very little about the first," said the banker.

They talked for some time after that. The old man asked the usual banker's questions, ending with, "But besides your jobs, what have you got for security?"

"My guts," said Paul. Well, who knows? Paul has since told that story to a great many interviewers, and some of them actually believed it, and all of them printed it.

The point is, he got the loan, bought the haberdashery, and hired two men, both older than he, to work for him.

When he was twenty, he not only owned that haberdashery, he had three others as well. Eventually, there were forty. There are still.

You can even now get a double-breasted suit and a free necktie in any one of the stores, though no longer for $11.98, but in each store there is also a section where the suits, while not quite Brooks Brothers, are of simple and good design. These are, it so happens, the most popular and the most profitable. The secret of Paul's success—is there ever only one?—may or may not be his belief that most people have instinctive good taste.

The same belief applied to the newspapers he owns. Before the Second World War, Paul decided that while certain people, mostly the poor and displaced, were moving into Chicago, the more prosperous were taking their families into the suburbs.

The latter, few of whom were lip readers, needed newspapers, and Paul Julian—Paulo di Cavalcanti was no more—provided them. They were brightly written, intelligently edited, and, within reason, courageous. Even at the height of the late inquisition in Washington, the newspapers published by Paul Julian Enterprises continued to point out that evil is evil, right is right, and tyrants tyrannical. Some few subscribers were lost, but for every one lost, two were gained.

There are now ten of the newspapers, most of them weeklies, all of them successful.

Is it a *saga*? Perhaps, although the word suggests something legendary, of a past age, something poetic even, and as Paul told Lydia, "In a saga, as I understand it, the hero makes something happen, and in my case, most of the time, that wasn't so. If I ever write my autobiography, which I doubt I'll be called on to do, the title will be *What Happened*.

"True, when I was a kid, I hustled. I ran, I pushed my way to the head of the line whenever possible, and if I had to knee somebody else out of the way, I did it. But mostly what happened was luck, chance, circumstance, accident, being in the right place at the crucial moment, and keeping an eye on the main chance."

That's about it. Paul did what he set out to do, and while the story may lack some of the romance of the journeys of Ulysses, it was far less hazardous, too. Paul had, as he says later, come home safe. And yet, on a hot night in July it all ended. Why? There is no easy answer to that. There is only the account of the night itself and of the day that preceded it.

That morning there was no warning of the coming storm, no dark clouds drifting across a hostile sky, no backstage roll of thunder, no hint of hurricane winds. To the contrary, the morning was peaceful and cool, with the suggestion of a breeze.

Paul woke up at a minute or two after six. He had been doing that ever since the newspaper route in Gary. It was no longer necessary, but the habit stayed with him, and he saw no reason to break it. He liked the ambivalent light of early morning, the pale sky, the sense of solitude.

He stood for a time at the bedroom window, looking out at the costly green lawn. The head gardener—there were three— was doing something or other near the row of neatly trimmed Japanese pines that separated Paul's backyard from that of his nearest neighbor. Could the gardener have been painting the roses red?

One of the Chicago papers once referred to Paul's place as a baronial estate. I am not a baron, thought Paul, and I never wanted an estate.

What am I doing here, then? Did anybody use force? No, I came of my own volition. The question is, why? And the answer is that I never gave much thought to where I wanted to be on a July morning at the age of forty-five. I was too busy running. But running for what? The brass ring, a crown of laurel leaves? Besides the money, that is.

He sighed. There are some questions it is better not to ask.

Paul felt suddenly heavy. I have, he thought, the greatest gift of all, the gift of a new day, but there is no joy in it.

At the time that was all, a certain feeling of heaviness and the realization that there was no longer any joy in the morning.

When Paul shaved, the familiar face stared at him with some hostility, or was it fear? And, afterward, when he swam across the baronial pool that was shaped like an accusing eye, Paul was perhaps more winded than usual.

He had breakfast alone at the graceful table that was said to have belonged to an Italian nobleman. The eggs, served by an Irish girl in a maid's uniform (at seven in the morning, mind you), were on a Wedgwood plate. The silver was from Florence, and in the middle of the table was a silver bowl filled with various exotic fruits, some of which were even edible. The bowl itself was from Peru.

Paul read the papers and went through various inconsequential documents that he would need during the inconsequential day ahead. At seventhirty his daughter came into the dining room.

"Oh, hi, Dad," she said. Always those same three words of acknowledgment, not cold, not warm, just casual. Paul made nothing of that fact; he simply noted it.

"You're up early," he said.

"Um," said Karen, and she asked the Irish girl to bring her some juice and coffee, picked up a copy of the paper, and started reading it.

Paul looked at his daughter proudly. Such a pretty girl; she looked much the way her mother had at nineteen, the shining black hair, the eager dark eyes, the generous wide mouth, the same graceful walk.

"What's your plan for the day?" he asked.

"The usual," she said, not looking up from the paper.

Karen has no doubt suffered rebuffs, sorrows, and disappointments, thought Paul. She surely has had her share of anguish, but she had never confided any of these to her father. None of her joys, either, not even when she was a child:

"Hello, Daddy. You're home early."

"I came home early especially. I thought maybe I could read to you. Here, I brought a book."

After she had unwrapped the book, "Thank you very much."

Noting the tepid response, Paul said, "You don't by any chance already have it, do you?"

"I'm afraid so, but don't worry. I can exchange it. Thanks again."

"Is it any good?"

"Not especially."

"Is there something else you'd like me to read to you?"

"Thanks, but I'd really rather you didn't."

And, more recently, many times this brief exchange:

"Oh, hi, Dad. Sorry, I've got to run."

"But I never see you. We never have a chance to talk."

"We will, doll. Don't worry (a peck on the forehead). But right now I've got to scamper."

After Karen finished her coffee and orange juice, she took out a cigarette, and Paul lighted it for her.

She thanked him; her manners were certainly proper. She had learned the manners and a certain way of speaking the English language as well as how to speak French and Italian and Spanish and, quite possibly, Esperanto. But how about a course in how to converse with the old man? Is that on any curriculum?

Paul thought of asking Karen if she felt joy in the mornings, but instead he said, "How about you and your mother and I having dinner at the Pump Room tonight? And then we might go to the theater. Is there anything you'd like to see?"

Karen gave him an indulgent smile. "It's sweet of you," she said, "but I'm afraid I'm booked up, and I think Mother is going to a meeting."

Paul nodded, and then, "Tomorrow night, maybe?"

"We'll see."

Paul picked up the documents he had been studying and started out of the dining room.

"See you later," said Karen.

I'm dismissed, thought Paul; my daughter has disposed of me. Run out and play now, Dad; some of us grownups are trying to read.

When he got upstairs, Paul, as usual, started past the closed door of his wife's bedroom. Then, it being the kind of morning it was, he thought of something that might not otherwise have occurred to him. He hadn't seen Fran for two weeks, not since the night they'd given a dinner for what Fran called "a bunch of the neighbors."

That may, thought Paul, sound as simple as a covered-dish supper in the basement of the First Methodist Episcopal. Not quite. How many times do the Methodists hire a six-piece jazz combo? Or serve vintage champagne as well as imported red and white wines? How often in a covered dish do you come across Chicken Kief? Or Crème à la Glace au Miel? How many Methodists can even pronounce it?

The conversation that evening wasn't quite up to the standard of the food. The rich don't have to take the trouble to be entertaining. The talk was about the necessity for upzoning, for upholding discrimination against dogs of uncertain lineage, babies with odd-sounding names, persons whose skins are not naturally pink.

Paul didn't agree with most of what was said, but he managed to listen in silence and without visible discomfort. Fran filled the neighbors in on the errors of their ways. She was accustomed to addressing large groups. She was a cause girl, a doer of good, a renouncer of evil, and as such she had won numerous citations and awards. Paul was proud of her. He contributed money to her many worthwhile organizations, and he voted the Democratic ticket. The exchange seemed fair enough.

Whether Fran ever changed anybody's mind by her flow of words, he wasn't sure. Himself, on the rare occasions when they were alone together, he had stopped listening.

So Fran, he felt, talked too much, but she, at the same time and no doubt with equal justice, complained that he talked too little. "It's like sitting down to dinner with a stone wall." Okay, once more no argument. Jack Sprat could eat no fat; his wife could eat no lean. And they lived happily ever after, surrounded by cupboards full of clean platters.

What kind of marriage did he and Fran have? Better than most? Worse than most? How do you ever know? Marriage isn't a balance sheet, this much profit, that much loss. Marriage is a delicate thing, as capricious as an April day. You either are married or you're not, and like most other things in life, it's either bearable or it isn't.

So far as he knew or for that matter cared, Fran had been physically faithful to him, and with some few exceptions when he was in one or another Pacific port during the war, he had been faithful to her, not because he was in that way especially moral. You make a bargain—a covenant, if you want to be fancy—and if at all possible, you stick to it. The other way is simply too much trouble.

And so it was that on a July morning Paul knocked on Fran's door. Her voice, even at that hour a public voice, said, "Who is it?" Her tone suggested an enemy at the gates.

"Paul. May I come in?"

"Oh, darling. I haven't put on a face yet."

"I've seen you without a face," he said, and, uninvited, he went into the enormous bedroom that was filled with furniture designed just before the French Revolution.

When she saw him, Fran leaped out of bed and, hiding her face, ran into the bathroom that had wall-to-wall carpeting and locked the door behind her. On the way she said, "There used to be such a thing as privacy."

She spent some time in the bathroom, and when she came out, she was wearing a red cashmere robe that became her, had gathered her dark hair into a loose swirl at the back of her neck, and had made up her face.

She was still, thought Paul, a good-looking woman. She had been a beautiful girl, and he thought of the first time he had seen her—the fresh, dark skin, the lustrous hair, the tall, hipless body, the eager look.

He had come into the office of the publisher of a suburban

weekly, and Fran was the receptionist. Paul had been twenty-two. When he asked to see the publisher, she said, "If you've come about the cub reporter's job, you should see the editor. He's in the other office."

Paul winked at her and said, "The paper's for sale, isn't it? I've come to buy it."

"You're a comedian, anyway," said Fran.

"If I'm telling the truth, will you let me take you to dinner?"

Still not believing him, she said, "Sure. As long as it's the Pump Room."

That night at the Pump Room they had shish kebab.

It was such a lovely evening, as if they had know each other forever. From birth on they appeared to have seen the same things and reacted to them in the same way. They were both the children of immigrants who had come to find the pot of gold and had failed, and they had both spent their childhood in slum areas—Fran's was in Springfield—and they were both ambitious, and they both felt an intense excitement for what life had to offer, all of it, and, and, and.

After dinner, as they were walking along the shore of Lake Michigan, Fran said, "Now that you're head of the whole she-bang, are you going to fire the receptionist?"

"Nope," said Paul, "I'm going to marry her."

Fran was, it so happens, the first girl Paul had ever taken to the Pump Room or indeed anywhere else for dinner.

"You don't have much time for girls if you're always in train-ing for the Olympics," Paul told Lydia. "Of course, what I didn't know then was that in the Greek Olympics, when their sons won, the fathers prayed to the gods that the punishment be light."

That first night Fran said, "And after we're married, could we have dinner at the Pump Room every night?"

"Of course," said Paul, "and lunch and breakfast, too."

"In her whole life," said Fran, "my mother never had dinner in a restaurant."

They were married a month later, and the best man was To-bias Waring, who was Paul's best friend.

Tobias provided the only cloud in the sky, and it was a cloud no bigger than a man's hand, nothing to worry about.

At the bachelor carousal the night before the wedding, Paul said, "Fran is convinced you hate her."

Tobias, even then the most discreet of men, said, "Now why in the world would she think a thing like that?"

He drank some more, and then he said, "Who do you suppose was the first man—I'm sure it was a man—who discovered the glories of the fermented grape? Because there ought to be a monument to him somewhere. As well as entire chapters in the history books."

"You do like her, don't you?"

"Who cares who won the Thirty Years' War?" said Tobias. "Who thought up Scotch whiskey?"

"Come on." said Paul. "I'd tell you."

Tobias said, "I like women who are soft and cuddly."

Francesca Julian, née Gillotti, on the July morning we're concerned with here, kissed her husband and rang for breakfast.

She seated herself on the queen-sized bed that could once have belonged to Marie Antoinette and said, "In one hour I've got to be at a meeting of the Foreign Policy Association. Now what's on your mind?"

"Nothing in particular," said Paul, "except that I just realized we haven't seen each other for two whole weeks."

"Darling, I don't have time to sit around and brood about things like that. I know meetings bore you, but some of us have to keep the world from falling apart."

"How about keeping us from falling apart?"

"Now what," said Fran, "is that supposed to mean?"

"How about us having dinner at the Pump Room? And then maybe going to the theater?"

"I'd love to, but the library board is tonight."

"You used to say you wanted to have dinner at the Pump Room every night."

"And I used to eat a lot of penny candy."

"How about tomorrow night?"

"Tomorrow night's the benefit for the freedom marchers. You'll agree that that's of some importance."

"I bought two tickets at two hundred and fifty smacks a week. It's *that* important."

Fran patted his hand. "Baby, I refuse to quarrel at this hour of the morning."

Her breakfast arrived, and she greeted the Irish girl like a long-lost friend. Fran was good with servants. She treated them as equals and was invariably heartbroken when they inevitably betrayed her.

After the girl left, Fran said, "I've got a big day ahead of me, Paul, a rather important day, not only to me but, if I may say so, to the city that's been rather good to both of us."

Paul didn't laugh, but he wondered what happened to her sense of humor, to her spirit of gaiety, to her eye for the ridiculous, and where was her compassion for small things, his own moods, to name one?

How long had it been since she had looked at him of an evening and said, "You've had a bad day, and you're worried, and you're to stop. Because everything turns out right for us, always, always, always. And I'm going to mix us a bathtub full of martinis?"

How long had it been since she had looked at him at all? Making it possible for the students to march through Mississippi next summer is important, but so is making it possible for me to get through the day. Or is that last my problem and no part of our marriage? Am I being selfish and self-centered?

He got up from the Louis XV chair, or else it was Louis XVI. "I certainly don't want to interfere with the destiny of Chicago, Illinois," he said.

Fran spread guava jelly on a still-warm croissant, and she said, "Maybe we'll have time to talk tonight, exhausted though I'll be. But right now I've got to concentrate on the day ahead. Did I ever tell you, Mrs. Roosevelt said that one of the secrets of her success was that she always had at least half an hour of absolute quiet and meditation when she got out of bed in the morning."

"And I've read," said Paul, "that she always took a handful of chocolate-covered garlic pills in the morning. If you'd like, I'll stop in at our friendly neighborhood druggist and see if I can pick you up a few of those."

"At heart you're a black reactionary," said Fran.

"I'll have to give some thought to what that means," said Paul, "and when I've finished playing, I'll try to remember to pick up my toys."

Fran was buttering the croissant and may or may not have heard him.

The rest of Paul's day was ordinary enough. After he got to the office he dictated a number of letters that could have been handled by a bright office boy, and late in the morning he attended a board of directors' meeting that was the same as a thousand others. But with this difference. He looked now at the successful, settled faces of the men around the table, and he asked himself if they had ever wondered what they were doing there. Had the excitement disappeared for them? Were they, too, going through motions? And what of the friends now gone? The ones who had recently died, unexpectedly and surely unwillingly? Had they in their final hours had regrets?

And from some half-forgotten day of his youth he remembered Browning's Bishop Blougram: "Just when we are safest, there's a sunset touch, a fancy from a flower bell."

Okay, he thought, I'm home safe, and now I'd like a little of the sunset touch. Yes, yes, I know they're expensive, but I can afford them. I'll take all you've got, as long as they're guaranteed not to fade or shrink. And where can I pick up a few flower bells? A call to the florist? "Two dozen, if you please, and be sure and put in plenty of fancy."

"It wasn't that I thought I'd wasted my life," Paul told Lydia, "no regrets in that way. True, I hadn't discovered a cure for cancer or written a symphony or composed a sonnet, but I'd done what I set out to do.

"At that meeting I said to myself, 'Maybe Fran and Karen are right; maybe we're all still playing childish games.' As for me, I'm forty-five years old, too old for marbles, too old for tag and I Spy. Now, where do you keep the games for grown-ups?"

That evening Paul had dinner with Tobias Waring, who had been best man at his wedding.

When Tobias came of age, a fortune of a hundred million dollars was divided between him and his sister Rosalie. She married an English earl. Or maybe it was a duke. No matter.

Tobias was a man of enormous energies and great enthusiasms—languages, higher mathematics, anthropology, genealogy, history, philosophy, religion, art. And people, of course, above all, people. It would be difficult to say what didn't interest Tobias. He was born with unquenchable curiosity.

Fran complained that he had never worked a day in his life, which was true enough if you consider work a punishment, but if work is what one does to please oneself, Tobias had never wasted a day.

He had returned a few days before from one of the Greek islands, where, he told Paul, he had succeeded in ruining a ruin.

He was five years older than Paul, but when he came into the restaurant, Paul felt, with some envy, that Tobias looked ten years younger. He was a man of medium height, small-boned, and thin, but he gave the impression of size. Perhaps it was the way he walked—the military stride, the straight backbone, the chin held high. His face had weathered, but it was a youthful face. Not boyish, that's something else again.

"Hello, old friend," he said.

Paul could never call anybody "old friend," not even Tobias. It was the kind of greeting you have to grow up with.

They ordered drinks, and Tobias said, "You look tuckered out. Is the world getting to you?"

Although it had been more than a year, you'd have thought they saw each other yesterday afternoon.

Tobias asked about Fran and Karen—fine, just fine. Paul did not ask about Jennifer, the girl who had gone to the Greek islands with Tobias. He always had a girl, and three times he had married them, and other times he had not. The girls were always pretty, intelligent, and amusing, and when Tobias grew tired of them (it was seldom the other way around), he settled handsomely, and that was that. Nobody was ever the worse off for knowing Tobias, and most people were better off, which is about the best you can say for any of us.

They talked of many things. Tobias told Paul of the peaceful, sunny days he had spent in the Greek islands and about the month with the Berbers in the Atlas Mountains and about the odd beauty of the city of Marrakesh. Wherever he went, Tobias enjoyed himself; in his entire life, he had never had a disenchanted day.

Eventually, Paul found himself describing his own day, the one that was just then ending.

When he finished, Tobias said, "In other words, you've started to think. That's dangerous. If you'd asked me, I'd have warned you against it."

"The trouble is," said Paul, "once you start, you can't stop."

"Who said you had to?"

Tobias remembered that when he and Paul first knew each other, Paul had said that when he could afford it, he was going to the village in Portugal where his father had been born.

Paul now could, God knows, afford it. What was to stop him?

"Go tomorrow morning," said Tobias. "Go by the first plane. That wise Roman, Horace, said, 'The man who puts off the day when he will live rightly is like the peasant who waits for the river to drain away. But it flows on, and it will flow on forever.' "

"I couldn't go tomorrow morning," said Paul. "That's foolish."

"Sometimes to be foolish is to be wise," said Tobias, "and, understand, I don't mean going for a month or so. I mean going for a year, three years, maybe the rest of your life, and I don't mean just Portugal. I mean everywhere you've ever dreamed about going."

"I'd be bored," said Paul. "People who don't work get bored."

"I'm not bored."

"But I'm not an intellectual. I don't have the—well, the resources you have. Intellectually, I mean."

"How do you know? When at the age of thirty-seven Montaigne retired to his country house to find out what made him tick, he didn't expect to stay."

"I wonder if Fran would enjoy it; she's always saying she never has any time to herself."

"Montaigne, as I recall, went alone," said Tobias. "It's true that he missed seeing the Massacre of Saint Bartholomew, which took place the following year, but I see no evidence that he minded."

"What's that got to do with Fran?"

"I don't think Fran would like missing a massacre," said Tobias.

For a wild, disloyal minute Paul felt like laughing, but instead he said, "You don't understand Fran."

"Do you?"

"I've lived with her for twenty-some years."

Tobias said, "Fran is an extremely worthy woman, and if it weren't for worthy ladies, we'd probably still be living in nice, cool caves."

"You're wrong about Fran," said Paul. "You always have been."

"It would be a pleasure," said Tobias.

Sometime later he said two things, neither of which at the time seemed to Paul to bear directly on the subject at hand.

He said, "Marriage is the only art in which we expect to turn out a masterpiece the first time around. It hardly ever works that way. Picasso had done quite a little painting when he got around to 'Guernica.' "

And he said, "Sherwood Anderson was forty years old and the manager of a paint factory in Elyria, Ohio, when he said to his secretary, 'My feet are cold and wet. I have been walking too long on the bed of a river.' Then he walked out and never came back.

"Now there are some people who, impossible as it seems, are perfectly happy in Elyria, and there are no doubt some who even like the smell of paint."

As they parted, Tobias said, "I'll see you in Europe. Let me know where."

"What do you think?" said Paul. "Will I be alone or with Fran?"

"You won't be with Fran, but you won't necessarily be alone either."

Chapter 25

❧   When Paul got back to the house on Lake Shore Drive, he sat for some time in the dark living room, and the more he thought about what Tobias had said, the more it appealed to him. But he still thought Tobias was wrong about Fran. Fran would be delighted. And wasn't it possible that Karen would go with them? She could postpone college for a year. What he wouldn't have given at nineteen to be able to spend a year in Europe!

He mixed himself a stiff drink, turned on the hi-fi, and when Fran came home—it was after midnight—he was still sitting in the dark, humming softly to himself.

Fran turned on the lights. The same switch controlled those in the yard, and there were spotlights on the swimming pool, on a sculpture that was shaped like an amoeba, on the nine-hole putting green that the landscape architect had insisted on, and on the topiary figures of characters out of *Wind in the Willows*.

Fran gasped when she saw him.

"What in the world are you doing here?" she asked.

"Thinking," said Paul. Surely she would sense the exuberance in his voice.

"Well, I wouldn't mind just sitting in the dark and doing nothing," said Fran. "What were you thinking about?"

"You. Me. The past. The future."

Fran smiled; it was a smile she had worked on. "My Italianate smile," she called it. She made no attempt to disguise her background and had been quoted in the newspapers as saying, "My father was a master plumber, and my ancestry is one hundred percent Italian." To her friends she said, "I'm a wop and proud of it."

She was still looking well. She was wearing a white Chanel suit, a string of black pearls that had surely cost more than Paul's father made in his entire lifetime, and was carrying a brown bag from Gucchi.

She kissed Paul on top of the head, yawned, and said, "Sometime when we've got a week to spare, you must tell me all about it."

"Right now," said Paul. "You're going to be pleased."

"I've got to go to bed; tomorrow's a big day."

As Fran took off her earrings, also black pearl, she said, "At the library board meeting, Mrs. Healy went on for forty-five minutes about *Last Exit to Brooklyn*. She said—well, you know, straight back to the days of the late Senator Joe. It wouldn't surprise me if she were a John Bircher, and I'm planning to do a little discreet investigating."

Paul, feeling capricious, said, "Would you do that if you thought she was a Communist?"

"It's too late and I'm too tired to argue politics," said Fran. She started toward the cherrywood staircase that seemed to be suspended in air. "Ma Healy didn't actually want to burn *Last Exit*. She wanted it to be restricted to what she called 'responsible adults,' whoever they are. I haven't read it. Have you?"

"That's exactly what I want to talk to you about. Reading books, among other things. Darling, please sit down."

"Tomorrow. Couldn't we please?"

"No," said Paul. "Tonight."

Fran looked at him with some annoyance, but she did sit down on the sofa beside him.

"Well, well, well," she said. "I've been thinking about what you said this morning, and you know what I decided? I decided you've gone and got yourself a girl."

It took some time, but Paul told her as well as he was able about what he had been thinking, about the questions that he had started to ask himself, about the doubts that were tearing at his mind, and, finally, about going to Portugal. He did not mention Tobias. Why complicate an already complex issue?

Fran was silent for the most part, but when he stopped to light a cigarette, she said, "It sounds to me as if you're going through male menopause." When he sipped at his drink, she said, "You don't think what you're saying is unique, do you? Most men have the same problems at your age." And when he rose to close a window, she said, "Darling, your trouble is, you don't have any suitable interests. The Art Institute wants you on the board of directors, but you turned it down. If they knew you were available now, I know they'd ask you again. For one thing, they'd think you might give them some more money."

Paul, swallowing his anger and surprise, made no comment on her first two statements, but to the third he said, "I don't want to be a director of the Art Institute. There are a lot of people who could do that better. I want to look at some pictures, study them. I want to find out why I like what I like, if in fact I like anything. Does that make any sense to you?"

"Not if you're eighteen years old," said Fran, and a moment later, "Of course, it makes sense to me. You're finally discovering what I've told you all along, that money isn't everything. But you don't have to rip up your whole life just to find out what Picasso is getting at."

"You didn't hear a word I said, did you?"

"To the contrary, I heard every word you said, and, although it wasn't wasy, I managed to keep a straight face throughout."

"But you don't agree."

"I'm going to get a glass of milk. How about you?"

"No, thanks."

Later Paul was to wonder if there had been any change in Fran's voice when she said that last. Had there been any indication of the destruction she was about to unleash? He decided not; at that point Fran had still thought she would win.

She must have, because when she returned to the room, she had changed into the red dressing gown and made up her face again.

She once more seated herself on the sofa, and as she put a pill in her mouth and drank some of the milk, she said, "The pills don't take effect for half an hour, so don't worry. I won't go to sleep on you. Now do go on. I'm fascinated."

"Are you all right?" said Paul. "You sound upset."

"I'm *wonderful,* absolutely, sensationally wonderful. We haven't had a good talk like this for years. Now let me be sure I've got it straight. You want us to pull up stakes, throw over everything, and take off for a smelly little fishing village in Portugal. We're to make friends with the natives, some of them your relatives, and they must be brilliant conversationalists, just like you. Now in addition, we're going to read and sit in the sun and study our navels. Study your navel, really, because I'm a little old for a bikini. And then, eventually, we're going to visit the Prado in Madrid and the Louvre. Am I right so far?"

"Fran, stop it."

"Stop what? I'm enjoying every minute of this. I told you, we've got to have oodles of little chats like this."

"Maybe you're right," said Paul. "You're tired. Maybe we should wait until tomorrow."

"No. You've managed at last to arouse my interest, but I do have a few little questions, if I may. First, what about Karen?"

And so, thought Paul, the charade begins. It's important. It has to do with survival, mine.

Paul was good in crises; his manner became calmer, his voice more controlled.

He said, "I'd hoped Karen might go with us, but if she doesn't, I don't think we have to worry about a baby-sitter. She's nineteen years old. She'll be in college. Next summer, if we're still there, she can join us."

"In other words, you don't care what happens to our daughter."

Paul walked to the French doors and looked out at the topiary figure of Mr. Toad, which he loathed.

"Let's get to the next point."

"The next point has to do with money. What about the papers, for instance? Are you planning to let them go to rack and ruin?"

Paul laughed. "Rack and ruin. That's a nice, old-fashioned phrase for you. Rack and ruin. I thought that went out with the melodrama of the late nineteenth century."

"If you're going to be angry, I see no reason for us to continue this farce."

"I'm not angry, but I wish you'd tell me what's bothering you. I thought you'd love the whole idea."

"I'm still up at bat. What are we going to use for m-o-n-e-y. And who is going to run the papers?"

Paul said that he intended to put the papers in the hands of a newspaper broker and had, in fact some time ago spoken to one who had told him that the lot would bring in the neighborhood of five and a half million dollars, after taxes. That was the papers alone, nothing to do with their other holdings.

"I think, if necessary, we'll be able to pig it out for the rest of our lives and still leave enough for a suitable dowry for Karen," he said.

"You're a clever man, aren't you?" said Fran. "You had it all planned, didn't you? You didn't want to talk anything over with me. You knew damn good and well I couldn't go with you. You didn't want me to."

"Why is that?"

"I can't really believe it has escaped your attention that next month I am going to become chairman of the Mothers' March of Dimes."

Paul knew then that both the battle and the war were lost, but he was not a man who gave up easily, not even when the odds were hopeless. He said, and there was a gentle sibilance in his voice, "Dear Fran, please believe me. I don't underestimate the importance of your wanting the position you've earned, and I know it's important, but I'm sure they'll put it off for a year. Not only that, I'll give them a check for ten thousand dollars."

"You think you can buy anything, don't you? You always have."

Paul looked at Fran's face, the face he had loved or thought he loved. He saw that the dark eyes had grown darker with hatred and that the mouth he had once found generous was thin and pinched.

"Who's the woman?" she asked. "I've always known there was a woman."

"There's no woman. There never has been."

Fran picked up the glass in which there was still a little milk, and as she started in the direction of the kitchen, she said, "I won't give you a divorce, not ever."

He called after her, feeling a moment of hope, "Do you love me, Fran? Is that why you're acting this way?"

She didn't turn; she didn't even stop walking.

She said, "I never loved you; I never liked you, either, not even in the beginning. I married you because you were the best meal ticket around. Any other questions?"

The scene rightly ends there, but afterward Paul stood for a time near the French doors of the house on Lake Shore Drive. It was once pictured in an October issue of a magazine called *The America Home*. One of the captions said, among other things, "A dream house, and dreams no longer come cheap. . . ."

The morning was as silent as a morning can be. There was not a ripple on the pool. Not a blade of grass stirred, and not a leaf in the trees was disturbed by the holocaust that had just occurred inside the dream house.

Paul, not upsetting the deathly silence, asked himself this: "Do all of us spend our lives with strangers?"

Then, for the first time since shortly before Christmas 1943, when at Pearl Harbor he saw the scarred survivors and the charred bodies of the dead from an aircraft carrier called the *Liscombe Bay*, he wept.

Later that day it rained, a rather gentle rain, and there was no thunder or lightning, except the internal kind, of course. Paul came down the cherrywood staircase carrying a handsome bag in which he'd packed all that he planned to take with him, except for some few memories.

His daughter was in the living room with a perfect young

man who could have made a good living posing for clothing advertisements, but that was hardly necessary; his father was a Federal judge. The young man's suit came from Bond Street, the tie from Sulka, and the sea-island cotton shirt from Marshall Field's. The tan he was wearing resulted from time spent in and around a great many swimming pools.

Both he and Karen were doing well with a bottle of King's Ransom.

"Oh, hi, Dad," said Karen. "Mother said you were leaving. You know Jere."

The young man showed no embarrassment. He said, "Hello, sir." The accent had cost the judge a great deal of money.

"I wonder if I could talk to you a moment," Paul said to his daughter.

"I'll be out by the pool, Karen," said the young man, and to Paul he said, "Good-bye, sir." Then, as if he were launching a voyager on the River Styx, he added, "And the best of luck."

Karen lighted a mentholated cigarette, took her glass of Scotch, and sat on a chair that was said to predate the American Revolution.

"Why don't you come with me?" said Paul.

"Thanks, Dad, but the sort of thing you have in mind just doesn't interest me."

"I wish it did," said Paul, and he said, "I'm sorry, Karen. I didn't mean for things to turn out like this."

"For Pete's sake, Dad," said his daughter, "it happens every day. What's the big deal?"

Until the morning in Paris that we're coming to, Paul didn't see Fran again.

The morning the end came she was up bright and early, early anyway, and she was gone until, once again, nearly midnight.

First, there was a breakfast meeting of the committee in charge of the Community Chest drive; Fran was vice-chairman. In the afternoon she was with a group planning a television

program to raise money for the study of the causes of leukemia.
She had dinner in a private dining room of the Blackstone
Hotel, where the problems of highway beautification were discussed. Afterward she went to the benefit performance to raise
money for a freedom march in Mississippi.

Fran, who was wearing a black Mainbocher dress, sat in the
third row center, one of the two-hundred-and-fifty-dollar seats.

That night Paul had taken a plane to New York and the next
day a second to Lisbon. By the end of the week he had found
the white villa and started furnishing not only its interior but
his own as well.

The first crates of books and records had been chosen with
the help of Tobias, but after those had been devoured, Paul
was on his own, and he went every few weeks to Paris to re-
plenish the supply.

To his delighted surprise, Paul discovered that he had inner
resources he had never suspected, certainly never exercised.
And, once again, he found joy in the morning.

Then came the day at the airport in Lisbon when he met
Lydia.

"I told you I'm a lucky man," he said, "but never so lucky as
I was that morning."

They were back at the apartment by this time, and Lydia
had make breakfast.

Paul said that Fran had had detectives following his every
move since he left Chicago, but he hadn't been aware of it until
he saw the Silent Man in the lobby of the hotel in Armação de
Pêra. A few days later, Fernando had come back to the villa unexpectedly and found the man going through Paul's private papers. Fernando had attacked the man and after the fight that
followed had been hospitalized.

"If I hadn't been such a coward," Paul said, "I'd have told
you at the start. I didn't for the most selfish reason; I was afraid
I might lose you."

"I selfishly wouldn't have let that happen," said Lydia.

"Besides, I thought I could *reason* with Fran. That's why I
went to Paris. I should have realized, I guess, that her heart is

on the good side of all the large causes and on the bad side of all the small ones."

At the meeting, Fran was surrounded by lawyers, American, French, Spanish, and, God and Fran alone knew why, two from England.

Paul was willing to give her anything she wanted so far as money was concerned, but, no, she wanted revenge. Revenge for what?

"I think she'll never forgive me for having found happiness," said Paul. "There are people like that, you know, people who have to destroy what they've arranged not to have themselves."

The choice her lawyers offered Paul was simple enough. Either he could stop seeing "that woman"—the description was hers—and return to Chicago at once. Or, and again the phrasing was Fran's, she would see to it that he would have trouble crossing the Illinois state line, with or without Lydia. Their names would be—that's right—mud. No wonder Fran was such a popular public speaker.

When the Paris meeting was near to an end, Paul said, "You don't want me, Fran. Why are you acting this way?"

"I don't want you," she said, "and when I've finished with you, neither will anyone else."

"I have no intention of going back to her now," said Paul, "if in fact I ever could have. It isn't that I hate her. I pity her, and that's an ugly emotion to feel for somebody I've lived with all the years I've lived with Fran."

Paul told Lydia about Tobias' contention that a longtime association with someone doesn't necessarily mean that you understand them. A man who spends his life as a guard in the Impressionist halls of the Louvre doesn't necessarily have the most reliable judgment as to the relative merits of Monet and Manet.

"I'll fight," said Paul, "and I'll probably win, but it will be dirty, no question of that, and some of the dirt always rubs off.

"It's like the boy whose watch was stolen, and his father advised him not to notify the police. When the son asked why, his father said, 'Because it will be in the papers, and for the rest of your life, whenever your name is brought up, some people will say, 'I don't know much about him, but I do know he had something to do with a stolen watch.'

"I can take the mudslinging. I'm used to it, but for you, my love, it won't be so easy."

"I never thought it would be easy," said Lydia.

Paul raised her hand to his lips and kissed it, and he said, "You could say good-bye now, and I'd still love you and admire you and cherish you.

"I'll leave if you say so, and no looking back, not even any prolonged good-bye. A quick hail and farewell, and for the rest of my life, gratitude for what we've had up to now."

"Now we need some sleep," said Lydia.

Paul could sleep; he always could, anywhere, anytime, five minutes, five hours, around the clock. In a bed, on a chair, a plane. The habit was one he'd taught himself early in life.

But, although she tried hard, Lydia could not sleep that sultry morning in Madrid. Tired she was, tired beyond belief, almost, she felt, beyond endurance.

Too much had happened too quickly. First Day, then Paul's wife, and, finally, the long night of talk.

Eventually she quietly rose, made herself some more coffee, and sat for a long time on the terrace. The roses were in bloom in the courtyard below, and their sweet scent drifted up to the terrace, but to Lydia that morning the smell was of festering lilies.

Perhaps, she thought, Candice is right; maybe the cheap, nudging in-the-ribs, ill-natured babble has already begun. Maybe they are already using the words—oh, *affair* will be the mildest of them. Affair, love nest, tryst (anybody been trysting lately?), illicit rendezvous, mistress, paramour.

All right, I can take it and no real damage done. Sticks and stones, and so on. True, I'm a coward. I prefer peace to a war, but when the malicious challenge is made, and it has been, I won't back away.

The malicious win through fear, and I've done nothing wrong, nothing I'm ashamed of, nothing I intend to apologize for, publicly or privately. You want a battle, ma'am, okay, you've got one. And when it's over, win or lose, I'll hold my head high. It's you who'll hide your face from the crowd, or from the mob if you arouse one.

But isn't it too bad—no more than that, isn't it an outrage that this late in this enlightened (isn't it?) century, the accuser has the upper hand.

There are, however, others to be considered.

As for Day and Ralph, it won't matter what is said.

What about Christopher, though? He can go far, I think, I have always thought, but will his journey upward be shortened by the harsh whispers about his mother? Her lover killed a man, you know, and she has something to do with a stolen watch.

Finally, Lydia's weary mind asked itself a possibly unanswerable question. Where does my responsibility to me end? Where does my obligation to my son begin?

She sat for a time longer on the terrace, listening to a mournful song from the boys' school up the street. Once she came close to falling into an uneasy sleep, but she roused herself, went to the phone, and called Christopher.

They arranged to meet in a café near the embassy.

Lydia dressed, and before she left the apartment, she tiptoed into the bedroom and kissed Paul gently on the forehead.

He stirred in his sleep but did not waken, and Lydia thought, Paul Julian is a good man, the best I've ever known or ever will, and from him I have at last learned the difference between the shadow of love and its substance.

And while we're on the subject, what is my duty to him?

The price of everything has gone up, she thought, the cost of loving along with the rest. But hating is still abundantly available at the usual bargain rates.

She left a note for Paul on the table beside the bed and then went out into the murderous morning.

Chapter 26

✿ The café where Lydia was to meet Christopher was tiny but cheerful, blatantly cheerful, insistently so. The blue and white walls looked as if they had been painted that very morning and everything else was scrupulously clean and polished —the white counter, the marble-topped tables, the great espresso machine, the ice-cream parlor chairs, the blue-tiled floor.

At the moment Lydia was the only customer, and the two shining young people in charge, the handsome boy behind the counter and the pretty girl in front acting as a waitress, gave the impression that they had spent the whole of their lives preparing for the pleasure of Lydia's company.

She started to light a cigarette, but the boy was at her side with a lighter before she could take a match from the folder, and when the girl brought the pastry and cake Lydia had ordered, she watched anxiously as the honored guest tasted, first the coffee, then the tiny cake with pink frosting. It was as if the future of the café depended on Lydia's reaction. And so, feeling something of a fool, she nodded too vigorously and smiled too broadly, *bueno, bueno.*

It was good, and anyway, all in a good cause. The boy and girl looked at each other with pleasure and relief.

While she waited for Christopher, Lydia tried to decide what she would say to him. She should, no doubt, have thought of that before. But she was not going to repeat the crime of which Simeon had said she was forever guilty: "Your worst fault is that you act first and think afterward. You're such a creature of impulse."

Think now, think, thou creature of impulse.

Suppose I said to Christopher, "I'm in love darling, and I am for the first time in my life—what? Happy? Content? Feeling necessary? Complete? Even serene? And I want to continue feeling this way as long as I am able. But there's trouble ahead —scandal, headlines, whispers. And they're making up a fresh batch of scarlet letters just my size, and there is talk of bringing back the stock."

What would Christopher say to that? How could she know? How can you ever know that of anyone? Even a beloved son?

One thing was certain. Christopher would not react emotionally, and, unlike his scatterbrained mother, he would think first and act second. He would speak the truth as he saw it. He always had, even when the truth was hurtful, as truth so often is.

Lydia thought of a brisk October night when Christopher was, say, twelve, give or take or year or two. She and her son had been together in front of the fire in the house in Briley. She remembered that there had been a complaining wind in the trees.

At one point Christopher looked up from whatever he was doing, his homework, his erector set, his chessboard, and said, "Mother, did you ever want to *be* anything when you were a little girl? What I mean is, are you satisfied with what you are?"

Lydia, feeling she was the failure of failures, the nonentity of nonentities, said, "I doubt if anybody is really satisfied, but there are compensations, you and Day, to name two."

"I know," said Christopher, "but Grandfather says you were so smart when you were in college."

"In my case," Lydia said, "senility set in about the time I reached puberty."

Christopher laughed, and he said, "I guess you're happy enough at that."

And another time, whether it was earlier or later, Lydia could no longer remember, only the snip of conversation itself:

Christopher, looking at her with a kind of puzzled amazement, had said, "I was just thinking, when you were young, you must have been quite good-looking."

"Some few people thought so," Mother Earth replied, "but, of course, even in my salad days, I could never compete with Snow White."

"To me you're still beautiful, of course," Christopher had said.

Ah, the cruelty of youth, the honesty of youth, and damn the truth, anyway.

Lydia ordered another coffee. Christopher was late, which was unusual.

She found herself thinking of a summer eight, no, nine years before, the last summer she had seen her son for any extended time. He was seventeen and would go off to George Washington in the fall. It was an ending for Lydia and a beginning for Christopher, and it was in the nature of things and to be accepted. The regrets, if any, were to be kept to oneself.

It was the summer she and Simeon and the children had shared a ramshackle house on Cape Cod, near Truro, with Sybil and Jack.

Such a beautiful summer, a peaceful oasis in time. There had been day after day of sunshine. Had it ever rained? Were there any storms? Lydia couldn't remember any, only the long, unsullied days.

In the mornings, she and Sybil had given the house a once-over-lightly. Actually, Lydia had done most of the cleaning. Sybil was more an overseer, a suggester of what needed doing rather than a doer. No matter. Some of us are queen bees, others drones. And who is to say which is the better off?

After an early lunch, Sybil, who had not yet turned her talents to encouraging Impressionist painters, would go off to the summer theater in Dennis. She had met a young actor who was appearing there, wildly talented, to be sure, and handsome. All his career needed was a little encouragement, and who was better qualified to give him that? Whatever happened to the actor? What, indeed, was his name? Where are the snows of yesteryear?

Lydia, the noble one, spent the early afternoons painting. Her seascapes, scores of them, hundreds of them, were now stacked in the attic of the house in Briley, and, if worst came to worst, they would make dandy kindling for the fireplace on a cold winter's night.

Simeon that summer had spent most of every week working in the libraries in Cambridge, and Jack was usually in the city.

It was the summer Christopher was involved, seriously, it appeared at the time, with a girl named Enid, the daughter of a man who had made millions in the whiskey business. Enid was a shade under six feet tall, was more handsome than beautiful, had magenta-colored hair, always seemed to wear canary-yellow dresses, and was a teller of anecdotes. The latter were never short, and should one's attention wander, just before she delivered the punch line, Enid always gave a gust of warning laughter. "And then *he* said . . . Don't you just *love* it?"

One agreed, one had to, that one had loved it. Otherwise, well—there had been times when Enid had felt that one didn't love it because one had not understood it. She then repeated the anecdote, word for word, breath for breath, including the warning laughter.

In addition to Enid, Christopher that summer found time to be on what he called a biography kick—Disraeli, Lincoln, Gladstone, Washington, Winston Churchill, Franklin Roosevelt.

Lydia remembered the late afternoon when she and Sybil were on the beach, playing a sandy game of canasta. Christopher was sitting a little away, reading, and Day was, as usual, at the water's edge, reflecting, as she could for hours, on the mysteries of the surf.

Once Sybil called out to Christopher, "From all that you've been reading, I gather you're planning someday to be President."

Christopher looked up from his book, the whiteness of his

teeth, the blue of his eyes, his blondness emphasized by his tan.

After considering Sybil's question, he smiled. The disarming smile always came first. Then he said, "I suppose you're making fun of me, but I have given the matter some thought, and it seems to me I might be a rather good President, but I'm afraid I'm not prepared to make the compromises that seem to be necessary along the way."

"I'll tell you one thing," said Sybil. "You already talk like a President, and you'd be the prettiest one we ever had. You'd certainly have the woman's vote sewed up."

" 'In politics, the purpose of words is to disguise the dead,' " said Christopher.

"Did you make that up?"

"La Rochefoucauld," said Christopher. " 'Silence is the best tactic for him who distrusts himself.' "

"Don't be personal," said Sybil.

"Enid would be a wonderful First Lady," said Day. "Dull enough, anyway."

"Enid happens to have a brain," said Christopher, "and she happens to be adult, neither of which certain people can understand."

Was it that afternoon or later, when Lydia said to Sybil, "Do you think Christopher is serious about Enid?"

"Christopher is serious about everything," Sybil had said. "The question that interests you is whether or not he's going to want to marry her, and I don't think so. Why? Because he never laughs at her jokes."

And sure enough, shortly before the Labor Day weekend, as Lydia recalled, she said to Christopher, "You haven't seen Enid for some time. At least, you haven't brought her around. What's happened?"

"Nothing's happened," said Christopher. "It's just over, that's all."

"Do you mind if I ask why?"

"You just did, and the answer is, I'd heard all her jokes."

And what did that mean? Lydia asked herself. It meant, did it not, that to Christopher, Enid was totally predictable, that there were no surprises, that she bored him?

And how, Lydia asked herself now, did I feel then? Relieved? Nonsense. How could I have been? Was Enid not, except for a perhaps too frequent lapse into an anecdote, an altogether perfect girl, totally acceptable? Was she not a graduate of Miss Finch's? Did she not later make a name for herself at Bennington, or was it Sarah Lawrence? One of those terribly progressive schools; I know that. I remember reading someplace that she had majored in finger painting. Or blocks, something like that. And her mother was a wheel among the university women. And her father was certainly not an American Legionnaire; very few members of the Racquet Club are.

Why, then, was my heart not warmer toward Enid? Had I, too, heard the jokes before? Or was it the magenta hair? Could it have been that I was not overly fond of any girl who had an eye on my son, and vice versa? Could that still be the case?

Oh, don't be silly, and I think now I'll have one of those delicious little cakes with the pecans. *Bueno, bueno.*

When Christopher came into the café, he looked tired. There were faint half-circles of purple under his eyes. He was pale, his face drawn-looking, and the inevitable smile was forced.

He kissed Lydia on the forehead and sat down at the tiny table across from her.

After he had ordered tea from the girl—she clearly adored him—Christopher said, "You look tired."

"I was just thinking that you look as if you'd lost quite a little sleep," said Lydia.

Christopher dismissed the idea; he was fine, just fine. And had Lydia heard anything from Day?

Lydia told him about Ralph's cable.

He was not surprised; Day was foolhardy, but she wasn't stupid.

"I love Day," he said. "You know that, and so, I think, does she. Beyond the normal sibling rivalries, mostly subdued, we've always been good friends. But Day still has the idea that the world was created for her special pleasure. She's so bright that she's never had to work for anything she wanted, including her marriage."

What Christopher said was undeniable and aptly put. Lydia, wishing she could have phrased it as well, said, "Is that the only reason she thinks the world is her oyster, just that she's bright?"

Christopher drank some tea, ate a bite of cake with orange frosting and said, "Day has been known to say, though never in your presence, 'I can get away with practically anything with Mother.' When you sent her home, that was one of the few times she didn't."

To that Lydia had no answer. Christopher's blunt remark had, once more, the ring of total truth, a truth she had not faced before.

"Do you mean that you think I spoiled her?"

"I've never been sure what that means," said Christopher. "Anyway, whatever you did or didn't do, Day is a nice person. But if Ralph wants my advice, he'll give her an occasional spanking or maybe a black eye or a good, hard right to the jaw."

Lydia, feeling like a child begging for approval, said, "Did I spoil you?"

Christopher, recognizing that for the moment he was playing Papa, patted his daughter's hand and said, "I was born less defenseless than Day. Now what else is on your mind?"

Lydia looked at her son's troubled face, and then impulsively—guilty, guilty, and proud of it—said, "I wanted to talk to you about Candice. Except for that first night when we had dinner together, we never really have."

Christopher turned away. He seemed for the moment intent on two giggling schoolgirls who had seated themselves at a table on the sidewalk.

Then, his face still averted, he said, "There's not much to talk about. We're just no longer engaged."

To a casual listener, Christopher's voice might have sounded as if he were reporting something as impersonal as the mineral resources of Outer Mongolia. But beneath the studied modulation, Lydia heard something she never had before, an unease, an uncertainty—oh, more than either of those. She heard the sound of suffering.

"Whose—?" She managed to say, "Whose idea was that?"

"Not mine," said Christopher.

When he turned, the familiar composure of his face was gone. Christopher had always seemed totally in charge of himself and able to deal with whatever crisis might arise. A death in the family, an errant sister, the affairs of the nation, the problems of the world, and, most difficult of all, his own destiny.

But not now. The "No Admittance" sign that he usually had in front of his eyes was gone; now his face begged for a friendly trespasser.

"But why?" Lydia asked, thinking, isn't this what I wanted? Answering, It was, but I've changed my mind, again. I was wrong, again.

"I don't really know why," said Christopher. "Everything seemed fine until two or three weeks ago, and then, all of a sudden, it changed."

In other words, thought Lydia, everything was fine and dandy until I arrived on the scene, wearing two left feet and acting as if I'd just been appointed God.

"Anyway," said Christopher, "she's resigned, and she's going back to Montana."

"Maybe she's been homesick," said Pollyanna, who seemed to have slipped into Lydia's otherwise empty chair.

"She hates Montana," said Christopher. "She always has."

Chapter 27

🌣 Who was it who said, "Question not where other people get their jollies—unless, that is, you've got a license"?

It sounded like one of Sybil's remarks, irreverent, brazen, not totally accurate, yet containing enough of the truth to cause it to stick in the mind, in Lydia's mind, anyway.

She recalled it now, sitting at the marble-topped table, listening to her handsome, her promising, her until-now predictable son. He was talking about Candice. No, he did not know why she had broken the engagement. Yes, he was sure she still loved him, and he was equally sure that he still loved her. How he knew he could not quite put into words; only the greatest poets could do that.

And even they, thought Lydia, have not often succeeded. Once, when much younger, and, heaven knows, more romantic, she had gone through all the quotations concerning love in *Bartlett's*—eleven columns of them, more than the entries under any other category; *death* had only six columns, *hate* but a column and a half.

None of the quotations about love had, as Lydia recalled, stirred her. None had come even close to describing the malady she had even then suffered and enjoyed. None had answered the tired, eternal question, "What in the world does he see in her? She in him?"

Best not to wonder, Lydia had decided, best to do that most difficult thing of all, keep your big mouth shut.

"Candice is the only girl I've ever known who needs me," Christopher was saying. "I guess maybe I want that. Does it sound foolish?"

"No, darling," said Lydia, and she did not add that it sounded familiar.

She remembered now a boy she had known when she was in high school and he was a freshman at Briley. His name was gone, and she could no longer bring to mind the circumstances of their meeting, not where, not when, not how.

He was from a farm near Grand View, Nebraska, was tall, had hair that was bleached by the sun, a harsh, unhandsome face, and he was suffering from being seventeen, from feet that were too large to lift, from hands that, like his hair shirt, he apparently expected to grow into, and a sweet shyness of manner.

He had asked her to go to a movie; the way he phrased it she would never forget.

"I don't suppose you'd consider going to a movie with me," he said.

Lydia, who at the time had been a somewhat backward fifteen, said, "Why, of course, I would; I'd like to."

It may have been kindness on her part, but, far more likely, the movie was one she wanted to see and nobody else had asked her. That happened a lot.

In any case, the boy said, "I've heard that people like you are always polite. That's the result of what they call good breeding, I believe."

"Has it ever occurred to you that I might enjoy going to a movie with you?" said Lydia.

"Frankly, no," said the boy.

They had gone to maybe a dozen movies after that, and Lydia had once asked the boy to go with her to a dance. He declined.

"Unfortunately," he said, "in addition to everything else, I don't dance very well."

That was about all. Summer came, and the boy returned to Nebraska, but before he left, he said, "I don't think I'll be able to get through the summer without you. I mean it."

"You'll be able to get through," said Lydia, and apparently, he had, because he never came back to Briley, and Lydia never heard from him again.

All right, then. That was a kind of need. But was it even remotely what Candice felt for Christopher? What he felt for her? Again, no answer.

Love, thought Lydia, must be one of the few diseases, if disease it is, in which the symptoms are never twice the same.

"I know it sounds conceited," Christopher was saying, "and maybe even a little ridiculous, but every other girl, almost every other girl, well, I always thought it was my body they were interested in, and not in me."

At the very least, thought Lydia, the panting desire that follows Christopher wherever he goes and always has must get a little tiresome. Myself, I could have settled for a little of that now and again, but then, it's true, I always thought I was the ugly duckling that would turn into a swan. I'm still waiting.

She watched as the pretty waitress poured another cup of coffee for Christopher. The girl's large, soft eyes never left his face, and now what Lydia earlier had taken for adoration was clearly lust.

And yet, thought Lydia, is lust so far from love? Are they really so different? Love, my sudden adoration, my great love. Lust, longing or intense desire, an eagerness to enjoy. Can there be one without the other? And which comes first?

As soon as we've settled the chicken-and-egg debate, we might get into love versus lust. Unless we're still hung up on how many angels can comfortable dance on the head of a pin.

Christopher rose, carefully not looking at the girl who lusted for him, and as he paid the check, Lydia thought—no reason, it just came to her—of a time when she and Simeon and the children had on a summer evening been returning from a late picnic.

Day had been in the front seat with her father, and Christopher in the back with Lydia. Was he going on eight?

Lydia said, "Darling, why don't you put your head on my lap and take a nap?"

Christopher did so, and, later, his eyes closed, half-asleep, half-awake, out of some dark depth, he said to his mother, "Don't let anybody hurt me."

"I won't," Lydia had said.

And I have tried, she thought now, but, recently, I'm afraid, I haven't tried hard enough. Time now to begin.

The sun had come out and shone hot and white. Lydia decided to walk back to the embassy with Christopher.

As they progressed through the leisurely streets, Lydia told Christopher what she had learned about Paul, about the encounter with his wife, and about the threats of trouble.

Christopher was unperturbed. He had known a good deal about Paul even before Lydia mentioned him. Paul, as she knew, had come to the embassy several weeks back. He had had in mind transferring a goodly sum of money from the States to Portugal, and since Portugal was a country of spies, almost as many spies as policemen, the Department had felt it necessary to look into Paul Julian. Prognosis, positive.

"I read quite a long report on him," said Christopher, "and while he's made a lot of enemies—a man doesn't get as far as he has without doing that—there was nothing very damaging."

And, ever the faithful public servant, he added, "I shouldn't be telling you this, you know."

Lydia, ever the upholder of privacy, said, "I'm not at all sure I approve of reports like that."

"I'm not sure I do, either, but if my mother is involved with a fellow and the report already exists . . . Anyway, a few newspaper headlines aren't going to affect my career one way or the other. There are a great many intelligent people in the Department these days.

"You love Paul, and, as I told you, I like him. So go thou forth. You don't have to ask my permission to try to be happy. But you do have my blessing."

They stood for a time in front of the embassy, and a great many serious-looking young men passed them, all wearing a look of dedication, all with the weight of the world on the shoulders of their seersucker jackets.

"Would it help if I went to see Candice?" Lydia asked.

"She admires you very much," said Christopher, "but you frighten her."

"I do? I didn't know I ever scared anybody but me."

Christopher, for some reason looking taller than usual, smiled down at her. "You're quite an awesome woman, you know," he said. "Everybody thinks so. I try to tell them that you're nothing but a bundle of indecision, but nobody ever believes me."

"I believe you," said Lydia.

Christopher said, "Candice told me, 'That first day, I was scared even before I saw your mother, and when I did I was even scareder—she's so *impeccable*. And the scareder I got, the more I talked and the sillier the things I said. And all about Missoula at that; I hate Missoula. I started packing to get away when I was about two years old.' "

"But why did I, do I, scare people?"

"Because you always look so damn sure of yourself," said Christopher. "You always look as if you've got it made."

Chapter 28

❧ " 'And the scareder I got, the more I talked and the sillier the things I said.' "

In the taxi on the way to the place Candice lived, that sentence repeated itself in Lydia's mind, not once but a dozen times, and there was another sentence, one she hadn't remembered in years. It was, "Oh, do you, my dear? One would not have guessed."

Nor had Lydia for some time thought of Jeremiah—never Jerry, never even that somewhat cozier diminutive, Jeremy—Kingsley. Some few close friends called him King, which was appropriate enough, and to the boys who had gone to prep school with him he was Pud. Lydia never knew why; she never asked. In the brief time they knew each other, she called him Jeremiah. As the name indicates, he was decidedly appointed or exalted by the Lord.

They met at a gala at the Plaza. Just why Jeremiah cast his monarch's eye on one of the leading wallflowers of her day is lost history. Perhaps he had glanced at her tiny instep and felt it would fit into a glass slipper he happened to have on him. In any case, and Jeremiah Kingsley could have played the Prince in anybody's Christmas pageant, he asked her to dance. The first time Lydia figured it was charity. The Kingsleys were always giving money to some underdeveloped group or other, why not a spirited minuet with an underdeveloped individual?

But then he asked her three times again, and Lydia managed to be both fleet of foot and to survive the killing looks of several of her inferiors. *Who's* underdeveloped?

Afterward, she and Jeremiah went riding in a carriage in Central Park, an activity which Lydia had read about, and the writers always seemed to think highly of it. Had any of them ever been? The horse could have used a bubble bath, the carriage had two square wheels of different sizes, the driver was drunk, and the night—it was late March—was chill. Lydia was wearing a burnt-orange chiffon dress with pailletes sprinkled all over the bosom area. In the store the dress had looked like something Norma Shearer would wear if she had a heavy date with Leslie Howard, but when Lydia got home, it looked more like Joan Crawford playing a role in which she is no better than she should be, the kind in which she wants to marry the scion of the family: "Do you know whom I am?"

Jeremiah Kingsley was a scion, all right; his family owned all the tin in Chile. Or was it Peru? Lots of tin, anyway, and that night, instead of waving a scepter in front of the bowing peasants, he had his arm around the Little Match Girl.

From where Lydia sat, shivered really, the whole thing looked like the beginning of a romance. Jeremiah towered over her; at least, he did when he stood up. He couldn't have been seven feet tall, could he? He had the body of a born tennis player, the grace, for that matter, and his face was—well, Lydia described him to Sybil as being "divinely handsome." True, he had a slight cast in one eye, but that minuscule defect only lent enchantment to his good looks and his charm.

He *was* charming. How could one not be who had gone to college in Bologna ("Nobody else I knew ever had"), who called the Prince of Wales David, who had gotten drunk with Scott Fitzgerald, had hunted in Africa with Ernest Hemingway, had gone sailing with Errol Flynn, who had been engaged to a Dutch princess and a widowed maharani.

That first dawn, after the hazardous ride through Central Park, they had breakfast at the St. Regis. Jeremiah had a suite on one of the upper floors and had urged Lydia to accompany him there. She declined, and when he asked why, she said, "Because I've never liked to box and eat at the same time."

"You're a funny little girl," said Jeremiah.

Unhappily, Lydia said back, "Funny peculiar or funny ha-ha?"

"Both," said Jeremiah.

To her credit, Lydia never asked Jeremiah why he had asked her to dance in the first place; she was afraid she might not like the answer.

They saw each other a few times after that, say half a dozen. Sybil said—well, surely you know Sybil well enough by now to know the kind of thing she'd say.

Was Lydia in love with him? She imagined so. How could she not be? Even when it was over, looking back on that time, Lydia sometimes managed to convince herself that Jeremiah had been the love of her life. Romances that, for whatever reason, don't come to much always in memory appear to be a good deal more glowing than the ones that do.

An evening came when Jeremiah and Lydia were going to the theater. He was once more in a suite at the St. Regis, and when Lydia phoned him from the lobby, he said, "I'm not quite ready. Come on up."

"I'll meet you in the King Cole Bar," said Lydia.

"Don't be so damned defensive of your virtue. My mother's here."

Lydia was even more frightened then. His mother? She'd rather meet the Wicked Witch of the North. In the first place, the dress was all wrong. Actually, it was Sybil's dress, black crepe, and since Sybil was wider than Lydia and shorter, the dress bagged in various unlikely places, particularly around the crucial bosom area. It was also too short.

"It's got style. That's the main thing," Sybil had said, "so what if it's a little roomy? Wear a belt."

In Lydia's room in Briley, Sybil's remarks made perfect sense; in the lobby of the St. Regis they sounded like dangerous lunacy. And Lydia's nutria coat looked as if the South American rodent from whose fur it was made had suffered a long, debilitating illness before calling it a day.

Lydia ducked into the ladies' room, made up her face in several different ways, all of them awful, then removed all of the makeup, assuring herself that she would have a scrubbed, school-girl look, which might have happened if she hadn't scrubbed so hard that she rubbed a chunk of skin off her nose and a portion of her forehead.

The woman who opened the door of Jeremiah's suite seemed to be even taller than her son. She had a large, disapproving nose, abrasive black hair, and lips that looked as if there had never been anything to smile about.

She said several things Lydia could no longer remember, courteous enough, no doubt; she was, after all, a lady. She invited Lydia to sit down, gave her a Coke, and then, missing not a detail of the dress, said, "How many sisters do you have?"

"None," said Lydia.

"Oh, I thought perhaps that charming dress belonged to an older sister," said Jeremiah's mother.

"Oh, no," said Lydia. "It's just that I have such a sentimental attachment to it. You see, Queen Marie of Rumania gave it to me during the several months that she spent at our country estate. She called our place her home away from home."

There was a good deal more. Lydia traced her family tree back to the Huguenots, although she wasn't really sure who the Huguenots were. She described the ancestral wealth as, one fears, incalculable, and she endowed Briley College with the age of William and Mary and the distinction of Harvard.

At one lofty moment, having described the army of servants scurrying around the manse at Briley, she found herself saying, "And I have my own personal hairdresser."

"Oh, do you, my dear?" said Jeremiah's mother. "One would not have guessed."

That was the end. She and Jeremiah went to the theater, but the glow was gone. He called once or twice again, but Lydia refused to see him.

The hurt he suffered was, apparently, not unbearable. Three months later he married a railroad heiress from San Francisco. Unfortunately, in addition to the money, the girl was beautiful.

When Lydia told her mother what had happened in the suite at the St. Regis, her mother said, "Mrs. Kingsley acted unkindly, and she's old enough to know better. You acted like a foolish child, a condition that some people outgrow."

And she said, "Did you really want to marry Jeremiah Kingsley?"

Lydia thought that one over with some care, and then she said, "No, but I wanted him to ask me to."

"That," said her mother, "is what causes most of the trouble in the world."

As the taxi stopped at the address Christopher had given her, Lydia remembered something else her mother had said, maybe not at that time, but she said it, all right. More important, she had as often as she was able practiced it as well.

She had said, "Darling, never be afraid to be merciful."

Chapter 29

❧ The exterior of the house was stone that once perhaps had been pink, and once the house might have been elegant, but that had been some time before. Now the stone was gray black; it was the unmistakable color of poverty and lost hope.

There was an elderly garbage can on the sidewalk in front, and a skeleton of a dog with a missing ear dispiritedly nosed through what had been spilled.

Candice's name was one of three on a finger-marked card beneath a bell. Lydia rang the bell, and then Candice's voice, harsh with the harshness of the West, and childlike, said, "Who is it?"

When Lydia gave her name, the silence was extended, but finally Candice said, "It's on the third floor." This time there was apprehension in her voice, too.

The stairs were steep, and the odor was familiar, rooming-house smell, as identifiable as the universal smell of a hospital. In this case, perhaps, a little more garlicky than most, but that was the only difference.

Candice was standing in the doorway of the room she shared with two other girls who worked at the embassy. For the first time since Lydia had met her, Candice's face was free of make-up; she had even washed off the disconcerting eyebrows.

She was still not beautiful, not even very pretty, but Lydia saw it was a hopeful face, a face wanting attention, wanting affection, wanting love and approval. Like my own, thought Lydia, and why is it I never noticed these things before? I'll tell you why. I didn't want to.

I took one look at Candice and, without a moment's hesitation, I decided she wasn't the girl I had in mind for my bright, my beautiful, my promising son. Without benefit of trial, without even specifying the charges, I condemned her. Did I make the slightest attempt to let my son go cheerily? Not the slightest. I acted selfishly, stupidly, neurotically, and now that we've gone this far, let's not mince words; I acted dangerously. I acted like a hundred, a thousand mothers I've known, some well, who can't bear to cut the umbilical cord, not to mention loosening their apron strings. In the nine years since listening to Enid's jokes I appear to have learned nothing.

This has been a day of revelation, a day when the furies have been working around the clock.

All right, furies, all right. I get the numerous unsettling messages. But why don't you all take a short vacation now, a nap, at any rate?

"It's nice of you to come and say good-bye," said Candice, "and I'm sorry the place is such a mess, but, you know, three girls and all, and I'm packing and all, and we're all sort of messy. The other girls, they never hang things up."

Lydia thought of the room on College Avenue that she had shared with Sybil. Among numerous other faults of Sybil's was the fact that she never hung up her toothbrush. Lydia, of course, then as always, had been faultless, not to mention being neat as a pin. A place for everything and everything in its place.

So what if her shoes were quite often in the middle of the floor? A thing like that simply gave a homelike quality to a room that was otherwise terribly drab.

Candice was wearing a dark housecoat, and her hair was piled in a loose knot on top of her head. She looked thinner than Lydia remembered, and younger, much younger. She looked younger than anybody has a right to be.

Her eyes were slightly red; she had been crying, but she appeared to have decided that she was done crying forever.

"Please to come in," she said, her hands uneasily trying to close the housecoat. The coat seemed to have developed a will of its own and was refusing to close.

Lydia stepped inside the front room, which was meagerly

furnished with an uneven table, a few relics of chairs, one over-stuffed and dirty, and a greasy couch. There was a small trunk in the middle of the floor, and Candice's clothes were scattered everywhere.

"I told you it was a mess," she said, and she giggled nervously.

"It looks very much like a room I used to share when I was a girl."

Candice giggled again, and her hand now reached for her hair, which was toppling around her shoulders.

"I didn't expect you," she said, giving up on her hair.

"I should have phoned," said Lydia, "but I didn't know how."

Candice greeted that remark with a burst of laughter, as if Lydia had said something unexpectedly witty.

"That's my room in there," she said, pointing to an open door. "There are some books. I mean, I'm sure you've read them all, but well, if you'd excuse me a jif, I mean, without any makeup or anything, I feel naked."

She started toward the bathroom. "I'm afraid there isn't anything to drink or anything."

She opened the door. "The thing is, with you, you never have a hair out of place or anything."

"In the mornings," said Lydia, "I have often been mistaken for the wife of the Abominable Snowman."

Candice giggled once again, "Yah, I'll bet."

The room that Candice had indicated as hers, more a cell, really had only a slit of a window, and the house across the dusky alleyway leaned forward slightly as if trying to peer inside.

The severe cot had been made somewhat more inviting with a bright green throw on which blue and red birds of no identifiable species had been embroidered. There was a wobbly bedside table with an exquisite green porcelain vase as well as a handful of books—the *Vogue Book of Etiquette*, soft-cover book of recipes, another modern poems, a two-volume *Don Quixote* bound in Spanish leather, a Spanish grammar, and several detective stories.

A few dresses hung on hooks in the minute closet, and none of the dresses was right, including the now-familiar one that was avocado-colored and was, no doubt, Candice's Sunday best.

But then, thought Lydia, at Candice's age I do not recall being on any list of the country's ten best-dressed ladies.

She recalled the black lace nightgown she had bought while her father and mother were in Europe. Sometime after their return, Lydia's mother had one day discovered the nightgown hidden deep in the recesses of the closet that her mother referred to as the black hole of Calcutta.

"What in the world is this?" her mother asked, holding the dress at arm's length as if it might be infected with a communicable disease.

"It's sort of what you might call a black lace nightgown," said Lydia.

"That is enlightening," said her mother, "but whose is it?"

Lydia considered several possible answers—that the nightgown belonged to Sybil, that it was being used for, say, a sociology experiment (but what kind?), and that she was going to wear it in the class play that year. But none of these answers seemed appropriate, the latter in particular, since the play was *Seventeen.*

Finally, she said, "It's mine; I thought it was sort of a hoot."

"A *hoot?*" said her mother. "Well, we'll have to dispose of it. Burn it, I guess."

"But couldn't you give it to the Salvation Army?" Lydia had asked.

"Those poor people have troubles enough as it is," said her mother.

When Candice came out of the bathroom, she had put on lipstick, not well, and she had changed into a dark print dress with a white collar. She probably wore it to work.

She had combed her hair and seemed more composed, but there was still in her eyes a plea. Please be nice to me, it asked, please don't let anybody hurt me. Including you.

All over the world, thought Lydia, everywhere, there are

people with a plea in their eyes, with outstretched hands, with beseeching hearts.

Why, oh why, are we—no, let's be specific. Let's get down to cases for once. Why, oh why, am I so reluctant to notice?

The fact that I'm frightened, too? True, true, undeniably true, but that's not good enough, not by half. I keep telling myself how grown-up I am. Why not try acting it for a change? If not now, when?

"It was nice of you to come to say good-bye," Candice said again.

"But I didn't come to say good-bye," said Lydia. "I came to try to persuade you to stay."

And then there they were, the two of them, their arms around each other and crying like babies.

Chapter 30

❧ There is a Spanish saying, "On the day of victory, no one is tired." Lydia remembered that after she left Candice. And it's perfectly true, too, she thought, and I should know. I have just won the most difficult victory of all, one over myself. I have triumphed, if only momentarily, over the hell in my heart. And as a result, the bone weariness of this morning has given way to a lovely euphoria.

I have learned something about myself, too. I have learned that the exterior I show to the world is not nearly as benign as I thought.

"The minute you looked at me," Candice had said, "I knew that everything about me was wrong. It was like one of those nightmares where you dream you're at a big party wearing your Maidenform bra, and nothing else."

It was then that Lydia told her about Jeremiah Kingsley and his mother and about wearing Sybil's ill-fitting dress and, "Oh, do you, my dear? One would not have guessed."

They laughed, and they talked, and after a time Candice decided that she would stay after all.

As Lydia went back to the apartment house—she walked a good part of the way—Lydia remembered a piece of advice she had given herself some time ago and was inclined to forget. It was this: You have to figure that most people goof most of the time, and you have to forgive them, even when it's you.

Paul took one look at her and said, "You're going to bed at once."

"Don't be silly," said Lydia. "I haven't been to bed in the

daytime for years, not since I had the measles, not to sleep, anyway."

And then she was laughing over nothing and crying over nothing, and then she was sobbing.

Paul picked her up, carried her into the bedroom, undressed her, put her to bed, and half an hour later brought her scrambled eggs, toast, and bacon.

"You have a thousand talents," said Lydia, "and you can cook, too."

"Of course. I used to work in a short-order joint. Scrambled eggs were our specialty."

He gave her a sleeping pill, and she yawned and told him about her conversations with Christopher and with Candice.

"And now you love Candice," he said.

Lydia thought a moment, sleepily. After the mutual tears with Candice had been mutually wiped away, Lydia had given that question some thought and had given herself an answer. It was not one she particularly liked. Nor, she felt, would Candice, but then Candice may have asked herself the same question about her prospective mother-in-law and may conceivably have come up with the same answer.

"I've accepted her," said Lydia, and she slept.

Two days after Lydia made her peace with Candice, Paul had to return to Paris for more conferences with the lawyers.

Lydia decided to remain in Madrid. The day for the wedding of Christopher and Candice had been set for three weeks away, and there were clothes to be bought, arrangements to be made, and Sybil was due to arrive at any moment.

When he got back, they were going to travel for a time—to Toledo, to Granada, to Córdoba, and, finally, to Seville for the Feast of Corpus Christi. After that they would go to London to meet Lydia's mother and then back to the white villa near Armação de Pêra.

Eventually? Why, eventually they would go home again. Lydia had not forgotten her promise to the hills in Briley, but there was time, so very much time.

It turned out not to be quite so simple, but then, whatever is?

"The trick," Paul once said, "is not to make too many agendas."

Late in the morning of the soft day Paul left for Paris, the phone rang, and a man's voice that Lydia did not at first recognize said, "Lydia? This is Jack."

"Who?"

"Jack Bernstein. How many Jacks do you know?"

"Only one of any importance," said Lydia.

"What are you doing?"

"I was waiting for you to call me."

Jack was at the Fenix; he had arrived the night before. He had a car and a chauffeur, and he had thought of going to El Escorial. Would Lydia be interested?

"I'll be ready in half an hour," said Lydia, and, knowing the answer, she nevertheless asked, "Is Sybil with you?"

"Not anymore," said Jack.

"I'll be out front in half an hour."

Jack had lost weight and was pale. The horn-rimmed glasses that he was forever adjusting seemed even more enormous than usual, but the smile was still wistful. The smile made you want to cry.

He kissed Lydia, and as she seated herself in the back seat of the Cadillac, he said, "You're the only person I know that I'm always glad to see."

The paved road they took to El Escorial is narrow and rutted, but in a Cadillac even the worst bumps are cushioned, and the driver, an elderly man with a limp, drove with care. He had been wounded in the civil war, he said, and when Jack asked on which side, the man side, "On the side of justice, the one that always loses."

The hills along the road were alternately red and green, and on some there were neat groves of olive trees. In a few places the almond trees were still in bloom. They passed through sevcral desultory villages with whitewashed houses and cobble-stone squares with a fountain and beds of pink geraniums and red and yellow roses.

Jack was determined to be amusing, and he talked about the New York theater, about concerts he had attended and books he had read. He didn't mention Sybil, and Lydia didn't ask.

At only one time was he serious, as they were going up the drive to the huge gray building that Philip II had built as a tomb for himself. Just before the chauffeur parked the car, Jack said, "I've thought a lot about Simeon lately. Poor Simeon, he wanted to be something he never could be, and maybe that's true of all of us."

The monastery and palace that the Spanish call San Lorenzo del Escorial is a defiantly ugly monastery and palace which even that bright morning was depressing.

Philip had been a man with a passion for pain, and the dark cell in which he spent the last fourteen years of his uneasy life had only one tiny window that looked out over an imposing altar. The walls of the cell itself were covered with frightening representations of the seven deadly sins.

"The man who had everything," said Jack, "and he couldn't stand it."

They had lunch on the terrace of the nearby hotel that was named after Philip but, happily, not influenced by his melancholy. The food was superb, and in the distance were the Guadarrama Mountains, green and blue in the comforting mist.

Over the desert, wild strawberries and kirsch, Jack said, "I had to come to El Escorial. I've been seeing pictures of it all my life, and I always had a notion, which turns out to be true, that it's very like the place I grew up."

The mansion in St. Louis was built with granite from Vermont and had a hallway of marble imported from Palermo.

" 'I dreamt that I dwelt in marble halls. With vassals and serfs at my side.' Except I never dreamt it. I was right there, and so were the vassals and serfs. The tutors and the nurses and the governesses and . . .

"On night at diner—I must have been twelve—I complained that I didn't have any playmates. My father, who was not a benign man, said, 'You're fortunate. That means you won't have anybody to make you unhappy.'

"My mother was really a sweet woman, and she said, 'Don't worry, dear; you will.'

"Sure enough, two days later a boy who lived a few streets away came to our house and asked if I'd like to come play with him and his sister.

"His name was Dale Wilmont, and he was, oh, I'd guess about eleven and was all the things I'd always wanted to be and knew I never could. He was tall for his age, graceful, and he was good at games and cheerful.

"His sister Cassie was thirteen and, I thought, the most beautiful girl in the world; it turned out she wasn't quite the most beautiful. When she was nineteen—as you will see, we were no longer friends—she got to be Miss Missouri, but I don't think she did too well in Atlantic City.

"Cassie and Dale and Jack. All for one and one for all. During those six months—that's how long it lasted, six months and two days—were the happiest of my life. I had two friends; two people liked me. I even began to like myself a little.

"And then one afternoon—it was October 12, Columbus Day,—and there was to be a parade downtown, and we were going."

Jack paused, and looking at the pale, drawn face, Lydia thought, what follows will not be easy, for Jack or for me, but if Jack wants to tell me, I, of course, must listen.

"I got to their place early that afternoon. It was a nice clapboard house on a good street. Their father was an executive in one of the insurance companies. They weren't poor.

"Anyway, I rushed into the house, slamming the front door behind me, but Cassie and Dale, who were in the living room, didn't hear me. They were working on a jigsaw puzzle. It was a reproduction of Gilbert Stuart's "Washington Crossing the Delaware." It's odd I remember that, but I do, and the exact sound of their voices is still with me.

"Cassie, my fairy princess, was saying, 'When is four-eyes going to get here?'

"And my friend Dale, that gentle, graceful boy, said, 'If we're lucky, maybe he won't come. Maybe he'll get run over by a truck, a Mac truck.'

"They must have fitted a few pieces of the jigsaw together, and then Cassie said, 'It's worth every cent his mother pays us to have to play with that fat little Jew.' "

Jack adjusted his glasses.

" 'I dreamt,' he said, 'that I dwelt in marble halls, but I also dreamt, which pleased me most, that you loved me still.' Shall we go?"

On the way back to Madrid the road seemed more rutted, the driver who had fought on the side of justice and lost seemed careless, and there appeared to be uneasy shadows on the hills and over the whitewashed houses and the flowered squares.

When the car stopped in front of Lydia's hotel, she said, "You're a dear man, Jack, and I love you."

"But you're not in love with me?"

"No, darling," she said, "I'm not in love with you."

That evening Lydia and Jack had dinner at the Caves of Luis Candelas, where the waiters dress as bandits. The food was superb. They had clams and roast lamb, tiny strawberries served with fresh orange juice, and wine.

The early conversation was general, that of two old friends remembering various pleasant times in the past—the summer on the Cape, another on the Jersey shore, the children.

Lydia told him about Christopher's forthcoming marriage. Yes, the girl was nice; yes, she was pleased.

She had not yet told him about Paul. She didn't quite know how, and yet, although it would not be easy, she realized she must. She was in fact on the verge of doing so when Jack, his face somewhat flushed with the wine, said, "I suppose you've guessed why I came to Madrid."

As a matter of fact Lydia had not given the matter much thought, perhaps deliberately, and she sensed now that what

Jack was about to say was not something she wanted to hear. What he was about to say he would later regret, and so would she. Their friendship would forever after be marred by it.

But before Lydia could say the warning word to stop him, whatever that word might be, Jack lifted her hand from the table, kissed it, and said, "I was going to ask you to marry me."

For a long moment Lydia could not have spoken if she had tried. She was close to tears, and she was angry with herself for not having earlier spoken of Paul. That would have prevented what had just happened. She hadn't, though, and now all she could say, hating the inadequate words, was, "I'm sorry, Jack."

But the worst was yet to come.

"You said you're not in love with me," he went on, "but there's a lot to be said for companionship, at our age especially. We have respect for each other, and we have many interests in common, and—"

"No, Jack," said Lydia, and the words sounded harsh, which was not what she intended. "No, I couldn't possibly."

Jack signaled for the check, and then he said, "That's the reason I married Sybil in the first place. I wanted to be near you."

Later, much later, after they had uneasily sat through a *flamenco* show that it seemed would never end, Jack said, "I'll take you home now."

At the door of the apartment house Lydia kissed him tenderly, and she said, once more unhappy with the inept words, "I cherish our friendship very much, Jack."

"I know," he said, but it was clear that the comfort he felt, if any, was cold. "Oh, yes, I do know that."

A moment later he said, "I think I'll go to Majorca for a couple of weeks, and after that, who knows?"

When Lydia got to her room, she undressed quickly and went to bed, but she knew that sleep would be a long time coming. She knew, too, that she would never tell Paul what Jack had said to her. She would never tell anyone, and she would never forget.

Chapter 31

🌸 Two days later a bellboy from the Ritz brought Lydia a note written on stationery with the welcome monogram *S.B.* The monogram was huge, defiant, and as awesome as a royal coat of arms. Sybil had just arrived; she was sorry she hadn't cabled; she had to see Lydia "but at once. I have carloads of surprises—good, bad, horrible. Hurry. Your aging aunt awaits you. Love."

Lydia's mood improved immediately. She had gotten up that morning feeling a sense of terrible isolation. "For two cents I'd get on a plane and fly to Paris. Paul and I are too old to waste time by being separated."

But, she thought, we are also too old to be so foolish. My presence in Paris at the moment would only add to the hostility and, for that matter, the tapes and photographs and innuendos.

Having made that virtuous decision, Lydia sighed. True, virtue is its own reward, but why can't there be an occasional dividend?

Lydia had started taking Spanish lessons, and while as a girl she had fancied that she a gift for languages, it appeared to have disappeared. Like her ability to compete in a hundred-yard dash.

Señor Davila, ordinarily the most patient of men, had that morning shrugged his shoulders in Latin despair. "But, *señora,* you must learn to listen with your ear."

Lydia, who had thought she was doing just that, said, "Maybe I'm just hopeless. I guess I'm too old."

"I have taught the language to a Yugoslav lady of seventy-two," said Señor Davila, but he looked at Lydia without much hope.

After he left, Lydia tried painting for an hour, but she could see that what she liked to think of as her new, free style was neither very free nor did it have much style. She put the incomplete daub in a far corner of a closet.

It was then that Sybil's note arrived, and Lydia started dressing. She decided on the blue shantung silk that she and Paul had found on the Gran Vía. No hat. She had been to the hairdresser only two days before. Why hide her chestnut blonde glory under a hat?

Lydia had already decided that she could not, would not, allow what Jack had said affect her friendship with Sybil. And she would say only that she had gone to El Escorial with Jack and that they had had dinner together. No more than that.

And she would not mention that the morning after that unhappy night she had received a note from Jack saying "It is not easy to forgive foolishness, but I hope you will try." At the bottom of the note was the name of his hotel in Majorca, and with it had come a handsome edition of the poems of Lorca.

Nor would Lydia say anything about the cable she had sent him, " 'And throughout all eternity/I forgive you, you forgive me.' "

A small, most elegant young man opened the door of Sybil's suite. The *señora,* he said, would be out in a minute, and he introduced himself. His name had a great many parts, but Lydia felt she'd have done her duty if she remembered only his first given name, Arturo. Forget the *José,* the *Roberto,* the *des.* Two of the latter. Forget the *Amado,* the *Orlando,* the *Zacarias.* Concentrate solely on Arturo, meaning valorous, brave, rock-like.

Arturo—was he twenty-five, twenty-six?—had a dark, melancholy face, glistening black hair that curled over his brown forehead, great knowing eyes, and a smile that would have made a fortune for a manufacturer of toothpaste. He was wearing a spotless white suit and shoes that looked as if they had never been worn before and likely never would be again. His exquisite wristwatch had cost somebody (S.B.?) a pretty penny, and so had the slim gold lighter.

Sybil walked to the open window and looked out at the faultless day. Then, as if making herself a solemn promise, she said, "We're going to have a lovely time."

She went to the phone, ordered a masseuse, then turned to Lydia and said, "Jack's left me."

Lydia said precisely what she had planned saying, and when she finished, Sybil said, "Was he alone?"

"He was alone," said Lydia, and she thought, oh, very much alone, perhaps the most alone man I have ever seen.

"He just packed up and left," said Sybil. "I didn't even know he'd gone. Of course, there must be somebody else; there has to be. Why else would he leave me?"

Lydia decided, wisely, to treat the question as rhetorical, no answer required.

"There've been times," said Sybil, a touch of archness in her voice, "when I've thought he was smitten with you."

No response to that one, either; Lydia concentrated on the dregs of coffee in her cup.

Sybil seemed not to expect a reaction. She sat down again, this time on the chaise longue beside Lydia.

"I don't know how I'll ever get along without him," said Sybil. "I mean it. I don't think I can exist without him."

"I'm sure you won't have to worry about money," said Lydia. "I'm sure Jack won't be selfish about that."

Sybil smiled patiently at her oldest, dearest friend. "You don't understand at all, do you? I love Jack. If I thought he'd take me back, I'd crawl on my hands and knees over broken glass to wherever he is."

Fortunately that was when the masseuse arrived, and Sybil sent her into the bedroom.

To Lydia she said, "Now I'll go and get myself beaten, and in an hour I'll go out to lunch with a pretty child who bores me, and I, as usual, will pick up the check. Any day now, people are going to start referring to me as a dirty old woman, and they'll be perfectly right."

"Would you like to have dinner?"

"I'd love it," said Sybil.

Lydia gave her the address of the apartment house. "I'll see you at seven."

Sybil nodded, and she said, "Neither of us did it quite right, did we?"

Chapter 32

When Sybil had finished repairing the damage the night air of Madrid had done to her face, she asked for a martini.

As Lydia prepared it, Sybil, smiling for perhaps the first time that day, said, "I think those blue silk pajamas in your bedroom closet are adorable, even though they do look a wee bit large for you, but then so are the gray cardigan and the Bond Street slacks. And since when have you started using the after-shave lotion and smoking cigars?"

Lydia gave her the martini, and Sybil said, "You always were a sly boots, but I knew good and well it wasn't just a change in environment that made you look the way you do. I knew it had to be love. Now tell Auntie all about it. Is he married? I'll bet he is. At our age they always are, either that or they paper their bathrooms with bullfight posters and are always showing you the doilies they're crocheting."

"Initials, *P.J.* Is he an American? And I hope he's rich. It's about time you took up with somebody with a bank account. Where in the world did you meet him? I knew something spectacular would happen to you. You were all ready for it, and I had a feeling that last night in New York . . ."

Eventually, Sybil quieted down enough to allow Lydia to tell her something about Paul.

When she had, Sybil kissed her on the forehead and said, "I'm glad; you had it coming. You've only been in love once in your whole life, and if your father hadn't kicked up such an unholy ruckus about that, you'd be Neil Gordon's wife right now. And being the wife of a Justice of the Supreme Court isn't exactly the worst thing in the world."

"You're perfectly right about that," said Lydia, "and only two things prevented it, really. In the first place, he didn't ask me, and in the second, I wasn't in love with him."

"Are you kidding?" Sybil rose to make herself a second martini. "He was so crazy for you he practically forgot how to play football. And you were mad for him. You'd just seen that Norma Shearer movie, whatever it was, and you kept repeating that ridiculous line of Shearer's, about Neil, I mean. You kept saying, 'I love him more than the earth, the moon, the sun, the sky, more than anything.'

"But your dear father—I know you think he was a great man, but I always thought he was a poop. Anyway, I never knew why he didn't like Neil. I guess maybe because Neil was always disagreeing with him in class, and your daddykins liked a lot of yes people around him.

"I'll never forget the night you came howling into my room. You and your father had had a big fight about Neil. He said Neil was one of those big men on the campus who'd never amount to a hill of beans."

"It was you who said that."

"That's one rap you'll never hang on me. I liked Neil. I could see that he had big possibilities."

"Shall we have dinner now?" asked Lydia.

"That night you said, 'I've promised my father I'll never see Neil again, and, of course, I won't.' And a couple of weeks later, Simeon called you for the first time. Talk about rebound.

"Naturally the great philosopher, Dr. Henry Lyman, approved of Simeon because Simeon was smart enough—weak enough, if you want to put it that way—to agree with everything the old windbag said."

"We're having braised duck with black cherries," said Lydia.

"Your father was always saying comforting little things like, 'If he'd lived, your brother would have been sixteen years old today, and I'd be sending him off to college.'

"The night of the ruckus about Neil, when you stopped crying, I'll never forget what you said. You said, 'In our family only the female blood is shed, mine and my mother's.'"

"Bring your drink with you," said Lydia.

"And when you told me you were going to marry Simeon, I said, 'You're marrying a pale carbon copy of your father, and while I have nothing against incest as such . . .' "

After dinner Lydia and Sybil sat in front of the fire, and Sybil, who was having that one Tío Pepe too many, was saying, "It's just like the old days. It's like when we had the room on College Avenue, and toward the end of the month when we were both broke, you'd cook supper on the hot plate, and we'd sit there blabbing away and eating hot dogs and pork and beans and all kinds of slops. . . ."

Sybil is once again mistaken, thought Lydia; it is not at all like the old days. And we've come a long way from College Avenue, both in distance and in time. She's wrong about Neil Gordon, too, and about my father.

"I'd give anything in the world to go back there and start all over again," said Sybil.

"I'd give anything in the world to avoid it," said Lydia.

Sybil laughed. She didn't for a minute think Lydia was serious. Perhaps she didn't dare.

"Dr. Manning says I'm an emotional alcoholic," said Sybil. "All the boys in my life, all that endless number of boys. I keep asking myself why. I keep asking Dr. Manning why."

Sybil was now on another of her favorite subjects, her latest analyst. She had been through half a dozen, one of whom was a fallen-away Jesuit. Another had specialized in Yoga, or was it Zen, and a third had, or so Sybil said, mixed in a little reading of the palm with his Freud. The latest was a woman.

"You know what she said about Arturo?" asked Sybil, and, not expecting an answer, she continued. "She said, 'Well, he doesn't sound to me like a split-level in Scarsdale.' And when I told her about Teddy Lipton, she said, 'Master Lipton and two or three others like him all rolled into one might make up something approximating a man.'

"And now, every time I go in for my fifty-minute hour, she

says, 'And what impossible situation have we gotten ourselves into today?'

"I don't think analysts ought to have a sense of humor, and they shouldn't be women. They ought to be dark, sad-eyed men with Semitic noses, and most of them are.

"The next time I pay somebody to stir around my brains with a wooden spoon, I'm going to make sure . . ."

Sybil's words rolled on, as endless as the sea, and you could listen or not. It didn't really matter, tuned in or out, off or on. It didn't matter to Sybil. She never missed a word she said.

"Arturo is the end of the line," Sybil was saying. "I'm afraid I've outgrown the ingenue roles. Could I ask you a direct question?"

"When have you not?"

"Do you know where Jack is? I told you this afternoon I'd crawl on my hands and knees over broken glass, and I meant it."

Lydia hesitated a moment. Then, hoping she was doing the right thing as well as the wise thing (They are not always the same), she said, "He's in Majorca, and why go on your hands and knees? Why not take a plane? It would not only be more comfortable, you'd get there faster."

Sybil picked up her coat, and she said, "He'll take me back. I know he will. All I have to do is ask him. He's sorry he went away, and he's miserable without me."

At the door she said, "I'm glad about you and Paul, and I can't wait to meet him."

She started out, but there was, of course, one more question, "You were in love with Neil Gordon, weren't you?"

"Yes, I was," said Lydia, and she added, not aloud, I loved him completely.

The next morning the phone rang at a little after nine; it was Sybil.

"Lyd? I wake you?"

"No, you didn't wake me."

Even then Lydia knew. She had been through something very

much the same many times before, and she no doubt would be many times again.

"Arturo and I are about to take off for Tripoli," said Sybil. "I need some time to think over what I really want, and there isn't any hurry, with Jack, I mean. I know he'll take me back. He may not realize it, but he loves me just as much as I love him. Don't you agree?"

"Good luck," said Lydia.

Chapter 33

❧   The time that followed was beautiful. Paul returned from Paris. Fran had agreed to an uncontested divorce. Under what terms Lydia never knew, and she didn't ask. It was enough that she and Paul were together.

Christopher and Candice were married as planned, in a small, American-looking island of a church not far from the embassy. The minister was an earnest young New Englander who spoke so softly that one had to strain to hear the familiar words. Candice was dressed in white Spanish lace, her face fresh and eager, her happiness clearly complete. And Christopher. He looked handsome, to be sure, the dark suit, the shining white shirt, and the single white flower in his buttonhole. But there was, too, in his face a look of achievement. Right or wrong, he had done what he wanted. Right or wrong, he had taken on the responsibilities of a man. And right or wrong, he would, as best he could, live up to them.

Kissing her second daughter and her son, Lydia felt some little pride in herself. She had started out all wrong, but, with some effort, she had had the good sense to admit her error and try to rectify it.

And in the end she had done the most difficult thing of all. She had not interfered, she had let well enough alone, she had succeeded in minding her own business.

And as she waved the last farewell, she did the only thing any of us can ever do. She hoped for the best.

The next day she and Paul started south. They traveled slowly through the villages and towns, finding pleasure in the red earth, in the hills crowned with olive trees, in the private, courteous people, in the hot tropical days, and in the soothing evenings that were filled with music.

It was not until they got to Córdoba that their journey was interrupted.

On that day they visited the Great Mosque, where there was a funeral in one corner and in another a baptism. They stood somewhere near the middle, listening to the two priests, one young and one elderly, one celebrating the beginning of life, the other lamenting its end.

Afterward they walked, looking into the elegant courtyards, watching the majestic afternoon drift silently into a tranquil evening.

When they got back to the hotel, the cablegram was waiting.

Paul read it through twice, then handed it to Lydia.

Mrs. Julian had suffered a severe heart attack, the cable said, and she was calling for her husband. Could he return at once. Question. Dr. L. Spencer.

As Lydia looked up, she thought, there would have been a time, and in the not too distant past, when I would have wept self-pitying tears, but that time is past. No tears amidst this alien corn. This calls not for weeping and the gnashing of teeth. It calls for fortitude. It calls for trust in Paul and, if I can manage it, myself. It calls for faith.

"I'm not going back," said Paul.

Lydia went to the closet and got out the brown bag made of Italian leather.

"If you'd asked me, I could have told you Fran would arrange something like this," he said. "If, in fact, she actually has had a heart attack."

Lydia opened the bureau drawer and took out his shirts, packing them neatly in the bag.

"In January 1942, when I told her I'd enlisted in the Navy, oh, my, the carrying on. You'd have thought I was the only man in the world who was going off to the wars. And all of a sudden she came down with *neuralgia*. I decided that was hardly a fatal disease and went off to San Diego anyway. A week later she had a miraculous recovery.

They had already said what needed saying, oh, many times, but at the station Paul repeated once again, "I'll be back."

He walked then to the train, a large, dark, indestructible-looking man with candid eyes and a hopeful smile.

As the train made its mournful departure, Lydia waved. Paul may have waved back, but, perhaps because of the rain, Lydia couldn't see well enough to be sure.

CODA

On the crest of a peaceful hill in the south of Portugal, there is a white villa. The hill is green the whole year round except for a few days in late January when the almond blossoms cover the earth like a fragrant snow.

It was on such a day that a man who had been absent for a time was seen to run up the hill toward the villa where the American woman had been waiting.

It is said in the village that in the late afternoon of that day the sun could be heard to sigh with gentle satisfaction as it settled itself for the night behind a distant wave.